Death By Irish Coffee

ALEX ERICKSON

Kensington Publishing Corp.
kensingtonbooks.com

KENSINGTON BOOKS are published by

Kensington Publishing Corp.
900 Third Avenue
New York, NY 10022

All Kensington titles, imprints, and distributed lines are available at special quantity discounts for bulk purchases for sales promotion, premiums, fundraising, educational, or institutional use.

Special book excerpts or customized printings can also be created to fit specific needs. For details, write or phone the office of the Kensington Sales Manager: Attn.: Sales Department. Kensington Publishing Corp., 900 Third Avenue, New York, NY 10022. Phone: 1-800-221-2647.

KENSINGTON and the KENSINGTON COZIES teapot logo Reg US Pat. & TM Off.

First Printing: February 2026

ISBN: 978-1-4967-5921-4

ISBN: 978-1-4967-5922-1 (ebook)

10 9 8 7 6 5 4 3 2 1

Printed in the United States of America

The authorized representative in the EU for product safety and compliance is eucomply OU, Parnu mnt 139b-14, Apt 123
Tallinn, Berlin 11317, hello@eucompliancepartner.com.

1

A sharp pain shot through the back of my arm, causing me to yelp and nearly spill the coffee I was holding.

"Careful, Krissy," Robert Dunhill said from behind, "or else the leprechauns will get you."

I rubbed at my arm and turned to glare at him. "I'm wearing green, Robert."

He looked me up and down. Not only did I have a big green shamrock in the middle of my shirt, the rest of it was a darker shade of green as well. "Oops. Sorry." The twinkle in his eye told me that he really wasn't.

Death by Coffee was hopping. It was St. Patrick's Day, and it seemed like everyone in town was there to get their morning jolt before taking part in the day's festivities. Our little town of Pine Hills was going all out this year. The streets were decorated for the occasion, full of green and gold, and a parade was planned for later that day. Afterward, the local bars would be hosting various events that would last deep into the night.

"Don't you have somewhere else to be?" I asked as the throb in my arm faded to a dull ache. He'd gotten me pretty good, and I expected to wake up with a bruise the size of a grapefruit in the morning. "Like, with your family or something?"

"I suppose you're right." Robert adjusted his golden bow tie. He was wearing a sparkling green hat and coat, complete with buckled shoes. I didn't know if he was taking part in the parade or if he'd simply chosen to dress like a leprechaun for the fun of it. "Trisha and RJ are waiting at home." RJ—short for Robert Jr.—was his baby son. "I only popped in to grab us some caffeine before we head out. I heard something about Irish coffee?" He looked at me hopefully.

"Not here," I said. "We don't have a liquor license."

"Oh." He frowned.

"But come to Bucky's later. That's where I'm off to now." I raised my coffee, as if the to-go cup should have made that obvious.

"That's the new place on Eucalyptus, right?"

I nodded. "Just opened last month. I'm working with the owner on a special Irish coffee brew for today's event. My coffee, his whiskey."

"Cool." A handful of customers entered and queued up in line. Robert frowned at them. "I'd best get moving," he said, before pointing at me. "And keep that green on. Wouldn't want you to get pinched."

Again, I thought somewhat unkindly as Robert slipped into line. While I'd been looking forward to the St. Patrick's Day parade all week, the tradition of pinching those not wearing green was something I could do without. Especially with people like Robert around, who took the opportunity to pinch you no matter what you were wearing.

"You're still here?" my best friend and co-owner of Death by Coffee, Vicki Lawyer, asked as she rounded the counter and entered the dining area, wet washcloth in hand, looking like a movie star, as she always did. "I thought you only stopped in to grab some coffee?"

"I was just leaving," I said, raising one hand in surrender. "I ran into Robert." I nodded toward his back. "He pinched me."

Vicki laughed. "I'll be sure to steer well clear of him, then."

The door jangled, and Rita Jablonski walked in. She was short, with round features, and an overly excited manner. She gave the long line a disapproving scowl before she noted Vicki and me standing off to the side. She headed our way.

"I'd best get back to work before I get dragged into a long conversation," Vicki said, nudging me with her shoulder. "You might want to hurry off too."

"You might be right." But it was already too late. As Vicki started wiping down tables, Rita approached, already talking.

"Oh my Lordy Lou," she declared, rubbing her hands together. "It's downright nippy out there this morning. You'd best make sure that jacket of yours is bundled up tight, Krissy Hancock, or else you're liable to freeze your tuchus off."

"I will," I said, taking in Rita's red cheeks and windblown hair. Strangely, I didn't think her appearance had anything to do with the weather, so I asked, "What have you been up to?"

"Oh, this and that." She waved me off. "Nothing for you to worry yourself over." She peered at my coffee. "Is that the Irish coffee I've been hearing about?"

"Yes, but that's not until later. At Bucky's Tavern. You know the place?"

"Of course I do, dear." She all but rolled her eyes at me. "Make sure they use Jameson with it, not any of the cheaper stuff. I'll know if they do."

I suppressed a smile. "I'll tell Bucky."

"See that you do." Rita nodded to herself and then looked toward the plate-glass window that fronted Death by Coffee. Shamrocks and redheaded leprechauns were pasted to the glass. She got a faraway look in her eye, and a faint smile graced her lips before she turned suddenly back to me. "Oh! I almost forgot to tell you. They're closing the library."

"What?" My eyes widened in shock. "Why?"

"They got funding. Well, not funding exactly, but a donation. The way I hear it, it's a big one. Not some piddly couple of bucks that might buy them a new bookshelf or two, but the real deal."

"Hold up. If they got a big donation, why are they closing?"

"You know that empty stretch of land out near the park?"

I nodded.

"Well, the town is developing it and is going to turn it into . . . honestly, I don't know what they're thinking. I like having everything here downtown. It's nice to be able to walk anywhere I need to be, you know? If you start putting businesses all the way out there, I'm going to have to drive all over town to do my shopping."

"Pine Hills *is* growing," I pointed out.

"Yes, well, I don't much care for it." Rita bristled a moment longer before her face brightened. "But I can't be unhappy about the fact that they are building a new library. It'll take a year or so to complete since they're starting from scratch, but I hear it's going to be a big one. Cindy told me that the plan is to have the building serve as a community hub. They'll host events and small groups and everything."

"That sounds good," I said, though I wondered why I hadn't heard about it yet. Death by Coffee often donated books to the library, so I'd worked with Cindy Carlton and her husband, Jimmy, quite a lot over the years.

"It is, dear. It is." Rita nodded sagely, and then, noting the line was mostly gone, clapped her hands together. "I'd best grab my coffee now, while there's a break. I'm sure I'll be seeing you around. That is, unless you plan on having a bit too much to drink later this evening." There was a strange twinkle in her eye that made me realize I shouldn't pursue that line of thought any further.

"Check out the books before you go," I said, gesturing toward the stairs that led up to the bookstore portion of Death by Coffee. "There's a St. Patrick's Day display just up the steps. We've stocked one of Dad's old Irish Detective titles."

"I might do that," Rita said, eyeing the display, before she turned and joined the line for coffee. She had a thing for my dad, James Hancock, who just so happened to be her favorite author.

"See ya later, Kris," Robert said, two coffees in hand, before he used his backside to push his way out the door.

Mildly annoyed at him using a shortened version of my name—and because of the earlier pinch—I decided not to follow him out, just in case he wanted to continue our conversation.

So, instead, I wandered briefly around the dining area, adjusting the St. Patrick's Day decorations we'd hung up. Nearly everything was green, with bits of gold speckled in. One of our employees, Eugene Dohmer, had handled the decorations, and I thought he'd done a pretty good job of it. If it had been me, I wasn't so sure we'd have had much more than a single window clinger. I wasn't much of a decorator.

Upstairs, Vicki's black-and-white cat, Trouble, watched me from atop a table often used by a local board game group. I vaguely wondered if Yolanda and her crew would keep playing here, or if they'd move on to this new library Rita had mentioned once it was built. While a bigger space would be nice for them, I'd miss having them around.

Once I was certain Robert was long gone, I headed for the door, feeling mildly guilty for leaving the inevitable rush to everyone else. Today was an all-hands-on-deck situation, though I wasn't planning on helping out until after the parade.

The morning was, as Rita had pointed out, on the chilly side, though it was supposed to warm up later. I held my coffee close as I hurried to my car. Eucalyptus

Street was within long walking distance, but with the parade coming through downtown later, there was a strict no-parking rule being enforced along the route, which I'd kind of, sort of ignored when I'd stopped in at Death by Coffee. I might be engaged to the son of the police chief—who was a police officer himself, to boot—but that didn't mean I wouldn't earn myself a ticket if one of the other cops were to spot my vehicle parked where it shouldn't be.

Apparently, none had, because there was no ticket pinned beneath my windshield. Not wanting to tempt fate, I hurriedly climbed in behind the wheel and headed for Bucky's Tavern.

I drove slowly, taking in the sights, even though I'd seen them hundreds, if not thousands, of times before. Pine Hills was beautiful and had a charm I had yet to find anywhere else. Eucalyptus Street had once been a mostly empty stretch of fields and a smattering of small, independently owned businesses that didn't fit in anywhere else. But now, brand-new buildings speckled the landscape, many of which were still empty, but soon wouldn't be as their occupants finally moved in.

Bucky's Tavern was smack-dab in the center of the new stretch of businesses, which would eventually make it a great location, though, right now there was very little in the way of traffic. The owner, Bucky Sweeny, had big plans for his little place once more shops and restaurants started opening around him, and he hoped to get things kick-started by making a splash with our Irish coffee.

I was nervous since I wasn't much of a drinker and had little knowledge when it came to alcohol, even alcohol mixed with coffee. But I'd tried it, and it seemed like it was good to my unrefined palate, so I trusted that people would be pouring in to try it. Bucky claimed he'd added something a little special to the mix that would make it our own, though he hadn't said what that something might be.

I parked out front and carried my coffee inside Bucky's. The wooden exterior of the tavern gave the impression of a cozy log cabin. The interior mirrored that, with rustic tables and chairs in the center of the room. There was a wood-paneled bar to the left of the entrance, and a warm fireplace surrounded by small, two-person tables on the right. A door behind the counter led to the kitchen, while a hallway near the fireplace led to the restrooms. Patrons could order food with their beverage of choice, and the menu included meals for kids. Bucky's might be a bar, but it was of the family sort.

No one was occupying any of the tables now since Bucky's was closed, but that didn't mean the place was empty. Bucky was standing at the bar, talking to three of his employees. I knew all three by sight, though I hadn't yet had the chance to get to know any of them beyond putting names to faces.

"Don't let anyone or anything distract you from what we're doing here tonight," Bucky was saying as I approached. He was a man of average size, with a trimmed beard and short-cropped brown hair that matched his eyes. "Make sure everyone knows where we get our coffee from." He tipped his head my way. "But don't tell anyone what we're putting in it. Same goes for the green beer."

"It's just—" Grant Price, a thirty-something former musician with a shaggy haircut that hinted that he wasn't quite done with the music scene, started to say before Bucky cut him off with a raised finger.

"Don't matter what it is. Just don't talk about it. The mystique is part of the appeal." He turned to me. "Hey, Krissy. You ready for this?"

"Me? Of course." I smiled. "But once I'm done at Death by Coffee later, I'm going to get to enjoy the rest of my evening. I'm not working my tail off like you."

"Lucky you," he said, matching my smile. "I truly hope that we can pull this thing off right. There's been some rumblings that . . ." He trailed off with a frown, hand going to his belly. "Never mind that. I just want to see people come in and have a good time. If they enjoy themselves, I'm hoping they'll be back."

I glanced around. Bucky hadn't gone all out with the St. Patrick's Day decorations, but I did spot a few shamrock window clingers. And there *was* the green beer and Irish coffee, of course. "I don't think you have anything to worry about."

"What he's not saying is how the other bar owners around town want to shut him down." One of his bartenders, Kandice Vaughn, leaned on the counter, hand brushing briefly against Bucky's forearm, as she spoke. She had long, worn features that spoke of a lifetime of hard work and little rest. "Dwayne was in last night and made his thoughts rather clear on the matter."

Bucky frowned as he massaged his stomach, as if the topic was turning it sour. "It was nothing, really."

"Oh?" From her tone, I could tell they'd already had this discussion, and like now, had differing opinions.

"I don't call Dwayne threatening to break your nose 'nothing.' I thought I was going to have to call the police."

"It's that bad?" I asked.

Bucky shook his head, while Kandice nodded. "Ruth put him up to it, I'm sure," he said. Ruth Camden was the owner of a place simply called, Bar, while Dwayne Morris owned the Whistling Wet Weasel. I only knew them by name, mostly from conversations with Bucky. I'd met neither.

"Don't forget about Ivan," the oldest employee of Bucky's, Jazz Day, said. His gray hair was slicked back from a sloping forehead, dimpled with acne scars. When he smiled, it caused his dark blue eyes to light up.

"I wish I could," Bucky said with a grimace. Ivan McGraw owned what many considered the skeeviest bar in town, Beers and Rears. The name said everything you needed to know about the place—and the man who owned it.

"What did Ivan do?" I asked, already dreading the answer.

"Nothing," Bucky said, shooting Jazz a warning look. The older man raised his hands in surrender. "Don't you three have work to do? I need some coffee, or else my head's going to explode."

"I can get that for you," Grant said.

"Me too?" I asked, lifting my half-empty to-go cup. "I could use a top off."

Grant smiled, took my cup. "Sure."

As Jazz and Kandice started setting up, and Grant turned to pour our coffees, Bucky and I leaned against the bar to chat.

"Cooks are coming in in an hour," he said. "When they get here, I doubt I'll have a moment to spare. This is going to be as stressful of a day as I've ever had."

"Are you feeling okay?" I asked, noting how his hand went to his stomach again.

He glanced down, dropped his hand with a grimace. "Nerves. It's nothing. When I get worked up, I tend to feel it in my guts."

"I don't think you need to be nervous," I said, tamping down my own nervousness. "People are going to love this place."

"I hope so." He glanced toward where Grant was finishing up the coffees. A trio of coffeemakers was set up along the back counter. In a cupboard beneath the bar, bags of the coffee we served at Death by Coffee were stacked and ready to go. "I'm afraid . . . No, ignore me. You're right. It'll be fine."

I considered pressing him, but it was clear that his worries were upsetting his stomach more than he was letting on.

Grant returned, sliding a mug over to Bucky and handing me my to-go cup. "Was that a cookie I saw in your drink?"

"Sure was," I said, taking a sip. "Chocolate chip."

His nose scrunched up in disgust.

"It's an acquired taste." And was something I'd done since forever. I loved the gooey bits left over after the coffee was gone.

"I think I'm okay *not* acquiring it, if it's all the same to you," Grant said, before heading to the back to help with setup.

Bucky chuckled, then pushed away from the bar,

coffee in hand. "I should get back there and make sure I'm not forgetting something. You plan on stopping by later tonight?"

"I am. I'll bring Paul."

"I look forward to meeting him." His eyes flickered to the engagement ring on my finger, before returning to my face. "He's a lucky guy." Bucky saluted me with his coffee, then turned and headed for the back.

I'm the lucky one, I thought.

And then, with that happy thought firmly in mind, I left Bucky's Tavern to get ready for the St. Patrick's Day celebration.

2

I shivered as I took a bite from my Irish cream and chocolate-chip ice cream. Out of the green-colored choices offered by Scream for Ice Cream, it sounded the most, well, St. Patrick's Day adjacent. Mint chocolate chip was usually a favorite, and pistachio was a flat no for me, so I'd opted out of those two. I could have also ordered plain old vanilla with green food coloring, but that was boring.

So, Irish cream it was.

I left the ice cream shop and started down the sidewalk, disposable bowl and plastic spoon in hand. It felt like the entirety of Pine Hills was out and enjoying the day. The sidewalks were packed, and since the road was closed for the upcoming parade, just as many people were walking down the street as well. The sun had come out from behind the fluffy white clouds it had been hiding behind earlier. Its warmth counteracted the chilly breeze, though my ice cream kept me huddled in my jacket.

My pace was leisurely as I ate. I didn't think I'd ever seen the town get so excited for a holiday before. And while green wasn't my favorite color, it was fun to see how everyone included it into their getups. Not everyone had gone all out like Robert, but there were a few leprechauns and a handful of women in what I took for Celtic outfits, with knots and very nature-centric themes dominating their attire. Mostly, I spotted green undershirts, ties, and more green ribbons than I could count.

"Hey, Krissy!" A woman who looked too young to be wearing a police uniform trotted over to me and gave me a hug. "This is nuts."

"Lena!" I returned the hug one-armed, as not to spill my ice cream. "It's hard to believe there's so many people living in Pine Hills."

"Tell me about it." She stepped back with a grin. Lena Allison had once been an employee at Death by Coffee, but had recently joined the police force. It was still odd to see her dressed without her skateboard and all the scrapes and bruises that came along with it. I *was* glad to see purple hair poking out from beneath her cap. It meant the department wasn't forcing her to change too much, though I'm sure some people didn't like it.

"I see they have you working," I said.

"Everyone is." Lena made a face, but brightened. "I get off early, so I'll be able to have a little fun tonight." Her eyes drifted to my finger, which was a common occurrence with people I knew these days. "You and Paul have plans for later?"

I smiled. "Now, what kind of lady would I be if I told you *that*?"

Lena snorted. "Well, he seemed like he was excited when I saw him earlier. He's around here somewhere." She glanced around as if she expected to spot him in the crowd. "Chief Dalton is wandering around here too. Maybe you can sweet-talk her into letting Paul off early."

I laughed. "Right. I don't think anyone has ever been able to sweet-talk her into anything."

"You're probably right." Lena shoved her hands into her pockets and hunched her shoulders. It made her look even younger than she had before. "I should get back to it. I doubt anything's going to happen this early in the day, but you never know. I've already spotted a group of guys carrying around water bottles I'm ninety percent sure aren't filled with water."

"Sounds like you'll have your hands full later."

"I hope I'm off before they get *too* tipsy." She leaned in close. "We can leave the drunks to Buchannan."

John Buchannan, my former nemesis–turned–police detective. He still sometimes liked to hound me whenever I got involved in one of his investigations, but he'd mellowed out on me over the years.

"I'm sure he'll love that," I said.

"I bet—hey! Stop that!" Lena gave me an exasperated look before she rushed over to where a group of teenage boys were trying to climb a light pole in a vain attempt to reach the shamrock hanging from it.

I chuckled as I left her to it. As the day went on, it would only get crazier.

By the time I reached Lawyer's Insurance, I'd finished my ice cream. I dumped the disposable cup into one of the many trash cans placed along the parade route and considered crossing the street to Death by Coffee for a warmup. Grant's refill was already gone, cookie goop included. Between the crowd and the window decorations, I could hardly see through the front window of the bookstore café. And what I could see showed me a nearly full dining area.

I opted against the coffee and instead picked my way through the growing crowd until I reached Phantastic Candies. An army of small leprechauns poured out just as I opened the door. They were followed by a harried woman dressed in a green nun's outfit. I stepped aside and held the door open for them as the kids scurried past, chattering about their sugar-infused finds. The woman thanked me before hustling after the kids, who weren't waiting on her.

"Krissy!" Jules Phan was standing behind the counter of his candy shop, dressed in a bright green outfit that was just this side of blinding. Literally. Every time he moved, the light caught the sequins, causing his every motion to flash, almost like a strobe. "In the mood for something chocolaty?"

"Always," I said, letting the door close behind me. "Been busy?"

"Always," he said with a grin. "How about you? I heard you were teaming up with Bucky Sweeny on his alcoholic coffee. How is that going?"

"Great, actually. Bucky's nervous, but I think it's going to work out."

"That's good to hear. Lance and I went to his tavern

the day after it opened. It's a nice place." Lance and Jules had lived together since I'd known them. They were my neighbors, and while I wasn't sure if they'd ever officially tied the knot—I was too much of a coward to ask, and neither wore rings—I thought of them that way. I couldn't imagine one without the other.

I crossed the room and peered into a shamrock-shaped tub placed by the counter. It was filled with more shamrock-shaped items. I looked a question at Jules.

"Green chocolate," he said. "Well, white chocolate with food coloring in it. Try one."

He didn't have to ask me twice. I scooped up a shamrock, unwrapped it, and popped it into my mouth. White chocolate wasn't my favorite, but it was still chocolate. Outside pure dark chocolate, I loved it all.

"Where's your fiancé?" Jules asked, propping his chin into his hands, elbows on the counter. "I figured the two of you would be attached at the hip."

I finished chewing and swallowed before answering. "He had to work or else we would be." Reflexively, I reached out and touched the ring on my finger, despite Jules not eyeing it like everyone else seemed to. I was struck anew by how *strange* it felt to wear the ring there. Butterflies flittered in my stomach, and my head did this little floaty thing, all while my heart pitter-pattered like I was a teenager thinking about her first crush.

Paul and I had dated for years, so I shouldn't have felt so goofy thinking about marrying him, but I did. I was pretty sure my dad thought that I'd never get married, that my lack of social skills would keep me from ever finding "the one." Heck, I'd thought much the same myself, and had contented myself with living alone with my cat, Misfit, for all eternity.

Yet here I was, engaged to be married, with what was quite literally the man of my dreams.

"Have you two figured out your living situation?" Jules asked, brow furrowing. "I can't imagine you not living next door to me, but honestly, that house of yours is too small for the both of you."

"Not yet," I said. "We're going to look at a place to-morrow."

"Serious?"

I made a seesaw gesture. "It's mostly just to see what's out there. It's one thing to look at pictures on-line . . ."

Jules nodded. "But another to see it in person. I get it. Every once in a while I take a peek at what's out there too. Not that Lance and I plan on moving. Just curious, you know? I saw this one house that looked huge online, but didn't look at the details. When I drove by to see it in person, it couldn't have been any more than seven hundred square feet. It's the angles. They take the photos so that everything looks bigger and better than it really is."

"And cleaner," I added.

He pointed at me and nodded. "You get the right person taking the pictures, and they can make any-where look like Buckingham Palace."

After I left Jules a few minutes later—with a bag of chocolates tucked under my arm—I worked my way back to Death by Coffee. I kept an eye out for Paul, though finding him in the crowd would be next to impossible. I could have texted him and asked him where he was, but that felt, I don't know, too clingy. Besides, we were due to meet up once everything died down. My house might be small for the both of us to comfortably live long-term, but it wasn't too small for a sleepover.

Death by Coffee was still hopping when I arrived, so even though it was early, I slid behind the counter and pitched in. There were lulls here and there, but they were just long enough to get things cleaned up before a new wave of green-clad customers would enter and the rush would start all over again.

It was a relief when music started from down the street and everyone poured outside to watch the parade go by. I stood with Vicki and her husband, Mason Lawyer, as it drifted past. The high school marching band led the way, dressed in Pine Hills High colors—green and white, of course. They were followed by the cheerleaders and then a group of men and women tossing green-wrapped candy—which I had a feeling was supplied by Jules and his candy shop—to the kids.

One leprechaun seemed especially raucous as he flung his candy outward, almost violently. It took me a moment to realize it was Robert in his leprechaun getup. His grin was infectious, and I found myself cheering him on as he passed, clicking his heels together as he danced and tossed his candy.

Next came trucks pulling trailers behind them. They moved at a glacial pace, so as not to upset the acts and displays riding on them. There were musicians, dancers, and in one instance, something that looked like a giant green cake. I kept waiting for someone to pop out of the top, but if they were in there, they never did.

I was watching a fiddler pass slowly by, playing an upbeat tune that had everyone's legs bouncing with the beat, when someone jostled into me. It took me a moment to realize the retreating back I was looking at belonged to Bucky Sweeny.

I frowned, checking the time. The parade still needed to wind around the town, but Bucky was supposed to be at his tavern, preparing for the flood of people that would descend on his place once it was done. He was walking quickly, bumping into people as he passed, hand massaging his stomach.

Vicki and Mason were lost in the parade—and each other, considering how his hand snaked around her waist—so they hadn't noticed Bucky passing by. I started to tell them that I'd be right back, but a crash of cymbals heralded an incoming drummer, so I didn't bother; they wouldn't have heard me even if I'd shouted.

Leaving them to enjoy the music, I hurried after Bucky, curious—and worried.

I didn't catch up to him until he paused to lean against a building down the street. He coughed into his hand, shook his head, and then lowered it briefly before taking a deep breath and starting forward again.

"Bucky!" I shouted. He didn't appear to hear me, so I sped up and then reached out to touch him when I was close enough.

He jerked like I'd pinched him, then spun around, eyes wide and startled. "Krissy," he said, my name coming out almost as a gasp. "It's you."

Who did you expect it to be? I wondered, but didn't say it. Bucky was looking decidedly green around the edges, enough so that my worry increased tenfold.

"Bucky? Are you feeling okay?" I asked him, though it was obvious he wasn't.

He started to say something, but ended up coughing instead. He sniffed, then cleared his throat, before wiping tears from his watering eyes. "I'm fine," he said. "That upset stomach is turning into a right bugger. I needed fresh air, so I went for a walk." He gestured around him with the hand not rubbing his stomach. "Really. I'm okay."

I didn't believe him. "Maybe you should go lie down," I said. "Or I could get you a cup of coffee at Death by Coffee." On second thought . . . "Or a water." Bucky looked as if anything stronger might do him in.

"I'll be fine." Even as he said it, his nostrils flared, and his cheeks puffed out as he suppressed another cough. "Stop by for some Irish coffee later, all right? We can talk about it then."

I nodded absently as he turned and walked away. He didn't quite stagger, but it was clear something wasn't right with Bucky Sweeny, whether it be an anxiety-induced upset stomach or a virus. He made it a few steps, then paused to cough into his hand, before he pushed forward and vanished into the crowd.

I watched him go, concern etched on my face. I turned to return to Vicki and Mason, and walked directly into someone hurrying in the same direction as Bucky.

"Sorry!" the man said without looking at me. I recognized his shaggy head of hair instantly, and was surprised to see him there. "Excuse me, please."

"Grant," I said, "it's me."

He blinked. "Oh, Krissy. I wasn't watching where I was going." He still wasn't. He was craning his neck, staring into the crowd where Bucky had vanished.

"What's going on?" I asked him, rising up on my tiptoes so that he had no choice but to look at me. "I just saw Bucky. He's looking rough."

Grant finally stopped searching for his boss and met my eye. He appeared as worried as I felt. "That's why I'm here and not back at the tavern," he said. "But I suppose he's gone now."

"You were following him?"

He nodded. "Kandice is worried about him." A crescendo of music swelled, then gave way to cheering. The tail end of the parade passed by where we stood, and people started filtering off for the next phase of their celebration. "I was told to keep an eye on him, but now I've lost him."

The "*thanks to you*" was implied.

"He seems sick," I pointed out.

"Kandice thinks it's something he ate." Grant frowned. "Though I'm not sure he had much to eat today. He's really worried about how things are going to go tonight. And with the other bar owners hounding him . . ." He frowned, as if he'd said too much.

"Grant?" I asked. "Did something happen after I left earlier?"

He bit his lip and looked like he wasn't going to say, before relenting. "It's Ivan. He called. I heard Bucky shouting through the door, but I couldn't make out what he said. As soon as he hung up, he left, looking like, well . . . *that*."

"And you followed him."

"Kandice told me to." He fidgeted. "I really should get back and let her know I lost track of him." Grant spun and speed-walked his way back down the sidewalk. I lost him quickly in the dispersing crowd.

Torn, I turned back the way Bucky had gone. If he'd gotten a call from Ivan McGraw that had upset him enough to walk away from his tavern on such an important day, then whatever they'd talked about had to have been a big deal. I didn't quite buy that he simply needed air. He'd been too determined—too distracted, even—for it to be that simple.

I hoped he wasn't going to get into a fight. Bucky and Ivan were both grown adults, so I'd like to have thought they'd hash out their differences in a more civilized way.

Then again, Ivan's place, Beers and Rears, was in the other direction, and it was nowhere near Death by Coffee. I expected Ivan was tucked away in his bar, prepping for his own St. Patrick's Day event, and not out wandering the streets somewhere.

But if Bucky wasn't going after Ivan, where was he going?

I headed back to Death by Coffee, doing my best to suppress my concern for Bucky's well-being. I hoped that when I went to his tavern later that evening, he'd be there, healthy and without a scratch on him.

Vicki and Mason were back inside Death by Coffee, which was hopping again, now that the parade had passed. I was about to head inside to join them when I finally spotted that certain someone who made my heart do flips and who caused my worries to flitter away.

"There you are." Paul Dalton's face broke into a wide smile, which caused his dimples to appear as he strode toward me. He was in uniform, though the undershirt peeking out from under his collar was green instead of his typical white. He gave me a hug that I wanted to fall into forever, before he stepped back. "I thought I'd stop by before I got back to work."

"I'm glad you did." I didn't add that his mere presence had lifted my spirits. I was pretty sure he already knew. "Once I head inside, I'm going to be swamped until we close, so this might be our only chance to talk until later."

"So, we're still on for tonight, then?" he said, a mischievous gleam coming into his eyes. "I just want to make sure so I don't exhaust myself too early."

The way he said the last caused a blush to flood my cheeks. "We're still on," I said, somehow managing to keep the squeak out of my voice. "I'll want to stop by Bucky's Tavern after I'm done here, but afterward, I'm all yours."

Paul leaned forward and kissed me on the temple. "Of course you are. Always will be."

And before I could respond to that, he turned and walked away, leaving me staring dumbly after him, wondering how in the world I'd gotten so lucky.

3

I cracked open an eye and immediately shut it again. Light pounded against my eyelids, almost a physical thing, and seared straight into my brain. A meow that sounded like it came from an inch away from my eardrum followed a moment later, accompanied by the tickle of long white whiskers in my nose. I groaned and pulled my pillow over my face to try to make the throbbing inside my skull stop.

It didn't help.

Paul had left sometime before I'd awakened, likely in far better condition than I was. I still had another ten minutes before my alarm would go off, yet I was already awake, and there was no going back to sleep. My body, despite its current state, still ran on an internal clock that refused to shut down and had me up like, well, clockwork. I was desperate for a shower, but the mere thought of dragging myself out of bed took a herculean effort. The actual act was, therefore, virtually impossible.

After I'd finished at Death by Coffee the night before, and before Paul was officially off duty, I'd paid a visit to Bucky's Tavern. The place had been packed, but Bucky was nowhere in sight, so I'd grabbed an Irish coffee, hung around for a few minutes to drink it, and then went in search of Paul. We'd later sat down to a fantastic St. Patrick's Day dinner together, which had included another drink or two, and before I knew it, I was back home, wondering where the time had gone.

A sudden weight pressed down on my pillow, which was still on my face, smothering me. A knee-jerk yelp and a flail followed. I cracked the back of my arm against the nightstand, which sent shooting pain through my entire body, as the heavy lump transferred from my pillow to my chest. I gasped for air, cracked open my eye again, and was rewarded by a blast of kitty breath as Misfit meowed in my face.

"Fine," I muttered, displacing him to the floor. "I'm up."

He led the way to the kitchen, tail swishing as if I'd made him wait well beyond normal breakfast time, which, for the record, I hadn't. I went to rub at my arm, but jerked back with a wince as soon as my fingers touched it. A quick look, which involved an undignified lifting of the arm and tugging on the underside flesh to be able to see, and I noted the bruise, complete with a greenish center. I hadn't gotten that on my nightstand, so what had actually happened?

It took all of two seconds to figure it out.

Robert and his pinch. I ground my teeth together. I *knew* I'd have a bruise, and sure enough, there it was.

Misfit meowed, peered into his empty bowl, and then slammed his entire body into my shins.

"It's coming," I groused.

I fed the orange fluffball and worked my way through my shower in something of a daze. When I finished my routine, I felt a little better, though every time I bumped my arm or moved it the wrong way, it twinged. A jolt of coffee—complete with the requisite chocolate-chip cookie—and I was out the door, ready to take on the world.

Or, at least, other hungover coffee drinkers.

A line had already formed outside Death by Coffee by the time I arrived. It was a good thirty minutes until we were due to open, but that mattered little for those jonesing for their morning jolt. Haggard faces looked at me hopefully as I slipped through the doors with murmured apologies.

"Hey, Ms. Hancock." Jeff Braun rose from a crouch from behind the counter as I entered. Coffee was already percolating behind him.

"Hi, Jeff." I removed my jacket and carried it toward the closet-sized space we called an office. "I might open a few minutes early if you think everything's close enough to ready?" I made it a question.

"Should be good," he said. "But I'll head to the back and check." He stifled a yawn, then vanished through the door that led to the back room. As the door swung closed, I heard Beth Milner say something to him that had the tone of being an affirmative, though I couldn't make out exactly what she'd said.

It was good enough for me.

It took ten minutes more before the register was set up and good to go, and then I opened the door to the ever-growing line of customers. St. Patrick's Day decorations were still up inside Death by Coffee, and would likely remain for the rest of the week. It would probably take that long for the town to recover after the parade and after-hours celebrations.

A man shambled his way up to the counter, still dressed in full green, though he now had a damp, rumpled look to him. Heavy-lidded eyes roved their way up to the menu board, then he muttered, "Coffee," as if it were the only word he could form. He then folded his arms on the counter, lowered his head onto them, and promptly fell asleep, half-standing up.

I retrieved his coffee, roused him enough to guide him to a corner table, and then returned behind the register, where I remained for the next hour and a half. Both Beth and Jeff ran orders, doing their best to keep the coffee coming, though with just the three of us, it wasn't an easy task, especially when one of us needed to clean the tables or take care of a customer in the bookstore.

"So much for everyone sleeping in," Beth said as she rushed past me, on her way to deal with a spill near the restrooms.

I grunted in response. When we'd created the schedule for the day, Vicki and I had assumed that most everyone would be too tired—and yes, hungover—to get up early. We figured we'd have the usual morning work crowd to contend with, maybe a few stragglers who'd spent the entire night out, but not *this*.

Thankfully, Jeff and Beth had been with Death by Coffee for a long time, so we worked well together, each knowing what to do and when to do it. Yes, another hand or two would have been nice, but we managed. Somehow.

Once the rush died down, I helped catch up with the cleaning, and then took a quick break before I collapsed on my feet. Beth and Jeff seamlessly shifted roles so they could serve the remaining trickle of customers and restock. I felt like a wimp as I dropped into a chair by the door, completely spent.

I'd no more than sat down when the door opened and a familiar face entered. Justin had long hair, cut to just beneath his chin, that hung down into his face, concealing his eyes. He paused just inside the door and ran a hand through his hair, pushing it back so he could see. He glanced toward the counter, frowned, and then turned my way. His eyes immediately lit up, and he headed over to my table.

"Good morning, Justin," I said, motioning to the chair across from me. "Would you like to take a seat?"

"Morning, Ms. Hancock." He hesitated with a nervous fidget before he sat.

"Call me Krissy," I reminded him. He had been for a while, so this sudden reversion to formality had me worried. Justin worked at Ted and Bettfast and took care of his younger sister, which had once included stealing from bed-and-breakfast guests to make ends meet. He'd stopped doing that, and had seemingly righted the boat when it came to his family life over the last few years. I wasn't used to seeing him here at Death by Coffee. "Did you get to watch the parade yesterday?"

A faint smile flickered across his face. "Yeah. Took Emily." I assumed that was his sister. Strange how I'd never gotten her name before, but it wasn't like Justin and I hung out. "We didn't stay long." His smile faded.

"Justin." I leaned forward. "What's wrong?"

He paused, glancing around the room. No one was paying us any mind. The dining room was mostly full, but everyone was too busy nursing their coffees—and headaches, in most cases—to care what we were talking about.

"Do you remember what we talked about the last time we spoke?" he asked.

"I do." Though, much to my dismay, that had been many, *many* months ago. Had time really gotten away from me that badly? "You were worried about what would happen if Ted and Bett were to sell the bed-and-breakfast."

He nodded, then chewed on his lower lip.

He didn't need to say anything. I knew what was wrong. "Robert fired you."

" 'Fired' might be the wrong word."

"Do you have a job at Ted and Bettfast anymore?"

He winced as if I'd struck him. "No."

A flash of anger shot through me. "Why not?" If Robert Dunhill were to have walked through the door right then, I would . . . well, I wasn't sure what I would have done. I wasn't a violent person. And with how I was feeling at the moment, I doubted I could do much more than give him the worst tongue-lashing of his life.

Justin picked at his thumbnail, but wouldn't look up.

"Justin," I said, sternly enough that he finally met my eye. "Tell me what happened."

"Nothing really happened," he said. "There's just no place for us anymore."

"'Us'?" My stomach fell as Justin nodded.

"Kari, Jo, and me."

"He fired *all* of you?" It took all my self-control not to storm out of Death by Coffee and drive over to Robert's place to yell at him. "Why?"

"Don't be mad at him," Justin said, a faint pleading tone to his voice. "I don't think he had much choice, and he's treated us the best he could under the circumstances. But . . ." He cleared his throat and looked away. "I was hoping that maybe you'd be willing to . . . you know?"

I worked my jaw, still angry with Robert. Justin took my silence the wrong way. He started to stand.

"I'm sorry," he said. "I didn't mean—"

"No, it's not that." I waved him back down. "I can't believe Robert would do this." Which wasn't exactly true. It was *exactly* the sort of thing Robert Dunhill would do. "You want a job."

Justin's nod was slow before he murmured, "All of us would like one, if possible."

I took a breath to calm myself. I'd promised Justin that if Robert were to let him and the others go, they could come to Death by Coffee, and we'd find a place for them. Originally, the offer was for Jo and Justin since Kari Collins was a bit on the cantankerous side. But if he was asking for her too, could I really say no?

"Okay," I said, and then, before he could get too excited, I added, "You'll have to apply. All of you."

His brow furrowed, but he nodded.

"I'm not backing out of what I told you," I said. "But I'm not the only owner here. Vicki will happily take you all on, but she'll want to do it right."

"So, applications?"

"Wait here a sec." I stood and went into the back. It took me a moment, but I found our applications stuffed into a desk drawer. I returned to Justin and handed three of them to him. "Give one each to Kari and Jo. The other's for you. You can stay here and fill yours out now if you'd like. I'll talk to Vicki and let her know what's going on. There shouldn't be any issues, just as long as you fill them out properly."

Justin blinked rapidly. If he started crying, I would too.

"Get these back to me as soon as you can," I said. "The sooner the better, all right?"

"Thank you, Ms.—"

I gave him a stern look.

"Krissy." Finally, a real smile crossed his face. "Thank you so much."

Justin didn't fill out his application there, but instead popped to his feet and hurried out the door. I wondered if he was heading straight to the others to give them the good news.

I liked Justin. And to some extent, Jo, though she'd soured on me over the years, thanks to some murders that had happened around Ted and Bettfast. But Kari . . . she'd be a challenge, one I was willing to take on, albeit with some reservations. She could be grumpy, and

I doubted she'd be good with the customers, so it wasn't like I could trust putting her on the register.

We could always put her on jobs that don't require her to talk to anyone. Organizing books. Cleaning up the back, wiping down tables.

I finished off my coffee as I mentally worked out how we could best manage the schedule with three new additions. I didn't want to cut anyone's hours, so that was out. But having extra hands around the place might mean that both Vicki and I could spend more time away from the bookstore café than we already did. Money wouldn't be an issue; we did great business, and Vicki and Mason were wizards with managing the expenses.

My short break had done me good. I was still irked at Robert, but I had some of my energy back and was ready to get back to work. I stood to toss my empty cup into the trash, but before I could do much more than reach my feet, the door burst open, and Rita Jablonski came flying in like her hair was on fire.

"Oh my Lordy Lou, can you believe what's happened? I've been on the phone about it all morning and was just able to get free!"

All eyes in the place swiveled her way. Many of them were narrowed in annoyance, considering how loud and boisterous Rita was being.

"Rita," I said, tapping my hand in the air, hoping she'd get the message and lower her voice. "It's early."

She didn't seem to notice, just plowed ahead at full volume. "When I woke up this morning, I just knew something was wrong. My head was all fuzzy, and I kept expecting my phone to ring at any moment. And you know what?"

I opened my mouth to answer, but she barreled on right over me.

"It did! Georgina was calling me to let me know all about it. You remember Georgina? She was all in a tizzy because it happened right down the street from her. She said all the noise woke her up, and at her age, she needs all the sleep she can get."

Georgina McCully was one of Rita's older friends and gossip buddies.

"What did Georgina say?" I asked, curious despite myself.

"She wasn't sure what was happening at first. You know, with the whole St. Patrick's Day stuff going on, she figured it might be some of the younger folks on her street getting back late." Rita paused. "Well, early, I suppose. I never know how to put it when someone comes slinking back home early in the morning. They're late getting home, but the time is early, and—"

"Rita!" I cut her off. "What happened?"

Rita bristled only slightly at my interruption, and then went right back to her story. "So, there she was, getting out of bed when she rightfully should have still been asleep. She said she looked out the window to see what the ruckus was about, but she couldn't see anything. She could hear it all right, but not see it, at least, not well enough to know what was happening. She got dressed as quickly as she could, which at her age, takes some doing, you know?"

A dramatic pause. I filled it with, "And then?"

"And then, when she finally made it outside, she realized that it wasn't just some kids, but rather, the police were milling around down the street, about five houses down. She wasn't sure what they were doing since her eyesight isn't what it used to be and it being so early in the morning and all."

The door opened, and Todd Melville walked in. He paused, took a deep breath, and smiled so wide, it lit his entire face up. He gave me a nod, then sauntered up to the counter to order. I watched him, amazed. Todd was allergic to cats. And while Trouble wasn't in yet, the fact that he'd ever been here at all was usually enough to set Todd's allergies off.

Yet, here he was, breathing in the air like everyone else, without a sniffle or a sneeze in sight.

"Are you even listening to me?" Rita said, planting her hands on her hips.

"Sorry." I turned my attention back to her. "You said the police were a few houses down?"

She gave me a disapproving look before continuing. "Like I was saying, everyone thought he'd had too much to drink and simply passed out. You know how some people can be? They can't hold their liquor, and the next thing you know, they're staggering down dark alleys, with no idea where they are." She sniffed, as if she'd never overindulged. "But he wasn't just passed out." She shook her head sadly, then finally lowered her voice. "He was dead."

Ghostly fingers ran up and down my spine. I glanced around the room, noted how the annoyed expressions had turned to ones of interest, so I pulled Rita aside. Not that there was anywhere private we could go, but I didn't want to talk about this while standing in the middle of the room.

"Who was it?" I asked, keeping my voice low.

Rita took my hands and squeezed them. "I'm so sorry, dear," she said. "I know you knew him."

Impatience made the "Knew who?" come out like a demand.

"Why, Bucky Sweeny, dear. They found him unresponsive in the bed of a pickup truck."

4

"Here you go." I handed the coffee across the counter. The woman thanked me, but I barely heard her. I was focused on the door, waiting for it to open and for Paul or one of the other Pine Hills police officers to walk in and ask me about Bucky Sweeny.

No, I didn't know what had happened to him, whether it was an accident, natural causes, or murder. Georgina—and, therefore, Rita—didn't know anything beyond the fact that Bucky was found dead in the back of a pickup truck. And the only reason Georgina knew it was Bucky was because someone in the neighborhood had caught a glimpse of him and had told her before she'd called Rita.

I kept thinking about when I'd last seen him, how sick he'd looked. He'd claimed it was an upset stomach—from nerves or illness, I didn't know—but one bad enough to kill him? It seemed far-fetched, but who knew? He *had been* stressed about the pressure he was receiving from the other bar owners about the tavern, which was so new that if something were to go horribly wrong, it could close them for good.

Horribly wrong, like Bucky's death?

With no further customers in line, I drifted into the back room and just stood there. I wondered what would happen to Bucky's Tavern now. He hadn't been married, didn't have family that I knew about. I supposed it was possible that his parents could still be alive somewhere, or that he could have a brother or sister waiting in the wings, but if so, he'd never talked to me about them.

Then again, I was just his coffee source. Why *would* he talk about his family to me? We might have been becoming friends, but we weren't quite there yet, at least not to the point where we'd feel comfortable sharing private information.

Still, I *had* known him, and now I desperately wanted to find out what had happened to him. I pulled out my phone, and after a brief debate with myself, I put in the call.

"Krissy," Paul said by way of answer. "I can't talk right now. There's . . . a situation."

"I know. I've already heard about Bucky."

A pause, and then, "Rita?"

"Who else?"

"What did she say?"

"Not much," I admitted. "She said that Bucky was found in the back of a truck. Georgina McCully lives just down the street from where he was found. She saw what was happening, and of course, called Rita to tell her all about it."

"I see." He sighed. Being a police officer in a town where rumor and speculation flew around at the speed of light had to make his job that much more difficult. "There's not much else I can tell you at this point."

Bucky's face flashed before my mind's eye. The cough. The constant rubbing of his stomach. "Bucky was sick," I said. "Like, really, *really* sick. I saw him at the parade and was worried about him."

"How sick are we talking?"

"He could hardly walk straight," I said. "I was afraid he might collapse, but he insisted he was fine. He said it was a stomach bug, but it looked like more than that."

There was a long stretch of silence as Paul absorbed what I'd said.

I couldn't stand listening to the dead air, so I filled it. "He kept coughing and rubbing at his stomach. It seemed to get worse throughout the day, but I only saw him twice, so that's just a guess on my part. One of his employees said they were worried he'd eaten something that didn't agree with him. And with the stress of the day, it might have made things worse. Could something like that actually kill someone?"

"Honestly?" Paul said. "I'm not sure what we're dealing with at the moment. We're still piecing things together, but it appears that he was indeed sick—there's evidence of that here, though I won't go into details. It looks as though he'd climbed into the bed of the truck on his own since there doesn't appear to be any signs of a struggle. There were minor wounds on his shoulder and head, but that looks to be from a fall, not any sort of attack. Currently, Detective Buchannan doesn't believe foul play was involved in his death. It's likely he overindulged and, well . . ." He left the rest unsaid.

I closed my eyes and leaned my head against the wall. "Does Kandice know? She works at Bucky's. I'm pretty sure they were close."

"No one has been informed as of yet, but you know how news flies around this town." My knowledge of the incident was evidence enough of that. "Look, Krissy, I've got to run. I'll stop by tonight, and we can talk about it, all right? I know you two were friends, and I don't want you to worry. We've got everything under control."

"Of course. I know you do."

We said our goodbyes, and I clicked off, unsettled. Bucky was dead, and I couldn't help but feel as if it was partly my fault. I should have stopped him when I'd seen him at the parade, forced him to come sit down for a few minutes. Maybe if I had, I could have convinced him to go to the doctor and he'd be alive today.

Stop it, Krissy. You don't know what happened, or when he died.

The door popped open, and Jeff poked his head in. "Ms. Hancock, someone is here to see you."

I took a breath and forced a smile. "I'll be right out."

Jeff hesitated, like he wanted to say something else, before he ducked back out the door.

I took a few deep breaths and steadied my features before I followed. I fully expected to find Detective Buchannan waiting for me on the other side of the

counter. Bucky might not have been murdered, but anytime someone died, especially someone I knew, Buchannan made it a point to warn me off of involving myself,
whether there was an investigation or not.

When I returned to the front, however, it wasn't Detective Buchannan standing on the other side of the
counter, but my friend Cassie Wise. She was dressed
in an all-green running outfit that she somehow made
fashionable. It helped that she was trim and fit and had
unblemished, dark skin that was the envy of any
woman who'd ever had a pimple.

"Cass!" I exclaimed, rounding the counter to give
her a hug I desperately needed. "What are you doing
here?"

She accepted the hug and then stepped back with a
smile. "I was in the neighborhood and thought I'd stop
by. We haven't had much of a chance to exercise together recently . . ." She gave me a meaningful look.

"Sorry about that," I said. "I've been so busy with—"

"You don't have to explain yourself," she said, eyes
flashing to my ring finger. "I get it."

"It's no excuse," I said. "Paul and I are still hammering out the details for the wedding, though you should
expect an invitation sometime in the very near future."
Or so I hoped. Sudden deaths had a way of getting in
the way of my plans, and I had a feeling that Bucky's
would be no exception. "How about we get together
later this week so I can give you all the juicy details?"

"You're on." Her Fitbit beeped. She checked it, tapped
something, and then gave me an exaggerated eye roll.
"I'd better get moving again. I just wanted to pop in
and say hi."

"I'm glad you did," I said. "Someone has to keep me honest." I patted my tummy, which had grown firmer ever since I'd started exercising with Cassie. It made me think of Bucky and all his stomach rubbing, and I forced myself to stop.

"Call me when you want to go for a run," she said. "I'll be sure you make up for lost time." She winked.

"You know it's not nice to threaten torture on a friend."

She laughed, and with a wave, headed out the door to continue her run.

I watched her go with some regret. I *had* been doing a poor job keeping in touch lately. Yes, I'd been busy with all the St. Patrick's Day stuff and wedding planning and everything that went along with getting married and changing everything about my life. But that didn't mean I should ignore my friends. It made me wonder when the last time was that I'd sat down and had dinner with Vicki and Mason. Sadly, I couldn't be certain. My days had turned into weeks, which had morphed into months, with me having no concept of how much time had truly passed.

I made a mental note to change that as I went back to work. I tried to keep my mind solely focused on the job, but I kept thinking about Bucky, about Kandice and Grant and Jazz. Like Justin, Jo, and Kari, the Bucky's Tavern employees could suddenly be out of a job, and this time, I didn't think offering them positions at Death by Coffee would help.

I went through the motions for a few hours more before saying my goodbyes. Jeff and the others had everything under control, so I wasn't needed anyway. I decided to head over to Bucky's Tavern to pay my condolences—or, if they didn't know, pass along the bad news. No, it might not have been my place, but I knew these people, albeit in a limited capacity, and it would probably be better coming from me. They deserved to know that their boss wasn't coming back.

Bucky's opened for lunch, so I expected there to be something of a crowd, yet when I pulled up, the door was closed, and Grant was standing outside it, peering through the front window. Every so often, he'd wince, shoulders hunching with the motion. I got out of my car and walked over to join him. My first look inside was accompanied by the sound of breaking glass. Kandice was behind the bar. Her face was red, and tears streamed down her face. She muttered something to herself, made a horrible, angry face, and then grabbed a glass from beneath the counter. She chucked it against the wall as hard as she could.

I joined Grant in flinching as it shattered.

"How long has she been doing that?" I asked him.

"Not sure. She's been at it since I got here ten minutes ago." He turned to me. "Have you heard about Bucky?"

"I have." I almost asked him how everyone was handling it, but one look inside answered that question.

"I can't believe it." Grant turned back toward the door and watched as Kandice tossed another glass against the wall. "No one can, really. Ruth Camden was here when I arrived, but she said she didn't have much luck talking to Kandice."

"Ruth was here?" I asked, surprised. The way they'd talked about her yesterday, I didn't think she'd much care about what had happened to Bucky.

"Yeah." Grant shrugged one shoulder. "She said Dwayne and Ivan had also come with her to pay their condolences, but they were gone before I got here."

I supposed I shouldn't have been too shocked that the other three bar owners had stopped by. They might not have gotten along with Bucky, but no one wanted to see someone else—even a rival—end up dead.

"She was in love with him," Grant said, nodding toward the window. Inside, Kandice was still raging. "It's really hit her hard because of where he was found."

I frowned. "In the back of a truck?"

"In the back of *Jaqueline's* truck."

I blinked at him. The name meant nothing to me.

"You don't know?" His eyes widened, and he ran a hand through his hair. "Oh man, I guess you wouldn't."

"Who's Jaqueline?" Though, looking at Kandice's reaction, I could hazard a guess. Grant's next words proved me mostly right.

"Jaqueline Lyon. Bucky's ex." He paused. "Though it appears as if he was trying to get back with her."

My heart sank. "He was cheating on Kandice with his ex?"

Grant shrugged, looked away. "That's the rumor. It's . . ." He shook his head. "Never mind."

"No, what?"

Grant took a moment to gather his thoughts before answering. "You remember when I ran into you yesterday?"

"Yeah." As if I could forget such a thing. "You were following Bucky. Kandice sent you because she was worried because he was sick and because Ivan had called, which had upset him."

Grant rubbed the back of his neck. "That wasn't entirely true. I mean, she *was* worried that he might have eaten something that disagreed with him, but that wasn't new. Bucky had some sort of condition that made it so almost everything he ate caused him to get sick. He never talked about it, and I don't know what it was called, but we all knew about it."

Everyone but me, apparently.

"Okay," I said. "Then, why were you following him if it wasn't because he was sick?"

"Kandice *did* send me," Grant said. "And she *did* say that she was worried about him. But . . ." He peered through the window. Kandice was no longer visible, having sunk down behind the bar. No more throwing of glasses. I didn't know if she'd run out, or if she'd gotten tired of the destruction.

"Grant?" I pressed. "Why'd she ask you to follow Bucky?"

He sighed, then turned to face me. "I think she was afraid he was going to see Jaqueline. I mean, she didn't say that then, but now, after what happened . . ." Another shrug. "I wonder if Ivan found out about it, and that's why he called that day. There's a rumor going around that Ivan was trying to blackmail Bucky. If he knew about Bucky and Jaqueline . . ."

Then it served to reason that he'd try to use it for his own personal gain somehow.

"Did anyone else suspect Bucky of cheating?" I asked, because I sure hadn't. "Jazz?"

Grant bit his lip, eyes flickering briefly away. "Jazz didn't say anything before today. He showed up for his shift like usual, but, well . . ." He motioned toward the door. "He started to say something about Bucky and Jaqueline, but then he got a call from his sister. She was upset—probably about Bucky. He was trying to talk her down when he left. I couldn't make out what she was saying, but whatever it was, she was saying it loudly."

Faint sobs came from inside. Kandice was in there, suffering alone. I didn't know her all that well, but I felt the need to go in and try to help if I could.

"Is the door unlocked?" I asked.

Grant shrugged. "Probably. I haven't checked. I don't think I'm strong enough to deal with this right now." He ran a hand over his eyes, then looked away. "I think I'm going to go home. I doubt we even open today." A brief pause, accompanied by a frown. "Or ever again, for that matter. Looks like I might have to start looking for a job. Again. I was really hoping I was done with that." He gave me a sad, weak smile, and then shuffled away, hands shoved deep into his pockets, shoulders hunched as if against a blow.

I waited until he was gone before I tested the door to find it was, indeed, unlocked. I entered Bucky's Tavern and walked slowly toward the counter.

"Kandice?" I called, keeping my voice calm and gentle. "It's Krissy Hancock."

A sniff and then she stood. Her eyes were red and

swollen, and her hair looked as if she'd been tugging at it for hours. She ran her fingers through it a few times to smooth out a few of the tangles, took a trembling breath, and then turned to face me.

"We're closed, though I suspect you figured that out already."

"I'm sorry about Bucky."

Kandice snorted. "Yeah, me too."

I came to a stop on the customer side of the bar. Shattered glass covered the floor on the other side. A few stray pieces lay atop the bar. Kandice brushed them away absently, and with the faintest blush of embarrassment.

"I talked to Grant outside," I said.

She gave me a side-eyed look, then went back to brushing more glass shards to the floor. She had a couple of small cuts on her hand and one on her cheek. She didn't seem to notice or care.

"He said you had been worried about Bucky."

"I was." She wiped her hands off on a towel she'd retrieved from beneath the bar. Only then did she notice the cuts. She stared at them for a long time before saying, "It appears as if I shouldn't have been."

"Because of Jaqueline?"

She flinched as if I'd struck her. "I can't believe he'd . . ." She took a trembling breath, looked as if she might grab another glass and throw it, but reconsidered. "She's married."

Once again, I was caught by surprise. "Jaqueline?"

"No, the queen of England." Clipped. "Of course Jaqueline."

I tried not to take offense at her tone. Kandice was hurting, and it *had* been a dumb question. "Do you really think Bucky was seeing her again?" I asked.

Kandice, seemingly calmer now, though I could see the anger still simmering behind her eyes, shrugged. "What else am I supposed to think? He was found in the back of her truck. At her *house*." The last was practically hissed. "Why would he go there if he wasn't seeing her behind my back?"

I had no answer to that, so I didn't try to provide one.

"I should have known better," she went on in my silence. "They were pretty serious before they broke up. Almost got married."

"You knew them when they were dating?"

Her nod was jerky. "It was, I don't know, fifteen years ago? Seems like a lifetime. They'd been together since they were in high school, which is an eternity at that age. When they broke up, it surprised me, but I couldn't say I was unhappy about it. I . . ." She cleared her throat, gave me another side-eyed glance. "Anyway, she started seeing Geno about a year after they'd called it quits. I could tell it broke Bucky's heart. He never got over her, I guess."

"They could have just been friends."

Kandice snorted. "Right. If that's all it was, why not tell me? It's not like I'd get angry with him for being friends with her. I'm not like that." Her jaw worked, and her entire demeanor changed. "I bet he did it," she said, voice growing firmer. "Geno. I bet he caught Jaqueline and Bucky together, and he killed him for it."

Her fists clenched, and her eyes blazed. She might be mad at Bucky for cheating—if he even *was* cheating—but that didn't mean she didn't still care about him.

"Do you think it could have been his stomach?" I asked. "The police don't think it was murder."

She laughed. It was a bitter sound. "His stomach hurt so badly, he decided to go to Jaqueline to make it better?"

"Bucky looked real sick when I saw him at the parade," I said, not taking offense at her tone.

"He sometimes drank too much," she said. Sudden tears filled her eyes as she continued to ride her roller coaster of emotions. "He'd start to get that discomfort in his stomach, and he'd grab a drink to ease it. When that didn't work, he'd try to drown it out, which often made him feel worse." She took a trembling breath, then went on. "And then, with the tavern opening, and his plans for St. Patrick's Day, it was all getting to him. The moment I saw him that morning, I knew it was going to be a bad one."

I thought back and wished I could have said the same. Bucky had been, well, Bucky. Yes, he'd incessantly rubbed his stomach, but honestly, I knew what it was like to worry so much that you made yourself sick, so it really wasn't all that strange. It wasn't until later, at the parade, that I'd noticed how bad he'd really looked.

"I'm sorry," Kandice said, cutting into my thoughts. "I really need to clean up this glass. We're not going to open today, but still . . ." She motioned for the door.

I wanted to stay and tell her that everything would

be all right, that the pain would stop and that her life would eventually get back to normal. But right then, that wasn't what Kandice Vaughn needed to hear.

What she needed was time.

"If you need anything, you can call me anytime," I said.

Kandice nodded and then turned toward the kitchen door, putting her back to me.

I watched her for a moment longer, and then I left her so she could grieve.

5

Paul didn't answer when I tried to call him a short time after leaving Bucky's Tavern. I wasn't surprised, considering the circumstances. Even if Bucky had died from food or alcohol poisoning combined with whatever stomach condition he'd been suffering from, there would still be a lot of work for him to do. I also didn't doubt the Pine Hills Police Station was packed full of hungover partiers who'd found themselves on the wrong side of the law for one misdemeanor or another.

As I drove back toward Death by Coffee, I kept thinking back to when I'd last seen Bucky. He'd looked sick, but not so sick that I'd thought he would *die* from it. There was no way I could have known what would happen to him, yet I felt as if I'd let him down somehow by *not* forcing him to sit down and talk to me.

The dining area inside the bookstore café was still relatively full of sleepy-eyed coffee drinkers as I entered. A soft murmur of voices filled the room as I made for the counter, where Beth Milner was leaning. She yawned as she straightened.

"Back again already?" she asked.

"Couldn't stay away."

"I'd say it's because of me and the rest of your fabulous crew, but I have a feeling it has more to do with the coffee than us." She smiled. "Want me to get you one?"

"That's okay, you can go back to relaxing. I can get it." I rounded the counter to do just that. "Is Vicki in yet?" I hadn't seen her car when I'd parked, but I hadn't exactly been looking for it either.

Beth resumed her relaxed pose, crossing her arms and ankles. "She's upstairs with Trouble. Book delivery came in, and she's sorting through it. Jeff's taking a break. I think he's bringing back some ice cream for everyone. I can share mine if you want to stick around and have some."

Ice cream sounded great right about then, especially with a hot coffee on the side. "We'll see," I said. "I'm not staying long."

Beth shrugged. "Suit yourself. More for me."

I watched the bubbles rise from the cookie at the bottom of my cup before taking a sip. I closed my eyes to savor it, then headed back around the counter and into the dining room. I didn't see Vicki from there, so I went up the three steps, rounded a bookshelf, and there she was, sitting cross-legged on the floor, a stack of books beside her. Trouble was curled up in her lap, contently snoozing away.

Just like Vicki was.

Trouble opened one eye, then covered his face with his paw. He looked like most everyone else in Pine Hills—tired and maybe a little hungover. I wondered if Vicki had broken out the catnip last night so he could partake in the celebrations. The thought made me smile as I came to a stop in front of where Vicki sat.

"You're in my light," she said without opening an eye.

"Rough night?" I asked.

She made a noncommittal sound.

"I take it Mason decided to stay home today?"

"The wimp could hardly climb out of bed. Tried to get me to stay there with him, but I wanted to make sure I got this done." She flopped a hand to the side and nearly knocked over the stack of books.

"Looks like you're making great progress."

Finally, an eye opened. She stuck her tongue out at me, then leaned her head back again. "Beth said everything went smoothly this morning. I was kind of worried when I saw how many people were still out in the wee hours."

"Like you?"

"Blame Mason. I wanted to be in bed by midnight. He wanted to tour the town or some such insanity. I practically had to drag him home from the bars."

A fleeting thought went through my head to ask her about Bucky. If she'd been out at the bars late, it was possible she might have seen him. If he was still alive by then.

Stop it, Krissy. He wasn't murdered.

And yet I kept thinking of it that way. It was as if my brain couldn't make sense of someone dying naturally, that if I were to somehow figure out what exactly happened to him, then there'd be some kind of justice. Even if there was no one to punish.

I figured that since Vicki was napping and hadn't immediately asked me about Bucky, she didn't know about him yet, so I opted to leave that conversation for later.

"There's something we should talk about," I said, shifting mental gears.

Vicki groaned and moved so she could sit up better. Trouble, annoyed by the motion, hopped off her lap and sauntered away, tail swishing. He was sometimes so much like Misfit, it amazed me.

"Ugh, thank goodness." Vicki stretched her legs out in front of her with a wince. "My entire lower half was going numb." A yawn, and she rubbed at her eyes before pushing her way to her feet, then she rubbed at her butt, which I assumed was part of the numb lower half. "Okay, I'm awake. What's happened now?"

"Nothing's *happened*," I said. "But Justin from Ted and Bettfast was in earlier." I briefly told her about his predicament. "He wanted to see if we might have room for them to work here. I might have told him that they could all have a job a few months back." I tried not to wince as I said it.

Vicki's brow furrowed. Annoyingly, despite her current half-awake state, not a hair was out of place. Somehow, no matter how she was feeling, Vicki Lawyer always managed to look like a movie star.

"There's three of them?"

"Maybe? I'm pretty sure Justin and Jo will apply. I don't know about Kari."

"Honestly? It shouldn't be a problem," Vicki said after a moment's thought. "I was thinking it would be a good idea to hire a few new hands anyway. With Lena joining the force, and Pooky asking for a few less hours next week, it should be easy enough to slot them in right away."

"Pooky wants less hours?" I asked, mildly alarmed.

"Just next week. Something about her brother and helping him with a new place? She was kind of vague on the why, to be honest."

Pooky Cooper's brother, Donnie, had been a problem for her for a while now. He'd taken advantage of his sister, using her home like a crash pad and treating her like his maid. Ever since she'd kicked him out, he'd been begging to come back. It sounded like he'd finally found a place of his own, which was a good thing.

"If I see Justin, I'll make sure he turns in the application ASAP."

"I'll keep an eye out for it." She yawned and stretched. "I suppose I should get back to these." She nudged the books with the side of her foot. "I fully intended to be done by now, but as soon as I sat down, Trouble was in my lap, and, well, you know how it is."

"A warm lap makes for a warm nap."

"Whether you wanted it or not."

She chuckled as she eased her way back to the floor and started sorting through the books. I fully expected Trouble to return to her lap the moment I was gone, and Beth would find Vicki passed out against the shelves again sometime within the next hour.

I headed back down into the dining room, waved to Beth and Jeff, who'd come back from his break with ice cream in tow while I'd been upstairs, and pushed my way out the door. As much as I would have liked to stay for ice cream, I wanted to get a few other things done today before I met with Paul to discuss what had happened to Bucky.

I paused just outside, a sudden sense of déjà vu overcoming me. I was standing almost exactly where I'd been when the parade had passed and when Bucky had bumped into me. The street showed little signs of it now—most of the trash had already been gathered—but I could still imagine the crowd, the sights and sounds and feeling of excitement that had thrummed through the town.

I turned, and without thinking about what I was doing, I started walking in the direction Bucky had been going. I passed by Fern's Perms and other businesses along the street, none of which seemed like a place Bucky Sweeny would have been heading, especially with an upset stomach and a business to run. Could he have been going to see Jaqueline? It seemed strange since I figured that if they were secretly seeing each other on the side, they'd want to do so somewhere private. Even if she worked at one of the businesses along the route, she wouldn't want him popping in where everyone could see.

No, I figured if Bucky really needed to talk to Jaqueline, he'd have done so through text or he would have called her.

But if his goal wasn't to see Jaqueline, then what had it been?

I was missing something. And while it really didn't matter why Bucky was there that day since he'd died of natural causes, it bothered me anyway. No, I didn't think it had anything to do with his death, but for my peace of mind, I wanted to know. I was obsessive in that way.

But walking up and down the streets of Pine Hills, looking for answers, would get me nowhere. I turned and started back toward my car, but I decided to make a detour along the way. I crossed the street and entered Phantastic Candies, desperately in need of something chocolaty to ease my mind.

Jules was standing behind the counter dressed . . . normally? It was a shock to see him in a normal pair of trousers and a green button-up shirt. He always dressed up for the kids who frequented the candy store, yet today he looked more like my next-door neighbor than the flamboyant character he played for his customers.

Speaking of children, no one was inside Phantastic Candies other than Jules himself. The candy bins were half full, and one of the cartons on the counter was completely empty, though I doubted I'd have wanted to try the "world's hottest chocolate," even if there had been some left.

Jules roused himself from the counter at the sound of the giant piece of candy being unwrapped, which served to alert him when someone entered his candy store. He saw it was me and then leaned back, a tired smile on his face.

"You look surprisingly chipper this morning," he

said before he frowned and glanced out the window. "Or is it afternoon already? I can hardly keep track."

"Wow," I said, snagging a bag of chocolate hearts on my way to the counter. "Just . . . wow."

Jules chuckled. "I admit, I'm not at my best today. Lance insisted on coming in with me this morning, but his argument fell flat when he passed out on the couch while I was getting dressed."

"I take it you two had a good time last night?"

"We did." Jules rang me up, then waved me off when I tried to pay. "This one's on me. Lance, as you know, is a wizard when it comes to mixing drinks. Once we got home, he decided to experiment with a few Irish-inspired beverages. I dare say, we tried them all."

Not being that big of a drinker myself, it was hard to imagine that there were *that* many variants, but looking at Jules now, I was probably wrong.

"Find a favorite?"

He shrugged. "Who's to say? I recall the first couple, but after that . . ." He waved his hand in the air like a butterfly fluttering away. "How about you? Did you have a good time with Mr. Paul Dalton? Oh! And how did the Irish coffee go?"

My spirits sank. He, like Vicki, didn't know about Bucky. It was strange that in a town like Pine Hills, where rumor and news alike spread at the speed of light, no one seemed to know what had happened to Bucky Sweeny. Though, I suppose after our first town-wide St. Patrick's Day celebration, it was no wonder. And I reckoned that the fact it wasn't deemed a murder helped dampen the gossip train's enthusiasm for the story.

I almost let the moment pass without telling him the news, but I changed my mind. Maybe it was the distress over not knowing if I could have done something to help. Maybe it was the need to have someone to talk to, someone not directly involved, like Paul would be, that made me tell him.

Whatever the reason, the moment I started talking, some of the weight was lifted off my shoulders as I shared the burden with someone else.

Jules listened with wide eyes before he slumped against the wall. "Bucky's dead? I'm sorry to hear that, Krissy. I know he was a friend of yours. But . . ." He trailed off with a frown.

I knew that look. "What?" I asked.

"I'm not sure," Jules said. "Keep in mind, I'm a bit foggy today, so I could be confusing things, but . . ." Once again, he trailed off, eyes going distant.

I waited him out. Jules didn't make a habit of being dramatic, at least not when it came to stuff like this. He needed a moment to think, and I was perfectly willing to give it to him, especially if whatever he said helped ease my mind.

"Honestly, it's likely nothing," he said after a moment. "You said the police think he collapsed on his own? He wasn't murdered?"

"That's what Paul told me. He was found in the back of a truck, and there were no signs of foul play." Or so I assumed. I really needed to talk to Paul and verify that was the case. Wounds, from a fall or otherwise, could point to violence. "When I saw Bucky last, he was looking pretty rough, so . . ."

Jules nodded slowly. "He was sick and wandered his way into the back of his ex-girlfriend's truck to die."

When he said it like that, it sounded too strange to be true. "Apparently so."

Jules didn't look convinced. Now, hearing him say it, neither was I. "I didn't know Bucky very well," he said. "But when you first mentioned he was found dead, I immediately thought about someone else. Another bar owner."

"Ivan McGraw?" I guessed.

"That's the one." Jules pointed at me. "You know him?"

"Not really. Only what Bucky had told me about him."

"Well, Ivan's a rather unpleasant man. I've had occasion to cross his path a time or two." He met my eye, gave me a coy smile. "Not at his place of business, of course." He shuddered. "That's most definitely not the kind of place I'd want to find myself, even if I was interested in that sort of thing."

"Me neither," I said. I'd never actually gone into Beers and Rears, but simply driving by had always made me feel icky. It wasn't like the bar had a big, flashing sign out front showing half-naked girls on a stage or anything of the sort, but the tinted windows and big bouncer types who hung around out front told me all I needed to know about what I'd find inside. And I was perfectly content on never verifying whether my suspicions about the place were correct.

"Apparently, I wasn't the only person to find Ivan an unsavory character," Jules went on. "Knee-jerk reac-

tion, I suppose. But last week, I saw the two of them together."

"Bucky and Ivan?"

He nodded. "It happened outside Bucky's Tavern. It
was rather late, and I was on my way back from a friend's
place when I drove by. I didn't stick around and watch
them, but what I did see looked heated." Jules frowned.
"I only noticed because as I drove by, Bucky pushed
Ivan."

"As in, they got into a fight?"

"Or had words and Ivan said something Bucky didn't
like. I didn't see what happened afterward because by
then, I was already past them. I'd forgotten completely
about it until now."

I considered it. Bucky and Ivan clearly had a history.
And based on what Grant had said, it wasn't too far-
fetched to think that the encounter outside Bucky's
Tavern that Jules had witnessed had something to do
with Jaqueline. Ivan could have threatened to tell
everyone about the affair. Bucky got angry and . . .

But Bucky hadn't been murdered. What happened
between him and Ivan didn't matter.

Did it?

The door opened, and a couple of teenagers entered,
looking suspiciously hungover. Jules met my eyes,
gave me a subtle eye roll, and then got back to work. I
left him to it, mind churning over what he'd said. It was
like my subconscious *wanted* it to be murder, because
then I could do something about it. If it was an accident or if it had something to do with his stomach condition, then it was over. Bucky was gone, and no one

could be held responsible but Bucky himself for not going to a doctor or being more careful about what he ate.

I walked back to Death by Coffee and climbed into my car. I tossed my unopened candy into the passenger's seat, wincing as my arm bumped against the seat as I did. Stupid bruise.

Stupid Robert.

Now, *that* was something I could deal with. Robert had fired Justin and Kari and Jo, leaving them without jobs. Sure, I'd stepped in and offered them a place at Death by Coffee, but that didn't change the fact that he'd let them go.

I could call him and give him a stern talking-to, but that wouldn't make me feel any better. Maybe it was because I felt inadequate because I couldn't do anything about Bucky, but right then, I wanted to look someone in the eye, say my piece, and hopefully, make a difference.

So, I started up my car and was soon on the way to Robert Dunhill's home, itching for a fight.

6

My phone rang as I pulled to a stop outside Robert and Trisha's house. The neighborhood was quiet and pretty, with trees dotting nearly every yard. A plastic baby pool was set up close to the front stoop. It was packed full of colorful plastic toys. It wasn't hard to imagine Robert and Trisha lounging out front, while RJ crawled—or was he walking by now? I didn't know—and played with the brightly colored toys. The thought brought a wistful smile to my face that vanished the moment I glanced down at my phone's screen to see who was calling.

Valerie Kemp.

My first instinct was to decline the call. Valerie and I had never truly gotten along. Even when I'd helped her keep her bookstore café in California afloat, she and I had butted heads. She was the popular girl in school, the bully who'd treated anyone and everyone as stepping stones for her own wants and needs. I had found myself under her foot more times than I could count, and I was still feeling the impact of her less-than-stellar treatment of me today.

But I had to admit, she was trying to improve herself, to put aside the past and move forward. Because of that, I felt as if I should do the same, even if a part of me still resented her for how she'd treated me all those years ago.

"Valerie," I said by way of answer. "I can't really talk—"

"I'm done." Stated flatly. "I can't do it anymore."

"Do what?"

"This place!" I could imagine her spinning in a circle, arm outstretched, inside her bookstore café, Death by Java. "First, half my employees up and quit on me with no warning. Then there's a power outage on the street that's somehow *my* fault, according to our less-than-grateful customers who were unhappy that we were closed. I mean, what was I supposed to do? Make a campfire and boil coffee in a tin cup?"

I was actually surprised she'd conjured such an image, but I chose not to be petty and comment on it. With Valerie, it was hard to resist. "Things like this happen when you own a business."

"Not to me, they shouldn't." There was a moment of silence, when I could feel her seething on the other end of the line. "I've taken some time and really thought things through. It's why I'm calling you, of all people."

I clenched my teeth to avoid saying something I might later regret.

Not that it mattered. Valerie plowed ahead without

giving me a chance to respond to her not-so-subtle swipe. "I figured that since you tried to help me with this place a few months back, I'd give you first dibs."

A strange tingle ran through my chest. "First dibs on what?" I asked, though I already knew.

"This place! Death by Java. Change the name if you want, I don't care. I'm done. Finished. The roof can collapse and the ants could take over for all that it matters to me."

I sat there stunned for a long couple of seconds. Death by Java was a Death by Coffee clone. Valerie had made some Valerie Kemp–like alterations, such as pink dresses complete with bows for her all-female employees to wear, but she'd come all the way to Pine Hills to take notes on how my bookstore café was run so she could do something similar.

"It's in California," I said.

"Well, duh." Her eye roll didn't need to be seen to be noticed. "You can, like, I don't know, commute or something."

"Commute from Ohio to California?"

"You know what I mean." She huffed. "All you need to do is fly out here, take this place off my hands, do whatever you want to it—hire a manager or whatever you need to do to keep it running—and then you can go back home. It shouldn't be hard to keep tabs on the place from there."

"Yeah, but . . ." I trailed off. But what? She wasn't wrong. I could take over, spend a week or so in Redwood Village training the new manager. Dad lived there—it was my hometown, and he'd never left—so not only would I have another reason to visit, but he could keep an eye on the bookstore café for me here in Ohio when I go back home to California.

"Crap, I have to go," Valerie said, cutting into my thoughts. "Yet *another* disaster awaits my attention. I swear, it never ends. Call me when you make up your mind."

A *click*, and she was gone.

I lowered my phone and just sat there. Death by Coffee was growing. Business was always brisk, and we were very likely about to hire three new employees. I wasn't needed for the day-to-day business much anymore. And Vicki and Mason handled the money side of things, so I wasn't needed there either. Even scheduling often fell on Vicki, who had a better head for it than I did.

It wasn't too far-fetched to think that we could manage another store, even one clear across the country. Hire the right people, set up the right infrastructure, and . . .

I climbed out of my car, dismissing the thought before it could go any further. This wasn't something I should think about on my own, especially with a wedding to plan. I needed to talk to Vicki and Mason, get their input, and *then* I could consider how it might be done, or even, whether it *should* be done.

One other car, besides my own, sat in Robert's driveway as I approached his front door. The curtains in the windows were slightly parted, revealing a busy living room, packed to bursting with children's toys and supplies. There was no movement or sounds coming from inside as I knocked on the door and stepped back to wait.

I could rename it Death by Coffee. A total rebranding. A franchise, even. Have a grand reopening.

I knocked again, mentally clamping down on the thoughts that refused to stay quiet. When no one came to the door after my third knock, I retreated to my car. No one was home, but I had a feeling I knew where Robert and his family were.

I made a slight detour on the way to Ted and Bettfast— or whatever Robert was going to call it once he finished remodeling. Since Ted and Bett Bunford had sold the place, it would feel strange to continue using their names, though I doubted I'd ever think of it as anything but the same old bed-and-breakfast I'd always known.

I drove slowly past Ivan McGraw's place of business, Beers and Rears, but there was nothing to see. It was too early for the bar to be open, and unlike Bucky's Tavern, they didn't open for lunch. This was the kind of place that only opened at night, and to the sleaziest customer base in town.

No, that wasn't fair. As far as I knew, it was nice inside, managed tastefully, despite the name. The building was relatively unassuming from the outside. You had the tinted windows, a lit-up closed sign, and a smudged brick exterior with a simple wooden door. There was no trash littering the front, no scantily clad women or hungover men in dirty clothes sitting outside. There were other places in town that looked far less appealing from the outside, so making assumptions on what kind of clientele frequented Beers and Rears was presumptive.

I put the bar behind me, both physically and mentally. I'd learned nothing from my detour, and dwelling

on what problem Ivan might have had with Bucky—
whether it be because Bucky was cheating on Kandice,
or simply because he'd opened a new bar in town—
would get me nowhere. It wasn't like Ivan had *killed*
him. Whatever troubles the two men had with each
other had died with Bucky, and they should remain that
way.

The winding driveway that led to what used to be
Ted and Bettfast looked somehow sadder than it had
before. There'd once been attempts to preserve the
hedge animals that lined the drive, but those attempts
had failed and eventually been completely abandoned.
Now the hedges were overgrown masses where they
weren't flat-out dead. It used to be a beautiful sight,
but now it was almost haunting, like I was looking at
the skeleton of a place I'd once known.

I wound my way up the driveway and parked in the
lot at the front of the old manor, noting the only other
car there was Robert's. I was surprised to see the exterior of the bed-and-breakfast had had significant work
done since the last time I was there. Boarded-up windows had been replaced, as had the siding. Say what
you want about Robert, but he *was* going through with
the restorations, though I did wonder where he'd gotten
the money to do so.

There was a quiet peace to the air as I walked up to
the front door. I pushed my way inside, walking in like
I always did, though before long, that might change.

"I know that, Robert, but don't you think it's too
much space for the three of us?" Trisha was holding RJ
as she squared off in front of Robert. She was thin,
blond, with wide, pretty eyes, and I was always amazed

that someone like Trisha had ended up with Robert Dunhill, of all people. Yes, my own less-than-savory history with him might have played a role in my disbelief, but even after all these years, I stood by it.

Robert paced away from her, clearly agitated. I'd walked in on some sort of argument, and from both of their expressions, it appeared to be one that had been going on for some time.

"I told you," Robert said, pacing back over. "That's why we rent out what we don't use. It's how we'll get a return on our investment, all while having a much bigger and better space for RJ to grow up in."

"With a bunch of strangers coming and going?" Trisha shook her head. "That doesn't sound safe."

"It's not like we'd leave him alone with them."

RJ was the first to notice me. He babbled something completely unintelligible and then reached toward me. Both Trisha and Robert followed his gaze.

"Kris?" Robert said, taking an abrupt step away from Trisha. "What are you doing here?"

"I'm sorry," I said, raising both hands in front of me, palms outward. "I didn't mean to interrupt. The door was open, and—"

"It's all right, Krissy," Trisha said with a tired smile. "You're always welcome here." RJ squirmed in her arms. "I need to get this guy fed anyway. You two talk." She turned to Robert. "You and I will talk later."

And with that, she turned and walked back toward what used to be Ted and Bett Bunford's office. She didn't quite slam the door behind her, but it was a near thing.

Robert had turned his back on me to watch her go. I walked up behind him and pinched the back of his arm.

"Ow!" he yelped, jerking away. "What was that for?"

"Remember when you pinched me?"

He rubbed at the back of his arm as he nodded.

"That's why. You *bruised* me."

"But it was St. Patrick's Day." As if that made it all right.

I could have continued to press the issue, but what would be the point? Besides, the pinch had done its job, and I no longer felt the need for revenge.

"Trouble in paradise?" I asked him, nodding toward where Trisha had gone.

Robert shrugged. "Not really. She's just concerned."

"About?"

"Money. This place." He sighed. "I floated the idea that we should move in here. Why keep paying on both houses when we have this big place? There's privacy, a pool. Even if we rent the place out, we can keep our private life separate from our guests. I mean, most people who come here do so to see the town before moving on, right? Or to get away. It's not like they'd be eating dinner with us."

"Are you planning on keeping it a bed-and-breakfast?"

He scratched the back of his neck, made a face. "I don't know. It'll be *something*. It's hard to explain, you know?"

Not really, I didn't, but I nodded anyway. "Might be hard to handle with just the two of you, having guests and all. You'd think it'd be easier with a staff." At Robert's blank look, I added, "I talked to Justin. He said you let everyone go."

"Oh. Right. That."

"Yes, Robert, *that*."

"I didn't want to do it, but I had no choice."

"No choice? Robert, there's always a choice."

"Not this time. There was nothing for them to do here. I mean, we're closed until renovations are complete. We're redoing the inside, as well as the outside. It'll take time. Money. Which, by the way, is starting to run a bit thin. I couldn't keep paying them without there being some sort of income." He gave me a pleading look. "Really, Kris, I couldn't."

I wanted to argue, but how could I? If the money wasn't there, then it wasn't there.

"What about later?" I asked. "After you reopen? Could you rehire some of them then?"

"I don't know." This time, he sounded like the old Robert, like he was hiding something. "I figure Trisha and I can handle things ourselves. And by then, I bet they'll already have found new jobs, so . . ." He shrugged.

I could have asked him, *"And if they haven't?"* but it would do no good. Besides, I'd already told Justin that he and the other two could come work at Death by Coffee, so he was right; they probably would already have jobs by the time he reopened.

A part of me was frustrated that I'd come here and hadn't accomplished my goal of . . . what? Getting Justin and the others their jobs back? If nothing else, I'd confirmed that Robert had no choice, that letting them go might have actually been the best thing for them. But I felt unsatisfied, much like I felt when it came to Bucky.

"Hey," Robert said, cutting into my thoughts. "How did that thing go?"

"Thing? What thing?"

"The Irish coffee thing. I stopped at the tavern for it, but I didn't see you."

"I was only there for a little while," I said.

"Oh." He looked off into the distance, before shaking his head. "That's all right. I was kind of wondering if you knew what was going on. When I was there, it got a bit sketchy."

"Sketchy how?"

"Like . . ." He thought about it with a frown. "It's hard to say. By the time I got to Bucky's, I'd already been around a bit. Things were getting a little hazy, if you know what I mean?"

I nodded and motioned for him to get to the point.

"At first, everything was cool. The bartender was paying me special attention, which shouldn't be much of a surprise." He winked at me. "Had to tell her I was married because I'm pretty sure—"

"Robert," I said, cutting him off. I seriously doubted Kandice had any interest in Robert Dunhill, no matter what he thought. "What happened?"

He gave a dramatic sigh, as if I'd hurt his feelings, before going on. "It was quiet at first," he said. "More like a restaurant than a bar, despite how everyone was there for a party. It was kind of nice, to be honest. Everywhere else was so loud."

I crossed my arms and gave him my best impatient stare.

"So, anyway, I was at the bar, chatting up the bartender, when I heard this big crash. I turned in time to see the owner pushing some dude out the door. He was practically carrying him by his collar, and if he'd been any stronger, I bet he would have chucked him out the door." He laughed. "But all he did was shove him. I'm pretty sure the guy face-planted outside, might have busted up his face. I didn't go out to check."

"Then what happened?" I asked.

Robert shrugged. "I turned around and finished my drink."

I blinked at him. "Did Bucky say who the guy was? Or why he threw him out?"

"I didn't talk to him," Robert said. "It's why I asked you if you knew anything. I was curious."

I thought about it. This had to have taken place after I'd seen Bucky at the parade, since Robert was *in* the parade and had said he'd already been to a few other bars before he'd gone to Bucky's.

"Do you know what time this happened?" I asked, not sure why it mattered, other than to sate my curiosity.

"Not really. It was still light out, I guess. I wanted to get home to tuck RJ in, so I made the rounds pretty early. But not *too* early."

It being light out meant it had happened *before* I'd gotten off work at Death by Coffee. When I'd arrived at Bucky's Tavern later, Bucky hadn't been there. Had he gone after the man he'd thrown out? Left to cool himself off?

"How had Bucky looked?" I asked. The man he'd tossed could have been Geno Lyon, Jaqueline's husband.

If he'd gone after him after throwing him out, it might explain why he'd been found in the back of Jaqueline's truck.

"Mad, I guess," Robert said. "Maybe like he'd had a few too many himself?" He shook his head. "Like I said, it's all a bit fuzzy. But I can say that whatever had happened between those two, Bucky looked mad enough about it to kill."

7

Misfit lay curled up against me on the couch, purring ever so softly. He'd started out on my lap, but ever since I'd gotten home, agitation had me jiggling my leg at a near-constant pace. Annoyed, he'd huffed once, then had chosen a spot next to me, where he'd fallen asleep.

Other than Misfit's purrs, the house was silent. I'd considered turning on the television, but I had no interest in watching anything, especially the news. What I really wanted to do was talk to Kandice about Bucky and what Robert had told me about him throwing someone out of his tavern. I found it suspicious that sometime later that evening, Bucky had ended up dead.

That doesn't mean he was murdered.

I picked up my phone and held it tightly in my hand, desperate to call someone—*anyone*—who might have information on what happened. What if Grant was right and Bucky was cheating on Kandice with Jaqueline? What if Jaqueline's husband, Geno, confronted him at Bucky's Tavern? Bucky ends up throwing him out, and then, later, Bucky decides to go after him again and . . .

And what? Geno upsets him so much that Bucky's body gives out? And then Geno up and decides to stuff Bucky into the bed of his wife's truck because, yeah, that made sense.

I all but growled in frustration. What was I supposed to do with myself without his death being a murder? I wanted to do something to help, yet what *could* I do? There was nothing to investigate.

I stood and walked to the kitchen. I set my phone down on the counter, then pushed it as far away from me as I could get it without chucking it across the room. No, there wasn't anything I could do for Bucky anymore. I had to accept that, as much as I didn't want to. I had a wedding to plan. An uncertain future that I should be worrying about instead.

Besides, Paul would be here shortly, and chances were good he'd be hungry after a long day at work. Heck, *I* was hungry.

I wasn't much of a cook—never was and never planned on becoming one—but I dabbled from time to time. My best dishes were usually things that could be cut up and tossed into a pot, but doing that wouldn't hold my attention long enough to keep me from stressing over Bucky's death.

Instead, I grabbed some chicken from the freezer,

rooted around until I found some spices that sounded like they might be good on it, added some broccoli to steam, cooked some rice, and got to work.

Misfit appeared a short time later, head cocked to the side as he watched me retrieve the chicken from the microwave, where I'd defrosted it—I didn't have time to thaw it naturally. I set the chicken aside and went back to veggie prep.

"Yes, I cook," I told him when he meowed. I then nearly sliced my finger on the knife I was using to cut the broccoli. "Just not well."

I eventually got everything cooking without cutting or burning myself, then retrieved one of the chocolate hearts I'd bought at Phantastic Candies as a reward for getting through the ordeal unharmed. I popped the chocolate into my mouth, then went to the window to check for Paul, though I hadn't heard him pull up.

As expected, there was no car sitting in my driveway.

But there *was* one sitting out by the road.

The car was red, with a rusty driver's-side door. It was idling out in front of my house, and as soon as I parted the curtain to get a better look, it sped off down the street in a cloud of black exhaust. I frowned as I watched it go. The car didn't look familiar, but I got the distinct impression the driver had been watching my place.

Sabrina Mayfield? I wondered. She was a reporter for the *Levington Online Herald* who'd taken an interest in me some time ago. And while Bucky's death wasn't murder, it *was* another sudden death in Pine Hills. That, in turn, might catch the attention of the out-of-town reporter.

But that wasn't Sabrina's car. At least, not the one I remembered.

I waited at the window to see if the car would return, mildly agitated. Minutes passed, and nothing moved, though Misfit did jump onto the back of the couch to join my vigil, curious as to what I was looking at.

"It's nothing," I told him. "It was probably—" I sniffed, brow furrowing. Something smelled . . . burnt?

My eyes widened as I dropped the curtain and rushed over to the stove, where smoke was coming from the broccoli pan. I yanked it from the burner and went straight to the faucet to add water since there was none. I'd put some into the pan earlier, but clearly not enough. The broccoli still *looked* okay, if not a little browner on the florets than it should be.

"See," I grumbled to Misfit, "this is why I never cook."

I returned the pan to the burner, turned the heat down, and spent the next fifteen minutes monitoring the food so I wouldn't burn anything else.

The sound of tires on my driveway had my anxiety spiking a short time later. I tamped down on the surge of emotion, turned off the burners, and ran my fingers through my hair to make sure I hadn't somehow gotten any stray food particles in it, before I went to the door. Paul was still in uniform, hair pressed down from a long day wearing his hat. I couldn't help myself. I reached out, and like I'd done with my own hair, used my fingers to reinvigorate it.

"Long day?" I asked him as he kissed me on the cheek and stepped inside.

"Very." He paused, sniffed the air. "What's that smell?"

"Sorry. I cooked."

"Why are you apologizing?" he asked, glancing at me askance. "It smells great. I'm just surprised is all."

I studied him, looking for deception, but he appeared genuine, which pleased me more than it probably should have. "I might have messed up the broccoli," I said. "So if it's burnt, just throw it away. I won't mind."

A smile flickered across his face. "I'm sure it'll be fantastic." He held up a hand when I started to say something else. "Really, Krissy, you didn't have to cook for me, but I'm glad you did. I haven't had a chance to eat much of anything today, so I'm starved."

We filed into the kitchen and filled our plates. Misfit looked on longingly, but at least she didn't try to hop up on the counter—or worse, on the stove—to snag a bite. As Paul sat down, I cracked open a can of food for Misfit so he wouldn't feel left out, before taking my own place at the table. While I sometimes gave Misfit table scraps, the older he got, the worse it was for him, so canned food it was.

"Try it yet?" I asked Paul, too nervous to take the first bite.

"Nope. I thought I'd wait for you."

"Afraid I might poison you?" I asked, picking up my fork and spearing a piece of broccoli. It *looked* okay, even smelled pretty good.

A strange look passed over Paul's face before he shook his head. "No. Though, if you wouldn't mind taking the first bite, it would ease my mind."

"Ha-ha." Deadpan. I popped the broccoli into my mouth, chewed, swallowed, and then opened my mouth to show him that I'd indeed eaten it.

Paul chuckled, and we both dug in. The first ten minutes were filled with eating and a little small talk about nothing important. I got up once to grab us each a Coke from the fridge, having forgotten to offer before we'd sat down. The whole meal felt like a tiny snapshot of what my life might soon be like. Quiet meals together after a hard day's work. Pets eating off to the side. Homey. Comforting.

I found my shoulders easing as I relaxed into the pleasant conversation. I hadn't realized how badly I'd needed this until that very moment.

"Don't forget, we have an appointment with a Realtor tomorrow morning," Paul said, scraping the last of his rice onto his fork. "Just to look. There's no pressure to buy." He paused. "You're still okay with that, right? I know we talked about it, but I'm worried I might have jumped the gun."

"Of course," I said, despite the slight spike of anxiety that shot through me. "Is the house far from here?"

"Not really. It's about a ten-minute drive from downtown, mostly because there's no direct route. You could probably walk to work if you wanted, especially if you cut through . . ." He trailed off, taking in my expression before he set his utensils aside. "Something is bothering you."

"What? No. I'm fine." I smiled, as if to prove it.

His brow furrowed. "If you don't want to go tomorrow, just say so. I won't mind. This is something we need to do, but not right—"

"It's not that," I said, cutting him off. "I won't lie and say I'm not worried about moving, but I'll get over that." I reached across the table and took his hand. "I want to get married and find a place we can call home, so don't take my neurotic behavior personally."

He squeezed my hand, though I could still tell he was concerned. "I just don't want you to feel like I'm pressuring you."

"You're not." I released his hand, sat back. "It's just . . . I'm going to worry and stress over things I can't control. I'm going to obsess over whether I'm doing things right, even when I know I am. It's how I am. I'll try not to upset you, but I'll probably say something at some point that will come out wrong and . . . and . . ."

"Krissy." He leaned over his plate to look me dead in the eye. "I understand."

My heart did a little hiccup, and a tear came unbidden to my eye. I'd spent my entire life struggling to make it so that others understood me. I was never the best when it came to talking to people. I tended to be blunt, to just blurt things out when I probably should have kept my thoughts to myself. A part of me was always nervous that I'd say or do the wrong thing, which often led to me doing and saying the wrong thing. People didn't like that, and yet, somehow, here Paul Dalton was, accepting me for, well, *me*.

Which meant I needed to be honest with him.

"It's Bucky," I said with a heavy sigh. "I can't stop thinking about him. I know he died of natural causes, but every time I talk to someone about him, they tell me something that makes me descend into my usual suspicious routine. I've been treating his death like a murder, even though I know it's not."

Paul picked up his utensils, set them carefully on his empty plate. "I see."

"I know I should let it go," I continued, needing to get it out. "But I can't. Something feels off about this whole thing, like I'm missing something vital."

Paul stared at his plate, refused to look up at me.

"Paul?" I asked, suddenly worried. "Did I say something wrong?"

"No." He took a deep breath, folded his hands on the table in front of him. "Tell me what you've heard."

My chest constricted. His tone wasn't one of curiosity. He made it sound like what I said next might be of extreme importance.

I took a moment to order my thoughts so I didn't leave anything out. "Bucky was dating one of his employees, Kandice Vaughn," I said, figuring I'd start with the easy details first. "I kind of figured as much, having seen them together, though nothing was made official until I talked to Kandice after Bucky's death."

"She's the bartender at Bucky's Tavern?"

I nodded. "The rumor is that Bucky was cheating on Kandice with his ex, Jaqueline Lyon, and that the owner of Beers and Rears, Ivan McGraw, found out about it. I guess the other bar owners were unhappy that Bucky opened his tavern, and this was Ivan's way of getting him to, I don't know, close or something? That part's not entirely clear."

"Did he threaten Bucky?"

I thought back to what I'd been told, then shrugged. "Maybe? Grant—another of Bucky's employees—said that Ivan called Bucky on St. Patrick's Day and that it upset him. Jules also said he saw Bucky shove Ivan, but this was last week. And then, sometime after the parade, Robert claims he saw Bucky throw someone out of his tavern, though he doesn't know who it was. I assume it was Ivan, but if the rumors are true, it's possible it could have been Geno."

"Or someone unrelated to all of this," Paul said. "There were quite a few altercations reported over the holiday."

I conceded the point. "Or it could have been Dwayne Morris. Kandice said he'd come in the night before the parade and threatened to break Bucky's nose, likely on orders from Ruth Camden. They both own local bars, and like Ivan, were unhappy about Bucky opening the tavern."

"I know who they are," Paul said with a frown. He was staring off into the middle distance and had a look on his face I would recognize anywhere.

"Paul," I said, trying to keep the desperation out of my voice. "What's going on?"

A beat passed when he didn't react to my question. Then his gaze swiveled to meet mine, and he said, "We're not certain Bucky Sweeny died of natural causes."

I slow-blinked. Spoke just as slowly. "You're not sure it was natural causes? What does that even mean?"

"It means that some things have come up." He sighed, sat back. "At first glance, it did indeed appear as if Bucky Sweeny had too much to drink, got sick, and then collapsed into the back of the Lyons' pickup truck. He'd sustained no wounds, other than the mild bruising on his shoulder and head that could be explained away easily enough, especially if he was so sick that he fell a few times. But none of his injuries could have accounted for his death, not even remotely."

I absorbed that, then asked, "And on second glance?"

"We think he might have been poisoned."

I stared. "Poisoned?" And then a new, panic-infused thought. "From the Irish coffee? I drank some of it that night. Nearly half the town did!"

"We don't know anything for certain yet," Paul said. "But I doubt it was the Irish coffee. At least not the same Irish coffee everyone else drank, or else we'd have seen other cases."

While it made sense, my mind still wasn't at ease. "How do you know he was poisoned?" I asked. "Was there evidence of some kind?"

Paul made a seesaw gesture with his hand. "The same evidence that pointed to natural causes could also point to poison. I don't know the details since I'm not a doctor, but the way I hear it, there were some tests done that indicated poison rather than intoxication. More tests are being run to be certain."

I sat back into my chair with a shocked *huff*. "Wow."

It was my turn to stare off into the middle distance as I thought about it.

Bucky might have been poisoned. Kandice would be an instant suspect, especially because of Jaqueline, who, I would assume, would be a suspect as well. Likewise for Ivan and Dwayne and Ruth and even Geno Lyon.

"Right now, John is investigating it as murder," Paul went on. "Better to play it safe and not waste time assuming otherwise. We wouldn't want the culprit to have time to dispose of any evidence that might still exist."

I agreed. "Will Buchannan want to talk to me?" I asked. "I worked with Bucky on the Irish coffee, which means I know a bit about his relationship with his employees." But clearly not enough. If Kandice *had* poisoned him for cheating on her, I hadn't seen it coming. And I doubted it was spur of the moment. I mean, who kept poison on hand? It felt more like something that had to have been planned, likely for weeks, if not months, ahead of time.

"It's likely," Paul said. "Until then, I'd like it if you kept your distance from his suspects. You know how upset it makes him whenever he finds out you've been talking to people in his stead."

I nodded, though I didn't say what I was agreeing to. I knew Detective John Buchannan hated my interference, but could I really sit back and do *nothing*? Bucky had been my friend. No, we weren't close, but I felt that if we'd had more time together, we might have grown that way.

I decided to change the subject. "So," I said, placing my elbows on the table so I could prop my chin into my hands, "tell me about this house we're seeing tomorrow."

Paul eyed me for a moment, as if uncertain about my sudden shift, and then he broke into a wide grin. "It's on Brushfire Road, which, if you ask me, is an awful name for a street in a town named after trees. But it's quiet. I think you're really going to love it . . ."

8

I was sitting on a too-small couch, squished between Paul, his two huskies, Ziggy and Kefka, and Misfit. The ceiling brushed the top of my head, and despite there being nowhere for it to go, it appeared to be getting closer and closer, so much so that I was having a hard time breathing.

"There's enough room for us all," Paul said. Both his dogs barked in agreement.

Across the room, Bucky was making Irish coffees at a wooden bar. Kandice stood behind him, along with shadowy figures I somehow knew were Geno, Jaqueline, and Ivan, despite not being able to see them clearly. A line of customers snaked across the room and out the door. The faces were all ones I knew, each and every one of them friends of mine. Rita stood at the front of the line, rubbing her hands in anticipation.

"Patience," Bucky said, before coughing into his fist. His eyes were bloodshot, and he had a bruise on his temple. "There's one final touch yet to be made."

He reached down beneath the counter and picked up a green bottle. There was a skull and crossbones on the label. He popped the cork and dropped a single bead of dark green liquid from the bottle into each of the cups as the customers filed past in a slow procession filled with parade sounds. Every time someone took a sip from their poisoned coffee, a cymbal would crash, and then they would fall forward, through a trapdoor in the floor.

Bucky smiled at me, black veins pulsing across his face. "Care for a cup?"

I woke with a start, not quite drenched in sweat, but close enough. My heart was hammering, yet already the dream was fading. Paul, who'd called his dog sitter last night after dinner to let her know he was staying the night with me, was sleeping on one side of me, Misfit on the other. I managed to slither out from beneath the covers without disturbing either.

Paul had stayed so we could get an early start on the day, but not *this* early. I went through my morning routine slowly, and as quietly as I could. By the time I was done, the dream had faded completely, and Paul was up and in the shower. A short time later, we were on our way to what could very well be the house of our dreams.

Of course, I couldn't fully shake the effects of my nightmare, even if I couldn't fully remember it. I kept thinking about Bucky, about the possibility that he'd been poisoned. I kept wondering if he shouldn't have tasted it, or at least showed more, I don't know, poisonous symptoms.

Then again, what did I know about poison? In the movies, the victim would take a sip of the poisoned wine, and would suddenly choke and collapse, and that would be that. The victim didn't go walking around most of the day, acting like they had an upset stomach, before finally succumbing to the poison. At least, not in the shows and movies I'd watched.

"Are you feeling okay, Krissy?" Paul asked from the driver's seat. And no, unlike the movies, he didn't recklessly turn to stare at me when he asked it.

I managed to smile nonetheless. "I'm fine. Just nervous."

He glanced at me askance, but didn't contradict me. He didn't have to, considering my words had sounded hollow to *my* ears.

We were about to take a major step in our lives. No, there was no pressure to buy this house now, but simply looking meant we *were* on the path toward our future. I couldn't be worried about what might have or might not have happened to Bucky Sweeny while trying to decide whether the kitchen was big enough.

We arrived at Brushfire Road a short time later. As Paul had said, the neighborhood was quiet, though the houses were much bigger than I'd expected. They weren't mansions or anything of the sort, but they were all easily twice the size of my current place, if not bigger. Each yard was at least an acre, maybe more—I wasn't a great judge of sizing land—and most were fenced in, including the house we were viewing.

Paul pulled in behind a Lexus already in the driveway. As soon as he shut off the engine, a woman with a mass of curly hair, streaked with artificial gray, got out of the fancy car. She was wearing a skirt and suit jacket, along with heels that were so thin, it was a miracle they didn't snap under her weight.

"Oh no," I groaned.

"What?" Paul asked. "You don't like it?"

"Not the house. *Her.*"

Even as I said it, Vanna Goff turned to face us. Her smile instantly froze on her face the moment she laid eyes on me sitting next to Paul. Slowly, it morphed into a scowl that could peel paint, and her hand found her hip and squeezed.

"I can call the real estate company and see if they can send someone else," Paul said, plastering on a smile of his own as he waved to a clearly unhappy Vanna.

"No." I sighed, resigned. "It's probably time I mended this fence anyway." Not that I knew *why* Vanna Goff disliked me so much. I understood that she blamed me for her inability to sell my neighbor's old house. No, her complaints weren't justified, but I recognized her belief that they were. Vanna's prickly personality likely had more to do with her clients finding a new Realtor than anything I'd done, but try to tell her that.

Paul and I got out of his car and approached Vanna, who glared at me the whole way. She was holding the listing in the hand not currently trying to squeeze a hole through her hip. She grudgingly handed it over to Paul when we reached her.

"Thank you for accommodating me on this," he said, turning on the charm. "I know you're extremely busy."

Vanna tore her eyes away from me, and her entire demeanor softened. "It's no trouble, Mr. Dalton." Her gaze flickered my way, then settled on him. "Please, let me show you inside."

As she turned, Paul shot me a wink.

I rolled my eyes, and together, we followed her in.

Once we were through the door, Vanna gave us the spiel, but I wasn't listening. The house was more than nice; it was immaculate. Granite-top counters were featured in a kitchen with space to cook for an army. The dining nook was small, which was fine by me, considering the island counter in the kitchen that was large enough to easily serve as an eating space. There was a living room, a family room, a small den, three bedrooms, two and a half baths. Spacious was an understatement.

I was standing at the back door, having lost Paul and Vanna somewhere along the way, staring into a covered back patio that led to an oversized fenced-in yard. I'd liked to have imagined what it would be like to sit out there, next to a firepit with Paul's huskies running circles around all my friends as we lounged under the stars, eating s'mores and talking about nothing.

But I couldn't. Every time I tried to envision it, I kept seeing Bucky's face that last time I'd seen him. How he'd coughed and looked as if he might be sick at any moment. What if I'd forced him to sit down inside Death by Coffee for a few minutes? Would I have been able to tell that his illness was more than just stomach issues? Would he still be alive now? If only I'd—

"Krissy?"

A hand landed on the back of my arm, squeezed.

I yelped and jerked away, immediately slapping a hand over the fading bruise.

Paul stood frozen, hand outstretched, eyes slightly wide in his surprise.

"Sorry," I said, managing a smile as I rubbed at the spot. "Robert pinched me. It left a bruise."

He frowned. "He pinched you? When?"

"On St. Patrick's Day. He claims he didn't see that I was wearing green." I forced myself to drop my hand, despite how it still throbbed. "It's nothing. It's healing already, though it's still a little tender."

Paul's lips pressed together, and I could tell he was contemplating on whether or not to go have words with Robert.

"Really," I said. "I'm fine."

"You don't look fine," he said. This time, when he reached for my arm, he went for the other one. "What's going on, Krissy? I know this is a big step, and if you're not ready, we can wait. Like I said before, there's no pressure to buy now. We have time."

"It's not that. It's . . ." I trailed off as Vanna entered the room, already talking.

"I should show you the basement next. It's not quite finished, but it's fully waterproofed, and with a little work, it could be turned into anything you want. A spare bedroom, a game room, or just extra storage. If you'd follow me, it's right this way."

"Would you mind giving us a minute?" Paul asked, never taking his eyes—or hand—from me. "Krissy and I need to talk privately for a moment."

Vanna narrowed her eyes at me like she thought I

was intentionally sabotaging the viewing before she nodded. "I'll be in the next room." She turned and *clack*ed away on her too-thin heels.

"All right," Paul said when she was gone. "Tell me."

I swallowed, suddenly embarrassed by my distraction. "It's . . ." I glanced out the door, back to his face. "It's just so big. Do you really think we can afford something like this?"

He didn't blink, didn't respond in any other way other than to stare.

"I mean," I went on, "there's room for the dogs to run around outside. And places for Misfit to hide until he gets used to them. And there's more than enough space so we could have quiet time on our own whenever we need it. And . . ." I trailed off. His expression hadn't changed an iota, but I could tell he wasn't buying it. I lowered my head as I said, "It's Bucky."

"You feel responsible."

"I saw him, Paul. I could have done something to help him, but I let him walk away."

"You didn't know what was wrong with him. We don't even know for sure he was poisoned."

"But it's likely." I glanced past him, to the other room where Vanna was waiting, and probably eavesdropping. "I can't sit still and do nothing. You know that."

Paul sighed. "I do." He pulled me in close and hugged me, careful not to bump my arm. "Let's do this another day, all right? I'll see if the results have come in yet about whether it was poison or not, and I'll let you know. We can always come back when things calm down."

"I don't want to mess this up."

He stepped back, gave me the kindest, most patient smile I'd ever seen cross a person's face. "You're not."

We stepped into the living room, hand in hand, a moment later. Vanna took one look at us, and her face fell.

"We're going to have to finish this another day," Paul said. "I'll call you and let you know when."

Before Vanna could object, or throw some obscenity at me for ruining yet another of her showings, we were past her and out the door. Paul was chuckling as we pulled away.

"What's so funny?" I asked.

"Just the look on her face," he said. "She *really* doesn't like you, does she?"

I don't know why, but I found myself laughing with him. "Not one bit."

Paul drove me home and dropped me off with a promise that he'd call the second he knew for sure what had happened to Bucky. I went inside and thought about sitting down and waiting for his call, but I knew I wouldn't be able to sit still. Even if I tried to look up information on poisons, I'd want to talk to someone in the know, rather than trust what I read on some web-site. These days, most of what you found online was questionable at best, especially now that fact-checking was often viewed as taboo.

Within five minutes of me setting my purse down, I was picking it back up, along with my keys. My hand had just hit the doorknob on my way out when my phone rang.

Paul already?

I checked the screen, and my heart did a little hiccup.

No, it wasn't Paul. It was Laura Dresden, my dad's girlfriend.

I answered, dread already forming in my gut. Laura never called, and since she and Dad lived in California, which was three hours behind me in Ohio, she most definitely never did this early.

"Hi, Laura," I said, doing my best to keep my tone light and unworried. "What's up?"

"Krissy." It was just my name, but the *heaviness* in her tone had me sitting down.

"What happened?" I asked. My voice came out sounding small, almost childlike. "Dad?"

"He's all right," she said with a tired sigh. "He didn't want me to call you at all, but I thought you should know."

"Okay?" I swallowed, imagining the worst. Dad was getting up there in years. And while he was never a smoker, nor was he overweight or anything like that, things *did* happen. "Know what?"

"Your dad fell last night. He tried to come to bed without turning on a light and ended up tripping over his own slippers, which he'd left sitting in the middle of the floor despite me warning him what could happen."

"Is he okay?" I asked, even though she'd already answered that. She wouldn't have called if he'd only fallen and bruised his ego.

"Mostly." She heaved yet another sigh. "He broke his hip."

I stood. "He's in the hospital?"

"I'm here now." There were no sounds in the background, so I assumed she'd found a quiet place to make the call. "Well, we both are. The doctor said he'll probably keep him for four days or so, then I can bring him home. James hates it, and he's already tried to talk his way out of it, but it's not like he can make a run for it."

"Which hospital?" I asked, already making plans. I could call Vicki, let her know I wouldn't be in for a few days, maybe a week or two. Jules could feed Misfit. And Paul . . .

"No."

I blinked. "No, what?"

"James said you'd want to fly out, which is why he didn't want me to call you. He said that if I insisted on calling that I should tell you 'no' even before you could finish the thought."

"Yeah, but—"

"No." Firm. "I called because you deserve to know, but there's nothing you can do here." Laura's voice softened as she continued, "James is okay. He's on some painkillers that have turned him a bit loopy, and I'm sure he's going to have a fit once I get him home and he wants to act like he's perfectly capable of moving around himself without assistance and finds out he can't."

I took a deep, shuddering breath, let it out in a huff. "He'll likely use the experience as research for a book."

Laura laughed. "You're probably right." A muffled

yawn followed. "I'm going to let you go. I think I managed an hour, maybe two, of sleep last night, so I'm
going back to James's room and taking a nap. The doctor told me to go home, but . . ."

"I get it," I said. "Call me if they tell you anything."

"Will do." Another stifled yawn. "Let me just say,
I'm not looking forward to the sponge baths your father is going to insist I give him."

And with that lovely image now firmly lodged in
my mind, she disconnected.

I stood at my dining room table, phone clutched in
my hand, and just stared. Misfit watched me from the
couch for a couple of moments before spinning in a
circle and lying down for a nap.

Dad had fallen, broken a hip. I was halfway across
the country from him. No, more than that. Two-thirds
of the way across. Somewhere in there, anyway, not
that it really mattered. What mattered was that I was
hours away, with no quick and easy way to get there if
something worse were to happen.

What if he'd injured more than a hip? What if he
fell, not because of carelessly placed slippers, but because something else was wrong with him? What if . . .

I clamped down on the thoughts and took a couple
of deep breaths. Dad was okay. Laura would have told
me if there was more to it. Or, at least, she would have
made Dad call me and tell me.

Focus on what you can control, Krissy.

And what was that, exactly?

Bucky's death, of course.

Yes, it was possible he could have died from natural

causes, but there was no harm asking around, just in case early indications of poison were accurate. If nothing else, it would keep my mind off of Dad, lest I soon find myself sitting on a plane on the way to California, no matter what he or Laura said.

Stuffing my phone into my back pocket, I pushed worries of Dad out of my head, then headed out the door to investigate what could very well turn out to be a murder.

9

Bea stared at me over her bifocals, a disapproving frown on her face. I fidgeted, gave her a nervous smile, and continued to sit and wait. When I'd entered the doctor's office, she'd merely glared at a chair in the corner, and I complied without complaint. While the elderly receptionist didn't like it when I showed up without an appointment—or at least when I didn't call ahead first—she always let the doctors know I'd arrived.

There were three other people in the waiting room with me. Two women were side by side, looking at something on the younger of the duo's phone. The other was a man with his hat pulled down over his eyes. I couldn't tell if he was asleep or just pretending to be so that no one would bother him. Or, perhaps, to avoid Bea's withering glare.

The door leading to the examination rooms and offices opened, and much to my surprise, Dr. Paige Lipmon poked her head out instead of one of the nurses. Her gaze swept across the room until it landed on me. Unlike Bea, she gave me a smile, though I could see the curiosity burning behind her eyes as she said, "Krissy, come on back."

I rose, noting the harsh look from beneath the man's hat. Clearly, he wasn't happy I got to go first when he'd been there before me.

"Thanks for seeing me," I said as Paige closed the door and led me down the hallway to one of the exam rooms. I almost told her that I wasn't there to be looked at, but an exam room would be private, whereas her office was shared with the other doctors at the practice, which meant anyone could pop in at any time.

"I assume this isn't a standard doctor's visit," she said as I took my place on the exam table. "You don't look injured or sick. Nor do you have an appointment for a checkup. With what happened, it's not hard to guess why you're here."

I swung my feet, suddenly feeling like a little kid again. "Do you know the details?" I asked. "About what happened to Bucky Sweeny, I mean."

Paige sat down, dark eyes scanning me. "I know that a man—Bucky, I assume—died, and that the police are treating it with suspicion."

"They think he was poisoned."

"Did you know him?"

"I did. Not well, but I was supplying the coffee for the Irish coffee he was selling during the St. Patrick's Day celebration." I bit my lower lip as I considered what

to say next. I wanted Paige's help, but I also didn't want
to put her in an awkward position. I didn't know if
Bucky was her patient, and with his death happening
the way it did, I wasn't even sure if doctor-patient con-
fidentiality mattered in this case.

Thankfully, Paige had a keen mind and knew what I
was thinking. Mostly. "You want to know if you should
be worried."

"I drank the Irish coffee." I shrugged. "Lots of people did."

She sat there a moment, as if debating on how much
to say, before, "I don't think you have anything to
worry about. No one else has come in sick with anything resembling a poisoning, not even food poisoning.
There've been a few people who'd overindulged, of
course, and a handful of injuries because of it, but that
was to be expected."

"Bucky complained about stomach pains," I said.
"He was coughing, looked as if he might be sick at any
moment. Could those have been symptoms? I was told
he had stomach issues, so it might have been normal
for him." Though, if it was, I hadn't noticed before that
day.

Paige frowned as she thought about it. "It's possible . . ."

"But?" I asked.

"It's hard to say," Paige said. "I don't have his med-
ical history, so I don't know if this sort of thing was
common for him."

"If his system was already compromised, could something he have eaten have triggered an episode bad enough

to kill him? Something that might appear as poison, but is really nothing more than a bad sandwich?"

She thought about it a moment before nodding. "I suppose it's possible," Paige said, sitting forward, folding her hands on her knee. "But I'm not an expert on poisons. No one here is. If the police are running tests, they're likely doing so through Levington."

My shoulders sagged. "I see."

"That's not to say I know *nothing*," she went on. "Many poisons take time to manifest symptoms. Some take a few hours, others days, depending on how the victim came into contact with it and how much was ingested or inhaled. I know you're interested in finding out what happened to this man, but it won't be as easy as finding someone who witnessed the crime, if a crime was even committed."

I continued swinging my feet a moment longer before hopping down. "I'm sorry I wasted your time."

"No, don't be." Paige smiled as she stood. "I get it. The police haven't talked to me, nor do I expect them to, but if you happen to speak with them about the investigation and it *is* murder by poison, let them know that they should go back hours, if not days, to look for their killer. Don't look at where the victim was when he was found, or even who he was with at the time. At least, not exclusively."

I nodded as she led me to the door. It made sense. Poisoning took time. Bucky could have ingested it or touched it anywhere, at practically anytime throughout the day, possibly even a day or two before. And there was still always the chance it was simple food poisoning gone haywire in a guy who already had troubles with his digestive system. I simply didn't know enough to be certain about anything.

We reached the door that led to the waiting room. I reached for it, but paused. "I have one more question for you, Doctor Lipmon. It's not about Bucky or poison. It's more . . . personal."

She crossed her arms and waited with a faint smile on her face.

"How bad is it for someone old enough to be my father to break a hip?"

Her dark eyebrows rose at that. "Someone old enough to be your father?"

"Okay, someone who *is* my dad. He fell. I'm worried. He's all the way in California and—"

Paige rested a hand on my forearm. "He should be fine. I won't lie to you and say there can't be complications, but if all he did was trip and fall, and if there are no underlying conditions that led to his imbalance, you don't have much to worry about. If he gets good care, and follows instructions when it comes to healing, he should be fine."

I left, not as reassured as I'd hoped I'd be. The man in the hat was gone from the waiting room, but the two women were still there, heads still bent over the phone. As I pushed my way out the door, I noted the poster on the wall about "tech neck" and wondered if the women had looked up from their own technology long enough to notice it.

I climbed into my car and then just sat there, unsatisfied. I considered calling Dad, but if he was still loopy on painkillers, I'd get nothing out of him. Perhaps once he was discharged, I could call and lecture him on following his doctor's instructions. Knowing Dad, he'd assume they were merely recommendations, and he could pick and choose which ones to follow.

I tapped my phone against my palm as I thought about what to do next. While I wasn't certain about what exactly had happened to Bucky or when, I *did* know of someone whose name kept coming up whenever I talked to anyone about Bucky: Ivan McGraw. And while going directly to Ivan would tell me *something*, it also didn't sound very appealing. Why not talk to someone who knew a bit about what might have been going on between Ivan and Bucky first?

I did a quick search and, before I could reconsider, put in a call, hoping I was doing the right thing.

The phone rang twice before it was answered with, "Jazz speaking. Who's this?"

"Hi, Jazz," I said, injecting false cheer into my voice. "It's Krissy Hancock."

"Krissy? What can I do for you?" The briefest of pauses before, "Never mind. I know why you're calling. It's about Bucky, isn't it?"

"It is," I said. "Would you mind if we met somewhere to talk?" I considered leaving it at that, but I wanted to pique his interest a bit more. "I want to talk to you about Ivan McGraw and his interactions with Bucky."

This time, the pause was long and heavy. When Jazz spoke, he sounded as if he'd aged twenty years. "I suppose it's prudent we have that chat. With how you and Bucky were getting along, you deserve to know what was really going on. I'll put on some tea." He rattled off his home address, and we disconnected.

The drive to Jazz Day's house from the doctor's office was relatively short. He lived in a small, slightly run-down house in the shadow of a larger apartment complex. He was waiting for me at the door in a pair of khaki shorts; a shirt that was red on one side, black on the other; and no shoes or socks.

"Today has not been the best of days," he said. His gray hair, which was normally slicked back, hung down across his forehead, concealing his acne scars. "I didn't hear about Bucky until . . . That can wait. Please, come in." He stepped aside. "Don't mind the mess. These old houses are difficult to keep up with sometimes."

The inside of Jazz's house was tidy and smelled faintly of pine. There was a small hole in the plaster wall calf-high just past the entryway, beneath a pair of hooks on the wall. Attempts had been made to repair it, but whatever he'd tried to use hadn't stuck.

"I'm always kicking that spot whenever I hang up my coat," Jazz said, nodding toward the hole. "You'd think I'd learn to keep my big feet to myself after all these years."

"It sounds like something I'd do," I said as Jazz led me to a small, circular dining table where a pitcher sat next to a pair of teacups. Cubed sugar had been placed in a bowl, alongside a small pitcher of milk. He motioned for me to sit, which I did. "I'm sorry to bother you with this."

"Don't be." Jazz poured before he, too, sat. He added a single cube of sugar to his teacup, and then just a dab of milk, before stirring it with a tiny spoon. "Sometimes it's best to talk about these things, even when you don't want to." He shook his head, took a sip, then motioned for me to do the same.

After adding a pair of sugar cubes, I did just that. "This is good."

Jazz gave me a polite smile and waited, so I dove right in.

"The police think Bucky might have been poisoned."

If Jazz was surprised by the revelation, he did well to hide it. "That so?"

"It's not been confirmed, but yeah, that's what they believe."

Another sip of tea before he set his teacup aside. "Suspects?"

"I don't know. I assume they'll look at Kandice since she and Bucky were dating."

Jazz nodded slowly. "Makes sense, though I'll wager they'll be wasting their time with that. Kandice wouldn't have hurt Bucky, even if she . . ." His brow furrowed. "No, she wouldn't have done it."

"You were going to say, 'even if she found out about Jaqueline,' weren't you?"

"No, but I suppose that fits too," Jazz said. "Kandice wouldn't have hurt him because she doesn't have that sort of violence in her."

"Poison isn't exactly violent," I pointed out.

"It isn't," Jazz agreed. "But it does take some pre-meditation."

I opened my mouth to respond, then closed it. He was right. And Kandice had acted like she hadn't known about Bucky cheating on her—if that was indeed what he'd been doing—until *after* his death.

"I see you understand," Jazz said with a nod. "Kandice didn't have reason to kill Bucky, at least one she knew about. You mentioned Ivan McGraw on the phone. He, like the others—"

"Ruth Camden and Dwayne Morris?" I assumed.

"They had more reason to get rid of Bucky than Kandice did. When I showed up at Bucky's yesterday, I saw Ruth leaving. Made me suspicious at the time, though I doubt she'd risk her own business by going as far as killing someone."

That reminded me of something Grant had told me when I'd talked to him. "Grant said you got a call from your sister," I said. "He thought she sounded upset. Was it because of Bucky?"

Jazz sighed. "Allie—that's my sister—can be . . . challenging. She has her troubles." He met my eye, held it. "She didn't know Bucky all that well, but her daughter, my niece, did. And let's just say that Allie's problems have trickled down into her daughter, and leave it at that." Jazz picked up his tea, but didn't drink. He swirled it slowly and watched the ripples it made.

I felt like I'd hit a nerve by bringing up the call, but I didn't press him on it. I doubted his family drama had much bearing on Bucky's death, and my asking further questions would only make him feel worse about it. It had to feel like the world was piling onto him.

"What about Ivan McGraw?" I asked instead. "Do you think he could have poisoned Bucky?"

Jazz considered it, then shook his head. "I don't know how he'd have much of an opportunity to do so. It's not like Bucky and Ivan ever broke bread together, if you know what I mean?"

I nodded. "Do you know why they didn't get along?"

At that, Jazz laughed. "Name a reason. Biggest of all would be Jaqueline Lyon, of course. But not in the way you're thinking. Ivan had nothing to do with whatever was going on between those two, mind you, other than wanting to cause Bucky as much strife as possible."

"Could he have found out about Bucky and Jaqueline?" I asked, thinking about what Grant had said about possible blackmail.

"Possibly," Jazz said. "Ivan may even have tried to use it against Bucky. That *sounds* like something Ivan would do. But poison? I doubt it. Hard to profit from murder."

Unless Ivan had something to gain. Though what that might be, I had no idea.

"Do you know how easy it would be to poison someone?" Jazz asked, almost thoughtfully. "You offer them something to drink. Then . . ." He reached over, picked up a sugar cube, and then dropped it into his tea. "Plop! Done."

My eyes widened as I stared down into my own teacup, where I'd added two cubes of my own.

Jazz spread his hands, as if saying, *"See!"*

I swallowed heavily. "I, uh . . ." I shoved my tea away, which caused Jazz to chuckle.

"I didn't poison you, Krissy," he said. "I just wanted to show you how anyone could have easily done it. If no one saw it happen, how will the police ever find the killer?"

Good question. "Do you have any idea who might have done it?" I asked.

"I do not." Jazz frowned. "At least, I don't know anything for certain. Kandice didn't know about him and Jaqueline until after he passed, so I find it unlikely that she would be responsible." A pause. "Unless . . ."

When he left the thought hanging, I pressed by repeating, "Unless?"

Jazz sighed. "I don't like speaking ill of the dead, especially a friend like Bucky. He gave us jobs—me, Kandice, and Grant—and we all appreciated him for it. I knew Bucky from before, but the job really brought us together."

I felt it, so I asked, "But?"

"But Bucky didn't have a mind for business. He often acted before he thought. He'd make an investment without really considering the consequences."

"Like with the Irish coffee?" I asked, only slightly offended.

Jazz chuckled. "That could have been one, but it wasn't. That turned out great. It was probably the single best thing he did for the place." The humor left him. "It's possible Kandice saw that we were running in the red, and she realized that something needed to be done about Bucky. I don't buy it myself, but I can see where the police might think that way."

"Okay," I said, thinking it through. I'd had no idea that Bucky's Tavern was losing enough money to be worrisome. But then again, that wasn't the sort of thing Bucky and I talked about. "If you don't think Kandice or Ivan poisoned him, who *do* you think did it?"

There was a long stretch of silence before Jazz said, "Bucky."

My brow furrowed. "Bucky?"

He nodded. "You know how I said he didn't think things through?"

"Yeah?"

"Well, Bucky and Geno Lyon have a history. I'm not sure if you know about it, but Geno was once poisoned."

I sat back in my chair, eyes wide, too stunned to speak.

"Everyone thought Jaqueline was responsible for it, and perhaps they're right." Jazz let that sit for a moment before continuing. "But I don't think so. I think that Bucky missed her, that he despised Geno, and so he tried to get rid of him."

"By poisoning him?" I asked.

"Like I showed you before, it's easy. Shooting someone leaves a lot of evidence. It's loud. Stabbing is messy. But poison . . . it's almost elegant."

My stomach churned. "It's still murder."

"That it is," Jazz said with a nod. "If it takes. Geno survived. No one was arrested for the attempt."

"But you think Bucky did it?"

"It's only a guess," Jazz said. "Like I said before, Bucky and I have known each other for a while now. He never admitted to poisoning Geno, but there were times, after he'd had a few too many to drink, that he'd lament about Jaqueline, how he hated that she married a man like Geno Lyon. It was clear he still cared deeply about her."

"Even after he started dating Kandice?"

"Even then," Jazz said. "I'm not saying he didn't care about Kandice—he did. But he still had feelings for Jaqueline. I'm worried that he attempted to remove Geno from her life once, but failed. Maybe he assumed that the first attempt would drive Geno away, that he'd be afraid that Jaqueline had tried to off him and he would leave her for it."

"But he didn't," I said.

"Bucky was unhappy about it," Jazz said. "There was also talk that Jaqueline and Geno weren't getting along, that she was sick of him, but she couldn't leave him for some reason. You know how it is. Bucky couldn't just leave her to fend for herself. He must have figured that he'd tried it once before and got away with it, so . . ."

"Why not try it again?" I supplied, heart sinking. "But you said you thought Bucky poisoned himself?"

"He'd been sick lately," Jazz said. "Far sicker than he let on. He was making mistakes. Dropping things." Jazz moved both teacups in front of him, held them there a moment, and then pushed *his* toward me. "Forgetting things."

The demonstration hit me like a brick. Could Bucky truly have tried to poison Geno Lyon, only to forget which cup contained the poison? It was almost too awful to believe.

"You see, Ms. Hancock," Jazz said, sitting back and crossing his arms. "The police should take a closer look at Bucky as being his own killer. When you know his history like I do, it's really the only thing that makes sense."

10

I drove, not quite paying attention to where I was going. I think, deep down, a part of me was trying to run away from the idea that a man I'd been getting to know as a friend might have been planning to commit murder.

But if he was, why hadn't I seen it coming? Why hadn't *anyone*?

A faded blue tarp fluttered in the wind, drawing me out of my thoughts long enough to realize I was about to pass the local library. A single car sat forlorn in the parking lot of what otherwise appeared to be an abandoned building. Just before passing the entrance, I yanked the wheel and pulled into the lot beside the car. I was curious about what was to become of the decrepit building now that the library had gotten funding, and since I recognized the car, I figured now was as good of a time as any to ask.

As I shut off the engine, the library doors opened, and Cindy Carlton walked out with an armload of books. The librarian was short and round, and she strode toward her car with a purpose. Her mouth moved in silent conversation with herself, and she didn't appear to see me as she loaded the books into the back seat of her vehicle.

"Hi, Cindy," I said as she stepped back to close the door.

"Oh!" Cindy's hand flew to her chest, and her eyes went wide. "Krissy! You startled me."

"Sorry about that," I said, suppressing my smile. "You seemed rather focused." I looked toward the library. "I take it you're closed today?"

She followed my gaze, and a sad, almost wistful smile crossed her face. "We will be closed off and on for the next couple of months. We have new hours while we prepare for the transition and all that. There's been quite a lot on my mind ever since we found out about . . ." She turned back to me, eyes brightening. "Have you heard? We've gotten enough funding to move to a new building!"

"I heard," I said. "Rita told me."

At the sound of Rita's name, some of the cheer went out of Cindy's expression. "Yes, well, I'm sure Ms. Jablonski gave you a skeptical view of what we're planning. She's already been in to complain at least a half dozen times." A sigh. "An exaggeration, but it sure feels like it."

"All she said is that you'll be moving locations," I said, figuring she didn't need the details, especially since she'd likely already heard them. "That you'll be building a new facility?"

"We will be, yes. But despite what Ms. Jablonski thinks, it's not necessarily a bad thing. This place is . . ." She frowned as she regarded the older library building once more. "I suppose *sour* is the only word that comes to mind. I don't mean it like in some horror-novel way. We had a good thing here once, but time and lack of funding left us with this." She fluttered a hand toward the old building.

Admittedly, the library *was* in a sorry state. The once-blue tarp was nearly gray now, barely held down as it flapped in the breeze. The brick exterior was stained, cracked, and crumbling in places. Even the parking lot was spiderwebbed with cracks and potholes that would soon be big enough to cause damage to cars that didn't steer around them.

I knew from experience that the inside wasn't any better. Water damage from the hole in the roof left sections of the place nearly unusable. Rooms that had once been big enough were now too small for the number of people living in town. Old outlets. Old fixtures. Uneven walls and floors that made the shelves sit not quite square.

"We've decided to close a good portion of the library permanently," Cindy went on. "The damage is too extensive, and it's been hard on the books. We're open three days a week, and only for a limited time, in just the main room. There's talk of opening a sort of temporary library in the church until the new building is open, but we'll see if that actually happens." She sighed. "I'll miss this place when we move, but at the same time, I won't. I'm hoping a new start is what we all need."

"Me too," I said. No, I didn't frequent the library much these days. Owning a bookstore café meant I had all the books I needed at my fingertips. "Do you know who donated the money?"

Cindy pressed her lips together before answering. "I best not say. At least, not yet. I'm sure there'll be an announcement at some point." She brightened. "We plan on turning the place into something akin to a community center. We're going to hire someone for outreach, to host events and so forth. Do you think your father would be interested in coming as a guest to a book festival if we were to host one?" She held up a hand before I could answer. "I don't need to know now. It'll be at least a year before we can even open, and likely a year after that before we'd be able to host such an event. Just keep it in mind. Maybe ask him about it when you talk to him next, okay?"

"I will," I assured her.

"Thank you, Krissy. You've done a lot for us over the years, and I hope that once we're settled into our new location, that relationship will continue. Jimmy is going to retire once we close here for good, but I'm going to keep at it." Jimmy was her husband, as well as a librarian.

"Good luck, Cindy," I said. "Tell Jimmy I said hi."

"Will do. This is so exciting. And sad. I really hope it works out."

"Me too."

Cindy climbed into her car, waved, and then drove off, leaving me standing alone outside the old library building. With her gone, the place truly did feel empty of life. I hoped that once they moved, the town would rally behind them and bring back the sense of community libraries often exuded.

I drove away, wondering what would happen to the space once the library was gone. I couldn't imagine anyone wanting to restore the building, but tear it down and rebuild? It was likely. The location was good, so why not?

Pine Hills was slowly getting back to normal after the earlier festivities. As I drove, I noted business owners removing their shamrocks and leprechauns and other St. Patrick's Day decorations. In some places, all evidence of the last few days had already been stripped away. It felt like everyone was moving on, and it seemed wrong to me. Bucky was dead, likely poisoned, and a part of me wanted the world to pause until his killer was found—even if that killer was Bucky Sweeny himself.

Since I had nowhere else to be right then, I decided to swing by Bucky's Tavern. I expected no one to be there, so I was surprised to find Kandice Vaughn standing in the parking lot with two men and a single, stooped-over woman. Kandice was gesturing angrily, but she stopped suddenly when she spotted me. She said something to the three others. They glanced over at me, then all filtered away, getting into three separate cars and driving off.

I got out of my car with a frown. "Who were they?" I asked, though I thought I already knew.

"Who do you think?" Kandice said. "Ruth, Ivan, and Dwayne. I can't believe they'd come here and . . ." She took a deep breath, let it out slowly. "Sorry. Was there something you needed, Krissy? I'm kind of busy right now."

"I guess I just wanted to see how you're doing," I said, gaze lingering on the street where the three bar owners had gone.

Kandice let out a harsh laugh. "I'm doing *great*." The sarcasm was heavy in her tone. "I—" Her cell phone rang. "One sec." She jerked it from her back pocket and checked the screen with a frown, before holding up a finger to me and stepping away.

The conversation was quick. Kandice's expression started as confused, but morphed into one of shock as she listened to whatever was being said. She barely spoke before clicking off and wandering back over to where I stood.

Curiosity had me wanting to ask her what the call was about, but it wasn't my place to ask. At least, not directly.

"Everything okay?" I asked her.

"I . . . Yeah." She shook her head, as if to clear it. "I have some things to take care of. I'm sorry, Krissy, but I really do need to go." She started to walk away, almost in a daze.

"Kandice?" I asked, following her a couple of steps. "I do have a question. It'll only take a second."

She stopped, turned back toward me. The stunned expression was still on her face. "As long as you're quick."

"I was told that Bucky threw someone out of the bar on St. Patrick's Day," I said.

"Yeah," Kandice said, some of her color returning. "I remember that."

"What happened?"

"I didn't see what *happened*," she said. "I only saw him drag the guy out and toss him."

"Do you know who it was?"

"No clue. He came in with a camera and was filming everyone." She thought about it a moment, then added, "He was a strange-looking guy, to be honest. I remember thinking how surprising it was that the dude's scrawny legs didn't give out from the weight of him."

I recognized the description without having to ask for a name: *Skinny Jefferson.*

Skinny was a photographer who liked to take photos of women, often in situations that were less than PG. If he'd caught Bucky in a compromising situation somewhere, it was possible Skinny had decided to show Bucky the photo to try to get something out of him. Money most likely. It was something I'd have to ask Skinny if and when I saw him.

"You're thinking that guy might have had something to do with Bucky's death," Kandice said.

"I don't know what to think," I admitted. "I've been hearing a lot of things, and at this point, I'm not sure what to believe."

She nodded as if that made perfect sense. "It's been a hard couple of days. I might look as if I have it all together right now, but truth be told, I'm a mess inside."

"I'm sorry, Kandice," I said. "I didn't mean to—"

"No, it's fine." She waved me off. "We all work through tragedies in our own way. Some of us internalize. Some break down and let their emotions show on their sleeves. Then there are some who need to go out and find answers, even when there are none to give." She eyed me at the last, telling me she knew of my reputation.

"What do *you* think happened to Bucky?" I asked, even though I'd said I only had *one* question and I'd already gone well past my quota. Sue me.

Kandice cleared her throat, then closed her eyes briefly before answering. "I think he made mistakes. I think he let the pressure get to him, and he went and did something he might have regretted if he'd survived. I think he was so worried about everything else, he let his own troubles build up until . . ." She spread her hands.

I bit my lip, desperate to ask whether she thought he could have poisoned himself while trying to kill Geno Lyon, but I didn't. For one, I didn't know if I quite believed it myself. For another, I didn't want to upset her any more than I—and seemingly everyone else—already had.

We stood in front of Bucky's Tavern, neither of us speaking for a long couple of moments. A car rolled down the street, vanished. The breeze blew past, bringing the scent of something cooking. It would have been peaceful if the tension between us wasn't so palpable.

"I was angry," Kandice said, breaking the silence. "My first thought when I found out where he was found was that he'd been cheating on me, so was it any surprise I got upset?" She didn't wait for an answer before going on. "But now that I've had a chance to think about it some more, I'm not so sure that was what happened."

"You don't think he was seeing Jaqueline?"

"I . . ." She sighed. "I'd like to say no, but how can I really know without asking her? And, even then, what are the chances of her telling me the truth if they *were* seeing each other? I want to believe that he was honest with me, that if he'd gone to see her, it wasn't a romantic hookup. People talk to their exes all the time, right?"

They did. But people didn't always end up dead in the back of those exes' trucks.

"Here." Kandice reached into her pocket and removed a key. She weighed it in her hand a moment before holding it out to me.

"What's this?" I asked, taking it.

"It's the key to Bucky's house. I haven't been able to bring myself to go past it yet. I left a few things there, but nothing I can't live without for now." She met my eye. "I've heard about you. You look into suspicious deaths. I want you to find out what happened to Bucky. Something was up with him lately. If there's anything at his place that would help you understand what that something might be, then it's better that you find it instead of me."

I looked down at the silver key. It looked like a copy, the kind you'd make for someone you cared about, especially if you wanted them to know you had nothing to hide, that they could come in at any time. *That* seemed like the Bucky I knew. Not someone who would go sneaking around behind his girlfriend's back with his ex. Not someone whose infidelity ended up getting him killed.

"There might not be anything there," Kandice went on. "But it would make me feel better if—" Her phone went off again, causing her to start. She glanced at the screen, brow furrowed.

From where I stood, I saw the name *Mara Wilson* on the screen. It meant nothing to me.

"I'm sorry, but I have to take this," Kandice said quickly. "Go to Bucky's place. See if there's anything there that says what might have happened to him."

"I will," I promised her.

She nodded once, then answered the call as she walked away.

I watched her go, grateful that she'd trusted me with the key, and confused at the same time. Kandice seemed conflicted, like she didn't know whether she should be sad about Bucky, or angry, or both. I supposed it was all the same thing when you got right down to it. His death was sudden, so conflicting emotions should be expected.

I bounced the key to Bucky's home in my hand a couple of times before pocketing it. I didn't know whether the police had been there yet, didn't know if it mattered one way or the other if they had. Bucky might have died of natural causes. It might have been poison.

Even if he'd met Geno somewhere else so he could poison him, he would have had to have kept the poison somewhere safe. Somewhere like his house.

But would he have wandered around town afterward, hoping he'd simply get over it if he'd known what was making him sick?

I doubted it. I was missing something—we *all* were. And if going to Bucky's house and snooping around would fill in that missing piece, then what was I waiting for?

I turned to head for my car when my phone went off, stalling me. I pulled it free, hoping it was Paul to tell me whether Bucky had truly died from poison or if it was natural causes like they'd originally assumed.

But it wasn't Paul.

It was Detective John Buchannan.

My heart sank as I accepted the call, already knowing this was going to be a conversation I wouldn't enjoy. "Hello, Detective," I said with only a mild anticipatory wince.

"Ms. Hancock." His voice was clipped, angry even. "Where have you been? I've been looking all over town for you."

I sighed and rubbed at my temples, where a headache was starting to form. "I was running some errands. Is there something I can do for you, Detective?"

Buchannan simmered on the other end of the line for a moment longer before he spoke, his voice softer, though it wasn't much kinder. "We need to talk."

"About Bucky?"

He didn't answer the question, only barked more commands. "I'm at the station now. Get here."

And then he was gone.

Great. If Detective Buchannan wanted to see me, I

was guessing that the cause of death had been confirmed as poison, which meant Bucky had been murdered.

Unless it was an accident, I thought. If that was the
case, chances were good that Bucky's death had *prevented* a murder before it could be carried out.

11

The Pine Hills Police Station parking lot was still decorated for the holiday. Green chalk outlines were speckled across the parking lot in the shape of leprechauns and even smaller shapes I took for fairies. There were others as well. A large, bulky humanoid. Something that looked like it was half human, half fish, or half snake. It was hard to tell for sure since that one had been drawn as if it had climbed out of a pothole that had been filled with water. The chalk had been smeared, so that most of it was an unidentifiable blob, though I was pretty sure the drawing was supposed to be a kelpie.

I wondered whose idea it had been to decorate the lot like a crime scene made of Celtic folklore creatures. For as morbid as it might be, seeing it brought a smile to my face. All in good fun, right?

The police station itself was decorated much like the rest of the town had been, with shamrocks and green streamers and such. Helium balloons sagged where they'd been tied, just inside the door, having lost most of their *oomph* over the last couple of days. When I opened the door, they bobbed lazily, bumping against the window and wall with hollow *bonk*s.

I stepped inside, and then stopped, suddenly unsettled. The police station was too quiet. A pair of police officers I didn't know sat at desks inside, eyes trained toward Chief Patricia Dalton's closed office door. The officers each wore stunned expressions and didn't so much as glance over at me as the door swung closed behind me.

My gaze swept the station, but other than the two officers, no one was immediately evident. I'd seen Paul's car in the parking lot, near the kelpie chalk outline, but that meant little if he was out on patrol in his cruiser. I'd also have expected Detective Buchannan to be waiting on me, the customary glower on his face, but he was likewise nowhere in sight.

I took a step forward and then stopped again, mouth parted as if to speak, yet something in the air told me not to. I felt like an intruder, as if I'd just walked in on a private moment and was expected to wait until whatever was going on had passed.

Thankfully, I didn't have to wait for long. Officer Becca Garrison strode down the hall, dressed in full uniform, with a slightly perplexed expression on her face. When she saw me, relief flittered across her features, and she hurried over.

"Hi, Krissy. I assume John called you?" she asked, voice kept low, as if she didn't want to break the heavy silence that hovered over the rest of the station.

I nodded. "He wanted to talk. I assume it's about Bucky Sweeny." My gaze flickered toward Chief Dalton's door, silently asking if he was inside. Buchannan, not Bucky. Obviously.

"John's waiting in his office," Becca said, jerking a thumb toward the hallway she'd just exited. "I think he's avoiding the rest of us."

"Oh." I didn't make a move to join him. "What's going on?" I asked. "Everyone seems so . . . somber."

Garrison was silent a long moment as she regarded the closed office door across the room. No one had come out from it, nor could I see any movement through it. "It's Chief Dalton."

My heart clenched. "Is she okay?"

A faint smile creased Garrison's features. "She's fine." The smile faded, and the perplexed expression returned. "But she's retiring."

"What?" It came out as a shout, causing the other two officers to glance my way before returning their attention to the door. I lowered my voice as I continued. "Why would she retire?"

Garrison shrugged. "No clue. It came out of nowhere, to be honest. Yesterday, she didn't make a peep about it. Nor had she so much as suggested that she was even considering it."

I opened my mouth and closed it a few times, too stunned to speak.

Alex Erickson

"But this morning, she walked in and dropped the bomb. Just came out and said it like it was no big deal. Blindsided the whole department." Garrison chuckled, though it was strained. "It even took Paul by surprise. He's in there now, talking to her. Needless to say, we're all pretty shocked about the whole thing."

Shocked was an understatement. Patricia Dalton, Paul's mom and the chief of police, was a constant around here. Paul and I had once joked that she'd never retire, that she'd keep working right up until she was unable, and quite possibly, even after. I couldn't imagine a situation in which she would *choose* to leave the police department on her own volition.

Did that mean the choice had been made for her?

Dread worked its way through me when I asked, "Is she sick?"

"Beats me," Garrison said with a shrug. "She didn't give anyone a reason, which is why we're all so surprised. But if she *is* sick, she's done a great job of hiding it." She frowned. "I hope she's just hit that point where she needs the break. Being a cop is hard enough on a day-to-day basis. Having to oversee the lot of us, *and* deal with all the politicking and pettiness that goes with the territory of being in charge, has to make it even worse."

"Wow," I said. I got it—I really did. But Chief Dalton had seemed so *strong*, like nothing could break her, let alone bend her. I felt like something had to have happened, whether it be in her life or within the department, that forced this upon her.

Garrison patted my shoulder. "'Wow' is right. It'll be strange without her."

We were both staring at the office door when a stern voice came from down the hall behind us.

"Ms. Hancock." Detective John Buchannan was standing just outside his own office door, looking as irritated as always. "This way."

"Good luck," Garrison muttered. She shot me a wink, and then joined the other two officers in their vigil. None of them spoke; they just watched Chief Dalton's door and waited to see what would happen. A part of me wished I could join them.

Buchannan turned and walked toward the interrogation room instead of his office. I wondered what kind of office a man like John Buchannan kept, but at least the interrogation room wasn't as scary as it sounded. Sure, it had a table with rickety plastic chairs around it where interrogations and interviews took place, but it also held a dartboard, a couch, and a coffeepot, making it more like a break room than anything else.

I noted that the pillow and blankets were gone, however. Becca Garrison had been sleeping in the room recently after losing her home due to a bad deal on her loans. The scam had been done legally, using loopholes in the contract, so there was little she could do about it but try to get back on her feet and start again. It appeared as if she'd finally done so.

"You've been hard to pin down today," Buchannan said as he sat down and motioned for me to do the same.

"Like I said, errands."

"Such as?"

I sat and ignored the question. "I assume I'm here about Bucky?"

Buchannan scowled at me, but answered, "You assume correctly."

"Was he poisoned?"

Another scowl. At this point, his angry looks didn't affect me. I almost welcomed them because they often told me I was on the right track.

"Right now, we're running on the assumption that he was. We're still waiting for test results." He leaned forward and pressed his hands flat on the table. "I don't suspect you had a hand in his murder—"

"That's good."

"—but I do know you were close to the victim."

"We weren't close," I said, probably a little too defensively. "We were just getting to know one another as friends and colleagues, but we hadn't quite gotten there yet. We only met after he came to me asking if I'd supply coffee for the Irish coffee that he planned on selling during the St. Patrick's Day event."

"Why would he come to you instead of just buying coffee at the store?"

"Cross-promotion," I said.

"Pardon?"

"Bucky wanted us to cross-promote. Small businesses sticking together and such. Death by Coffee provides the coffee, while Bucky's Tavern provides the whiskey and then sells the resulting beverage. He'd make it clear where the coffee came from, and we, at Death by Coffee, would send people over to Bucky's to sample it. Cross-promotion."

"I see. And did you work closely with him when it came to the creation of the Irish coffee?"

"Close enough, I suppose," I said. "But I didn't see who poisoned him, if that's what you're asking."

He flashed me an unamused smile. "Perhaps not, but you may have seen something that would help us find the poisoner." A pause. "If there is one."

I didn't comment on the last, considering Jazz's suspicion that Bucky had poisoned himself. That was a can of worms I wanted no part of. At least, when it came to discussing suspects with Detective John Buchannan.

"Such as?" I asked.

He shrugged. "What was his personal life like? Did he ever talk to you about someone he might have been having trouble with? Enemies? Annoyances?"

"Have you talked to Kandice Vaughn? She's a bartender at Bucky's." I paused, once more not quite sure how much to say. I opted for the full truth this time. "She and Bucky were dating, though I personally never saw them together in that way. She would know more about his personal life than me."

"I have spoken with her, yes," Buchannan said. "But I wanted to get *your* insights."

"I don't have any," I said. When he glared, I added, "Really, I don't."

"So, you have no idea who might have wanted to harm Mr. Sweeny?"

I opened my mouth to tell him no, but realized that wasn't entirely true. "Ivan McGraw," I said. "There's a rumor going around that Ivan might have discovered that Bucky was cheating on Kandice with Jaqueline Lyon and was blackmailing him. And since Bucky was found in the back of Jaqueline's truck . . ." I spread my hands.

Buchannan frowned. "You suspect Ivan killed him?"

"Or Jaqueline. Or her husband, Geno." *Or Kandice.* Although, would she have given me the key to Bucky's house if she was guilty? I suppose if Kandice had made the poison herself, she could have planted it at Bucky's to mislead me. She might even have sent me there to find other "evidence" that she'd left behind for the same purpose.

I hated to admit it, but Kandice Vaughn was as much of a suspect as Jaqueline and Geno and Ivan. Maybe more so, considering the fact that he might have been cheating on her.

"Ms. Hancock?" Buchannan snapped his fingers in front of my face. He'd been speaking, and I'd completely missed what he'd said.

"I'm sorry," I said. "That's all I know. Bucky and I had a business relationship. I liked him, but I knew little of his personal life. I didn't even know Jaqueline was his ex—or that she even existed—until recently."

Buchannan sighed and rubbed at his temples. "Are you telling me that these errands you had to run had nothing to do with you poking around town, looking for answers to questions you shouldn't be asking?"

"Well . . ."

He glared, waited.

"I've talked to some people, yes," I said. "But really, there's not much I can tell you. I'm not sure if any of it is important."

"How about you tell me what you've heard, and I can decide if it's important or not."

Still, I hesitated. If I had something concrete, I'd

feel better about telling him. But so far, all I had was assumption and rumor. No facts. No actual evidence.

But Detective Buchannan needed to know.

So, I told him. I explained what Jazz had told me, about Geno getting sick and Jazz's belief that Geno had been poisoned by Bucky. I told him about how it might be possible that Bucky had tried again and had accidentally poisoned himself in the process. I talked about Ivan and the other bar owners, Ruth Camden and Dwayne Morris, about how they didn't like that Bucky had opened his bar in what they viewed as their territory. I even passed along Paige's warning that poison took time and that he should be cognizant of that when looking at Bucky's timeline.

Buchannan listened and didn't interrupt, even when it was clear he was skeptical of what I was saying. I admit, I was having a hard time believing most of it myself, especially when I talked about Jazz's belief that Bucky might have poisoned himself. It simply didn't make sense, not with what I knew of the man.

"I see," Buchannan said when I was done. He didn't sound happy. Big surprise there.

"I told you it might not be important."

"You believe Mr. Sweeny once tried to poison Geno Lyon, making the other man sick, but not killing him. And then, years later, he decided to do it again, but somehow ingested the poison himself?"

"I didn't say *I* believed it," I said. "I don't even know how much of it is true, if any of it. Like I tried to warn you—rumor and hearsay."

Buchannan's jaw worked as he regarded me. He

knew as well as I did that what I'd told him wasn't actionable. He could ask around, sure, but what were the chances anyone would tell him the truth? Ivan, Ruth, and Dwayne might not even admit to being upset about Bucky opening his tavern now that he was dead. They wouldn't want to appear as if they'd had reason to kill him.

The same went for Kandice, Geno, and Jaqueline. No matter what Bucky's relationship was to them, they'd downplay it so as to minimize the possibility that they'd be looked at for murder. Or they would make their association with him appear idyllic.

"I suppose that's it, then," Buchannan said, pushing his way to his feet. "I would appreciate it if you were to leave the rest of the investigating to me. I'd like this to be the last time we speak on the matter, if it's all the same to you."

I rose. "I know you don't have confirmation that it was poison yet," I said, "but do you know what kind it might have been?" Because if I knew that, it might help determine who had poisoned Bucky—and if it was possible he might have accidentally done it to himself.

"What kind?" Buchannan asked with a frown.

"Of poison. Arsenic. Ricin."

He sighed, then walked over to the door. He opened it and motioned for me to precede him. "No, Ms. Hancock. I do not. And if I did, I wouldn't tell you."

Miffed, I left the interrogation room. Buchannan followed me out, but turned toward his office, rather than escort me to the door. I was okay with that, because right then, I didn't have much else to say to him.

Garrison saw me heading for the door, so she rose

from where she was sitting with the officers in their vigil of Chief Dalton's office. She joined me just as I stepped outside into the blessedly cool air. The interrogation hadn't been warm exactly, but the topic of conversation had me feeling stifled nonetheless.

"How'd it go?" she asked, crossing her arms over her chest and hunching her shoulders against the breeze.

"As well as it could go, I suppose," I replied. "I told him what I knew, and like usual, he didn't care for what I had to say."

"That's John for you." She smiled. "But honestly? I think he likes having you around. He might not show it, but he appreciates your help. He may not approve of how you get your information, but it does keep him from having to find it all out on his own."

"Well, a thanks every now and again would be nice." I sulked a moment longer before a new question popped into my head. "Hey, do you know if anyone's been to Bucky Sweeny's house yet?"

She gave me a curious look. "We have. Why?"

"I was just wondering. Do you think it would be okay if I checked it out? I have a key and—"

Garrison held up a hand, cutting me off. "Don't tell me. I don't want to know how you got a key or why you want to look around his place. Just go ahead and do it. But if you find anything . . ."

"I'll tell Buchannan."

"Good. That's all I need to hear."

She turned and went back inside the police station before I could say something more that she'd be obliged to take to Buchannan.

I returned to my car and pulled the key Kandice had

given me from my pocket. I bounced it in my palm a few times, thinking, before pocketing it again.

The police might have already been to his house, but that didn't mean they'd found what they were looking for. The evidence might not be, well, *evident* to the police. Heck, even I might not recognize it when I saw it. I knew nothing of poisons or how Bucky had lived. Going to his place was a long shot, and I knew it.

But even if I didn't find anything that specifically pointed to him poisoning himself or someone having reason to kill him, going to Bucky's would tell me *something*. No, I didn't yet know what. Often that was how it went.

And if I *did* find evidence of poison after the police had already been through Bucky's house, I had a feeling it would tell me more about *Kandice* than it would about Bucky.

12

Bucky's house was in a part of Pine Hills often referred to as the "old part of town." No, the nickname wasn't original or inventive, but it did describe it accurately. It was where the town began, where the first houses were built, and where the first business had opened. But as time passed, so did preferences, and the downtown area eventually migrated to where Death by Coffee sat today, leaving this section of Pine Hills as a relic of a time long past.

As I pulled up in front of the old, boxy house, I wondered if our little town was about to experience another such shift. With the latest planned expansion, I feared it was only a matter of time before the streets I knew became less frequented, and would soon be speckled with closed shops and forgotten businesses, as everyone migrated to the newer—and quite possibly subjectively better—section of town.

I shut off the engine and then took a moment to take in the atmosphere. The gutters were sagging from the weight of years of leaves and debris. It appeared as if they'd never been cleaned since the house had been built. Trees that appeared just as ancient as the house—and were likely far older than that—dotted the yard. Branches reached out, their clawed tips resting against the shingles, which were raised in places from where they scraped in time with the gusting wind.

Much like Bucky's Tavern, there was no police tape on the door of his house or any indication that anything was amiss other than the emptiness. The neighbors weren't standing at their windows or on sagging porches, watching me. It was quiet—a place forgotten. It made me sad to think that before long, Bucky's memory, just like this part of town, would fade away to nothing.

Shaking off the unsettling thought, I climbed out of my car and approached the front door. I kept expecting someone to call out, to demand to know why I was there or threaten to call the police. I gripped the key Kandice had given me, eyes forward, as I quick-stepped my way up a sidewalk so cracked and segmented, grass and other plants were poking through and would soon take over if left unchecked.

My first instinct when I reached the door was to knock. Strange how, even when I knew that no one would be home—or ever would be home again—I still felt the need to respect Bucky's privacy.

The lock was a smidge stubborn due to rust on the knob, and the door creaked and listed slightly to the side when I pushed it open. When I tried to close it behind me, it didn't quite fit the frame right. I didn't want to make too much noise, so I left it only partially closed. I'd wrestle with it once I left.

The inside of Bucky's house didn't appear as run-down as the outside, though there were indications of its age still evident. The walls were freshly painted, though one wall appeared as if it was made from plaster, while the other three looked to have been more recently replaced with drywall. The bumps and irregularities felt somehow *right*, with the smoother walls feeling out of place, though I didn't know why.

"I'm here," I muttered, voice pitched low so as not to disturb the eerie silence. "Now what?" The front door led directly into an oddly shaped living room that was too long and narrow to decorate properly. Everything seemed squished in place, angled ever so slightly so that there'd be a walkway to the dining room, which was square-shaped. A small, galley-sized kitchen sat off of that. The counters were green and unappealing, but the stove and fridge were stainless steel and relatively new.

A staircase off the living room led upstairs to where I assumed the bedrooms and bathroom were located. Another set of stairs off the kitchen led to the basement. The door hung open, and a damp, heady smell oozed from it, telling me that it hadn't been waterproofed.

"If I were making poison," I whispered to myself, "where would I do it?"

The good news was that there was no evidence of poison immediately evident, making me think that my earlier concerns that Kandice might have planted evidence for me to find were less likely. It was entirely possible that she'd hidden it just enough not to make it too obvious, but not seeing it staring at me the moment I was through the door did feel like a relief.

The floor creaked and groaned as I crossed the living room, then passed through the sparsely decorated dining room and into the kitchen. An old mug sat in the sink. It had been turned upside down, so if there'd ever been anything in it, it was long gone by now. Otherwise, everything else was in place. A calendar on the wall had St. Patrick's Day circled with a green Sharpie, which was clipped to the top of the calendar alongside a black one. There were no other notes written on the calendar, hinting at clandestine meetings or anniversaries.

I frowned as I scanned the rest of the kitchen. Buchannan had said the police had been here, yet the mug was still sitting in the sink and nothing else appeared to have been disturbed. Even the living room didn't have that ransacked look to it that I expected to find whenever I thought of police rifling through a home for evidence. The remote to the television had been sitting on the armrest of the recliner, drawers had been closed, the floor relatively spotless. I hadn't even noticed smears in the dust that had gathered on shelves and the TV stand, though I hadn't looked closely.

They weren't looking for poison.

As far as I could tell, they weren't looking for *anything.*

Determined not to leave any stone unturned, I got to work.

The fridge was half full, organized in a way that was almost OCD-like. Cleaning supplies resided under the sink. The cupboards were packed with various boxed

and bagged food items. Pots and pans and cooking utensils were right where I expected them to be. The ancient dishwasher was partly filled with clean dishes, as
if Bucky, who lived alone, hadn't bothered to put anything away before taking it out to use it.

Other than the cleaning chemicals, nothing appeared
poisonous to my untrained eye. I even picked up the
mug from the sink and sniffed it. Old coffee, as far as I
could tell.

I went down too-soft wooden stairs, into the damp,
barely used unfinished basement. An old washer and
dryer sat in a corner, an empty clothes basket next to
them. The center of the room was dominated by the
water heater and furnace. That was it. No table or empty
containers or anything that indicated Bucky ever came
down here, other than when he needed to do his laundry.

I headed back upstairs and made a quick pass through
the dining room and living room. As I'd noted before,
there was dust on the shelves and the TV stand, but it
was your standard house dust, not something dangerous, like residue from some sort of crafted poison. There
were no mysterious baggies of an unidentified substance. No scrawled instructions on how to make an
untraceable poison. Nothing.

As I reached the front window, I peeked outside. No
one was bothering my car, nor were they watching the
house. It made me wonder how difficult it would have
been for someone—Jaqueline, perhaps—to sneak in
and clean up after Bucky, if he had indeed made the
poison and accidentally poisoned himself like Jazz believed. I'd seen no indication that anyone else had been

here—the police included—but I couldn't rule it out either.

I let the curtain fall back into place and then ascended the stairs to the second floor. A tight hallway led across the length of the house, with four doors, two to a side. The bathroom was the first on the right. I figured that out of the remaining rooms, it would be the most likely place to store—or hide—poison, so I started there.

Like the rest of the house, the bathroom walls showed the house's age, but the tub, toilet, and sink were new. A peek in the closet and beneath the sink revealed the usual bathroom supplies, cleaning and otherwise. There were a few half-full prescription pill bottles, but I didn't recognize the names of the medications, only that they were prescribed for Bucky. I snapped a quick picture of the labels with my phone, just in case they could have been what had killed him, and moved on.

The room across the hall—a spare bedroom so dusty, I don't think it was ever used—was likewise empty of evidence. The last two rooms consisted of Bucky's bedroom and a small office with a desktop computer and monitor sitting on a small, single-drawer desk.

I paused at Bucky's bedroom door, not wanting to invade his private space. I could see a few feminine items at the bedside farthest from the door. I assumed they were Kandice's, which made my heart ache a little for her. I considered boxing them up and giving them to her the next time I saw her, but decided that was something she should do on her own. It would help her grieve, give her closure, for as hard as it might be.

A quick pass through the bedroom showed me nothing more than what you'd expect out of a sleeping space. Blankets, clothing, half-finished books. I didn't check under his underwear or poke through a drawer that looked as if it contained personal items he'd saved over the years. It didn't feel right, and while it meant I wasn't as thorough as I could have been, I already was pretty sure that if Bucky *had* poisoned himself, he hadn't done it here in his home. I was also starting to believe there was no evidence of any kind that might explain why someone might have wanted him dead.

I entered the final upstairs room, which turned out to be Bucky's office, expecting to find nothing. A cursory glance into the closet showed me printer supplies, along with a stack of old CDs so covered with dust that I'd have to brush them off to see the artists' names. I turned on the computer, figuring I could check his browser history and then leave. As I waited for it to boot up, I opened his desk drawer, but all I found was a single pen, missing its cap.

Bucky kept his computer desktop bare. Only the recycling bin icon sat in the upper-right corner. And the taskbar only held his start menu and Chrome browser icons. I clicked on the browser button, and it took me directly into his email. No password needed.

"Huh," I said. I supposed it shouldn't have been *too* surprising since Bucky lived alone, but so did I, and I still had two-factor authentication set up on my shiny new laptop.

I was moving the mouse pointer to the upper right, where I could check his search history, when I noted a name I recognized on one of the emails. Brow furrowed, I diverted to the subject line, which simply read, "Keep the faith," and clicked it.

> *Bucky,*
> *I know the others are dead set against you and will stop at darn near nothing to keep you from accomplishing what you wish. They don't understand, and I'm not of a mind to teach them. Now, optics prevents me from speaking out on your behalf, but know that I would never do anything to risk what we have forged. We should meet and discuss our options sometime in the very near future.*
> *Keep the faith.*
> *Until then,*
> *Ruth*

I reread the email twice, then hurriedly closed it and scoured the rest of his emails, looking for another that might give me more insights into what exactly she'd been talking about.

But if there had been any other emails from Ruth Camden, Bucky had deleted them. *Or someone else had.*

But who? And why?

No other names leapt out at me as I skimmed the rest of his inbox, which he seemed to clean out regularly. He had subscription notifications, an email from Kandice that talked solely of their plans with the Irish coffee, and the message from Ruth. Nothing from Jaqueline or any of the other bar owners or anyone else whose names I recognized at all. I clicked on a few random

emails and found most of them to be spam made out to
look like friendly correspondence.

From there, I finally got around to checking his
browser history, but as expected, there was nothing interesting to find. Like the basement, it didn't appear as
if Bucky spent much time on his PC. Just as most people these days, he had a phone for that.

I turned off the computer and headed for the stairs,
my mind a million miles away.

Hadn't Bucky been the one to mention Ruth when
we'd talked on St. Patrick's Day? I thought he was, and
he'd done so as if she was just like the other bar owners, if not more so. Hadn't he said that she was likely
the one who'd sicced Dwayne Morris on him?

It didn't make sense. The tone of Ruth's email made
it sound like she was siding with him, that they might
even have been friends to some degree. Or was I misin-
terpreting her words somehow?

I jerked to a stop, halfway down the stairs, as a sudden thought hit me.

What if Bucky wasn't cheating on Kandice with
Jaqueline?

What if he was cheating on her with *Ruth*?

A *creak* interrupted my thoughts as the front door
slowly opened. I immediately dropped into a crouch.
The railing wouldn't hide me completely, but it *would*
obscure me from casual view. The angle was awkward,
so I couldn't see who entered, only that whoever it was,
they were moving cautiously and quietly.

They stepped into the living room, leaving the front
door hanging open behind them. They didn't call out,
only took another step into the house.

My legs were throbbing from my crouch, so I shifted my weight ever so slightly.

The *creak* that followed was so loud, it could have been heard next door.

The intruder spun around with their arm raised in a way that told me they had a weapon of some kind. A beat passed, and then they started my way, stride quick and determined.

Panicked, I tried to scramble back up the stairs, but my foot slipped out from under me. I cracked my shin *hard* on the step. Instant agony shot through my leg, and I cried out, positive I'd broken a bone, or at the least, cracked it.

The intruder rounded the banister, weapon raised. Wild, terrified eyes met mine, and then, "Krissy?"

I sucked in a shocked breath and let it out with, "Grant?"

We stared at each other for an excruciating long moment before he lowered his weapon, a half-rotted branch he must have picked up from just outside the front door.

"What are you doing here?" he asked.

Heart hammering, I retorted with a less-than-kind, "What are *you* doing here?"

Grant leaned against the wall and massaged his chest, as if *I'd* been the one to come at him and scare him half to death. "I was thinking of Bucky and decided to drive by his place. I saw the door hanging open and thought someone had broken in." His face flushed. "I thought . . . honestly, I don't know what I was thinking by coming in here like that. I should have called the police and let them handle it."

"I'm glad you didn't," I said, stretching my leg out in front of me. Now that the initial shock of it had passed, it barely throbbed, though, like Robert's pinch, I was sure I was going to bruise. "Kandice gave me a key."

"Why would she do that?" Grant asked, face scrunching up in confusion.

I considered how much to tell him, then opted for honesty. "I was looking for evidence. If someone was after Bucky and he knew about it, he might have written something down, or perhaps they'd left him an angry letter. And if he was poisoned—"

"Poisoned?" Grant paled as he cut me off. "You think he was poisoned?"

"It's a theory," I said. "Did you see anyone give him anything to drink or eat on St. Patrick's Day? Maybe the day before?"

Grant considered it, then shook his head. "I don't recall anything like that. Bucky's stomach had been bothering him for a few days, but that wasn't anything new. I suppose it might have been worse than before, but honestly, with the stress of the holiday, it was no wonder."

Which jibed with what others had told me, so I opted to change the subject. "What was Bucky's relationship with Ruth Camden like?"

Grant looked confused by the question. "They didn't get along. I mean, I never saw them together or anything, but Bucky always gave the impression that he was fighting with her, just like he was with Dwayne and Ivan. Do you think Ruth poisoned him?" His eyes widened. "Will she come after the rest of us next?"

"I don't think you have anything to worry about," I

said. Though, honestly, how could I be so sure? I didn't know who had poisoned Bucky Sweeny or why. It was entirely possible that something at Bucky's Tavern was the source of the poison, which *would* put the other employees at risk.

"Oh man." Grant ran his fingers through his hair. I noted his hand was shaking, and was it any wonder? Bucky was dead, and none of us knew why it had happened or who might be next, if anyone.

I stood and tested my leg. Only a slight twinge. "We should probably go."

Grant nodded and picked up his stick, which promptly broke in half from the rotten center. The laugh that followed was nervous and half-crazed. "I guess this wouldn't have helped me much if someone dangerous *had* been here."

Grant led the way out the door. As I exited after him, I was forced to pull up on the doorknob so the door would rise enough to close properly. Even then, it took three good slams before it latched.

Grant had his hands shoved into his pockets, shoulders hunched, when I turned around, exhausted from fighting with the door. "I'm going to go," he said, scuffing his shoe across a weed growing through the cracks in the concrete. "I'm sorry I scared you like that."

"It's fine," I said. "I'm glad it was you." Then, because he looked so vulnerable, "Are you okay?"

He tried to smile, but it faded before it could fully form. "Not really. Bucky gave me a job when no one else would, and now . . ."

"And now he's gone."

"And now he's gone," Grant repeated, though his tone held far more melancholy than my own. "I'm not sure what I'm going to do. Money has been tight for a while, but without a job, it's nonexistent."

"Do you have any family who could help?" I asked, thinking of Jazz and his sister.

Grant laughed. "Right. I mean, yeah, I've got family, but they won't help me. Before I landed this job, I was a mess. Burned those bridges years ago, then went back and tried to burn them a few more times. I told them that I'm better now, but they won't hear it. I think they expect me to do more than get a job at a bar. If I owned it, now, that might get their attention."

I almost told him that he might want to try to buy it now that Bucky was gone, but he'd already established he didn't have the money. All I managed was a pathetic, "I'm sorry."

"Me too." He flashed me a sad smile, then slunk over to his car, which was parked behind mine.

I turned to face the house, not wanting to watch him go. I felt bad for Grant, but at the same time, he was still alive. Bucky wasn't. The house would remain empty until someone came along and bought it, brought life back to it. The same went for Bucky's Tavern. What a mess.

A rumble of Grant's car engine started and then faded as a new thought hit me. I spun around, but it was already too late.

What color was his car?

I wished I'd paid better attention because my mind

supplied the red vehicle with the rusty driver's-side door. Could Grant have been the one who'd been lurking outside my house last night?

As I climbed into my car, I realized something else. Someone *had* given Bucky something to drink the morning of the St. Patrick's Day parade. And that someone was none other than Grant Price.

13

Misfit sat on the floor, tail swishing back and forth as he waited for me to take notice of him. I knew he was there, of course. I also knew that if I acknowledged him, he'd insist I feed him by making sure I couldn't do anything *but*. And no, his partially filled dish of dry cat food was not enough to sate him. He wanted wet food. And maybe a few dry treats. And a wet one. Then he'd want me to sit on the couch where he could take a post-meal bath on my lap before curling up for a nap.

Normally, I'd be all for a relaxing few hours doing nothing but petting my cat and dozing while half-watching a forgettable show on TV, but right then, I was too wound up to relax.

I was sitting at my dining room table, laptop open before me and a mostly empty cup of coffee cooling next to that. I'd been there for the last two hours, scan-

ning website after website, trying to come up with
some indication as to what could have happened to Bucky
Sweeny. I'd looked up his medications and found that
none of them were likely to have been the cause of his
poisoning. They were for anxiety and a variety of stomach issues, which, knowing him, wasn't a surprise.
And, sure, if he'd taken a bunch of them, it would have
made him sick, might even have killed him, but he
would have shown other, more severe, symptoms before he'd succumbed.

I soon moved on to researching specific poisons.
And when that didn't yield results, I looked at other
substances that could be poisonous.

Unfortunately, *poison* was a relatively general term
when you got right down to it. Common chemicals
could be poisonous. Insects. Venom from spiders and
snakes could be used as poison. There were natural
poisons, manufactured ones. Some people considered
certain foods poisonous due to allergies and other conditions that made food that everyone else could eat
deadly in the right circumstances. Even if the substance
wasn't *poison* per se, to those ingesting it, it acted that
way.

It also didn't help that I didn't know any of Bucky's
symptoms beyond an upset stomach and coughing.
Bucky had appeared sick, like he'd had a bad cold
combined with a stomach bug. Yes, he'd looked terrible. But did he have a fever? Was he reacting in any
other way? Nausea? Vomiting? Hives? Could he have
had a cold, and most of the other symptoms I'd seen
were irrelevant?

I didn't know. Nor did I have any way of finding out.

I closed my laptop with a snap and sat back, frustrated.

The assumption was that Bucky had been poisoned. At this point, I wasn't disputing that. But as I noted before, poison could be nearly anything. Did someone manufacture it? Was it accidental? A severe allergy that was being termed *poison* because it was the easiest and quickest explanation? I'd seen what a severe peanut allergy could do to a person. And while the peanuts weren't poison in and of themselves, the act of lacing a drink with peanut dust could be considered poisoning someone who had an allergy.

Grant served Bucky a coffee that day.

He'd also served me, and I hadn't gotten sick. Coincidence? Targeted? I didn't know.

I rose, which caused Misfit to jump to his feet and make a beeline for his food dishes. I went the other way, much to his consternation, but he could wait. In fact, he could probably stand to lose a few pounds now that he was getting older.

Asking Grant about the coffee would get me nowhere. If he'd poisoned Bucky, he'd say that he gave him his coffee, and that was it. He'd point out that I'd had some coffee from the same pot as well, which he'd use to prove his innocence. And if he *was* innocent, he'd say the exact same thing, which would make my questions pointless.

Kandice might know whether Bucky had an allergy that wouldn't affect anyone else. So might Jaqueline, and by extension, Geno. Would Grant know about such a thing? And would he risk serving Bucky a coffee laced with a poison—or an allergen—in front of everyone?

For now, I had no answers for that line of questioning. And no amount of sitting around and dwelling on it would help either.

But there *was* a thread I could tug on, one I'd yet to pursue.

I retrieved my phone from the table, did a quick search online, and then dialed the number I found. It rang twice before a tired, slightly annoyed woman's voice answered with a terse, "Yeah?"

"Hi," I said, uncertain. "Is this . . . Bar?" I floundered. "The one near Hotel?" Boy, did I ever wish they'd have given either one of those places a real name. It didn't exactly roll from the tongue.

"You got it."

"Could I speak to the owner?" I asked. "Ruth Camden." As if the person on the other line wouldn't know whom I was talking about.

There was a slight pause before, "You got a complaint?"

"No," I said, putting casual cheer into my voice. "It's about something else."

"Uh-huh." Clearly, the woman didn't believe me.

"I haven't been to your establishment," I said. "So, there's no reason for me to complain."

"Uh-huh."

"I just need to talk to Ruth. It's about . . ." Here, I paused to consider what to say. I didn't want to scare Ruth off, but at the same time, I didn't want her to ignore me either. So, I opted for the truth. "It's about Bucky Sweeny."

Something *clink*ed on the other end of the line. It sounded like beer glasses. "You with the police?" Pronounced with a long "o."

"I'm not." Though I wondered why she would ask such a question. "My name's Krissy Han—"

"I know who you are. I'll be here for the rest of the day, on into the evening. Tell Lou your name, and he'll send you back."

"Thank you—" I was talking to dead air.

I pocketed my phone, and then took pity on Misfit. I gave him a handful of treats, along with a fresh catnip toy mouse from a stash I kept hidden from him. The mouse would last all of ten minutes before he'd lose it under the stove or behind the couch or wherever toy mice ended up. As long as I doled them out one at a time, a single package could last weeks.

That done, I headed for the simply named Bar at the far end of town. The wooden building appeared sad from the outside. Dirty windows. A listing picnic table, already occupied by early drinkers, sat out front next to a couple of motorcycles. The inside looked a bit better, though not by much. Dark brown, glassy deer eyes watched me from the heads on the wall as I approached the bar, where a haggard man in a flannel shirt was lounging with a tattered paperback bent from cover to cover in hand. He glanced up at me as I entered.

"I'm—"

"Back there," he said, jerking his head toward a door in the corner, next to the bar. He didn't watch to see if

I'd follow his instructions, instead turning his gaze back to the tortured book in his hand.

All righty then. I made my way across a floor that was alternatively squishy and hard, as if decades of spilled beer had weakened some of the boards but left others intact. It was a rather unpleasant feeling, so I was happy to note that it firmed up as I approached the closed door the bartender had indicated. I knocked.

"Yep," came the answer from the other side.

I took it for an invitation and opened the door.

Ruth Camden was sitting behind a desk, an open beer bottle in front of her. She was flipping through her phone, index finger curled unnaturally as she swiped. Her gray hair was pulled out of her face in a messy bun that was coming loose. She was frowning in concentration, jowls almost quivering as she focused on what she was doing.

"Dang it," she said, slamming her phone down onto the desk hard enough, I jumped. "I swear these dang games cheat." Gray eyes met mine when she looked up. "You're Krissy Hancock, then?"

"I am," I said, entering the rest of the way. After a moment's hesitation, I closed the door behind me. "I'm here because—"

"Yeah, yeah." She waved me toward a chair. "Bucky."

I sat. "I own Death by Coffee with my friend Vicki. We provided the coffee for his Irish coffee on St. Patrick's Day."

"Good for you," Ruth said, leaning back in her chair, though she remained stooped forward, as if her back didn't quite straighten. I also noted that it wasn't just her index finger that was curled oddly, but all of them.

When she laid her hands across her slight paunch, her fingers pointed every which direction, as if they'd all been broken at some point. She noted me looking, and smiled. "Arthritis, along with some other joyous conditions I won't bore you with." She wiggled her fingers, which was rather disconcerting. "You should see me try to type. Takes near half an hour to finish a single paragraph, and that's if I haven't been drinking." She laughed.

"I'm sorry," I said. "Does it hurt?"

She shrugged. "Probably. I'm used to it by now. And, well . . ." She leaned forward and tapped the beer bottle with a fingernail. It *tink*ed in a way that told me it was empty. "So," she said, easing back again. "You wanted to talk about Bucky? Not sure what I can tell you, being that we didn't much get on."

"Because of his tavern?"

"I suppose." She shrugged, gray eyes flicking away from my face before returning. "We don't need the competition."

"'We' being you, Dwayne Morris, and Ivan McGraw."

Another shrug. It seemed to be her go-to gesture. "That'd be us."

"You went to pay your condolences."

"Sure. It was the polite thing to do." Once again, spoken with the elongated "o."

"I was also told you sent Dwayne to Bucky's before his death, and that the two men almost got into a fight."

Ruth smiled, revealing a missing canine that she prodded at with her tongue before answering. "Dwayne's a hothead. He likes to tussle whenever he can, often without much reason for it beyond his own amusement, so I'm not surprised they got into it. I didn't send Dwayne after Bucky, however. You best check your information on that."

It was my turn to smile, all sweet and innocent. "Is that because you and Bucky were seeing each other behind Dwayne and Ivan's back?"

She blinked, expression going neutral. "I don't know what you're talking about."

"I saw Bucky's email," I said, suddenly wishing I'd forwarded it to myself, or at least taken a picture of the screen so I could show her. And possibly the police, just in case they hadn't seen it. "There was an email from you there. You said something about the others not understanding what the two of you had."

Another blink, then sudden realization.

Ruth Camden burst into laughter. "You . . ." She wheezed. "You think . . ." More uncontrollable laughter while she grunted a few other attempts at words, but she didn't have the air to speak.

I sat there and fought against the rising blush I could feel coming on as I waited her out. I'd expected a reaction from her, but *this*? It made me feel like I'd wildly missed the mark.

"Woo, boy," Ruth said, wiping her eyes as she finished. "After everything that's happened, I needed that." She cleared her throat, and when she looked at me, she was still grinning. "You think that Bucky and I were screwing around behind everyone's back?"

"Were you?" I asked.

She snorted like she might burst into laughter again, but restrained herself. "No, miss, we weren't. We had . . . an understanding."

"About?"

"What do you think? This place. His place. There was no reason for us to be at one another's throats. No, I didn't much care for the competition, but Bucky assured me that he'd work with us, rather than against us. We had talks. Compromised, I suppose you'd call it."

"What about Ivan and Dwayne? Were they in on this compromise?"

This time her snort was one of derision. "What do you think? Those two are a couple of boneheads. Both are too volatile to be responsible. They thought Bucky was going to steal their customers, when we all know that we each serve a different breed of clientele. Bucky was going for families, which is the polar opposite of the crowds those two served."

"And you?"

"What about me? I'm way the heck out here, where barely anyone knows I exist. I get bikers and people who stay at the hotel next door. I've got a few other regulars, and that's about it. I'm not worried they'll go somewhere else. I'm convenient for my clientele. I'm not serving some specialty Irish coffee or what have you. I've got beer, and there's a place to crash next door for those who imbibe more than they should. For some, that's all that matters."

"You could have talked to Dwayne and Ivan about Bucky," I said.

Ruth sighed, shook her head. "I could have, sure, but I didn't want to."

"Why not?"

"Why else? I told you Dwayne was volatile. And honestly, Ivan's no better. Get the two of them together and . . ." She mimed an explosion with her crooked fingers. "If they found out I was buddying up to the 'enemy,' I'd never have heard the end of it. They'd have made my life miserable, and well, I think I've had enough misery for one lifetime, thank you very much."

Outside, a motorcycle revved. It felt like the entirety of the building trembled at the sound. Glasses didn't exactly shake, nor did Ruth seem to mind—or notice— but it was loud enough that I didn't bother speaking until after the sound faded into the distance.

"The police think that someone poisoned Bucky," I said. "Any idea who might have had reason to do such a thing?"

Ruth prodded at that gap in her teeth with her tongue as she considered it. "If you're thinking Ivan or Dwayne, I'd say you're on the right track, but perhaps on the wrong trail."

"What do you mean?"

"I can't see either of those two twits poisoning any-one. They'd happily use their fists or cause a scandal if they could get away with it, but poison?" She made a doubtful *click* with the side of her mouth. "I don't think so."

I could feel it coming, so I prodded with, "But?"

"But that doesn't mean one or the both of them aren't involved in it somehow. I may be all the way out here in the middle of nowhere compared to everyone else, but that doesn't mean I don't know a thing or two. Bucky had his secrets. I'm not wont to share such things, especially with you, considering our fledgling relationship. But he had 'em. We all do."

I immediately thought of Jaqueline and Geno and about Bucky possibly cheating on Kandice with his ex. "And if Ivan found out about those secrets?"

"He wouldn't hesitate to use them," Ruth said, pointing at me. Kind of. "He'd use it against Bucky, would make his life a living hell. If he could go to someone, use them to hurt Bucky, even better."

"Someone like Jaqueline Lyon?"

"Perhaps. Or Kandice Vaughn."

Something in the way she'd said Kandice's name made me think she knew a lot more than she was letting on. I mean, she'd all but said as much when she'd talked about secrets, but this felt bigger somehow, like she was telling me who'd killed Bucky without saying it outright.

"Just know this," she said. "Bucky wasn't as innocent as he tried to let on. To be frank, none of us ever is. He might not appear as if he has much in the way of enemies, but like my interactions with him, sometimes public appearances aren't telling you the whole truth about how someone truly feels about someone else." She picked up her empty beer bottle, swirled the dregs around. "As they say, appearances can be deceiving."

"And you think Bucky was deceiving someone?" I asked. "Who?"

Ruth smiled, eyes landing on me. "The question you should be asking isn't who Bucky might have had cause to lie to. If you ask me, the bigger question, the one you really should be asking yourself is, *why.*"

14

"Hey, Krissy." Pooky Cooper beamed at me from behind the counter at Death by Coffee. Blond-haired and blue eyed, she stood all of five feet, and that was with her shoes on. "Can I get you something?"

"A coffee would be great," I said. While I could have gone around and poured it myself, right then I was too distracted by what Ruth had said. And besides, it was okay to let someone else wait on you once in a while.

"Did you hear about Donnie?" she asked, glancing over her shoulder as she poured. "He's finally found a place of his own. I'm helping him move next week."

"That's great." I smiled as I said it. Pooky—whose real name was Claire, but she hated it when anyone called her that—had been having troubles with Donnie for so long, I'd been wondering whether it would ever end. "Is he staying in Pine Hills?"

"He is." She handed over my coffee, which had a cookie bubbling inside it. "I'm glad too. He can be annoying, but I don't like the idea of him moving away. I just don't want him living with me, you know?"

I nodded, though I had never had a sibling of my own. "I'm glad it's worked out." I sipped my coffee, relishing the heat of it.

"We'll see how long this lasts, but I'm hopeful." Pooky crossed her fingers.

I took a moment to relax and enjoy my coffee before asking, "Is Vicki here, by chance?" I hadn't seen her when I'd come in, though I thought I'd spotted her car when I'd parked.

"She's upstairs." Pooky snatched a rag from beneath the counter. "I suppose I should get back to work. Once Eugene's back from his break, I might go find somewhere to take a nap. This Donnie stuff has me feeling exhausted."

"Don't wear yourself out *too* much," I told her before I headed toward the stairs that led up into the books.

On the way, I noted that the St. Patrick's Day decorations had been taken down, something I should have done myself, but I'd been too distracted as of late to do so. Life was getting back to normal for the rest of Pine Hills, yet I felt as if I was stuck in a rut. Between Bucky's death, my upcoming wedding, and now Dad's hip, I felt torn in twenty different directions, with no idea which way to go first.

Vicki was sitting cross-legged on the floor against the back wall, between a pair of bookshelves. She had a pen in hand and was scouring a sheet of paper on the floor in front of her. Trouble was dozing nearby on his own page, which crinkled slightly with every rumbling breath.

"Hiding from work?" I asked.

"I wish." Vicki sat back and winced as she rubbed at the back of her neck. "I'm going over the schedule for next week and trying to slot everyone in without messing with anyone's hours. I figured it would be more comfortable to work out here rather than in the office, but it's putting a kink in my neck."

"Did Justin and the others turn in their applications?" I asked.

"Justin and Jo have. I still haven't gotten one from Kari Collins."

"I'm not surprised. I'm not sure she's right for us. I wouldn't turn her away, but . . ."

"I get it." Vicki's gaze dropped back to the schedule in front of her. "But if she does decide to come work for us, I hope she waits for another week. By then, I'll have a better plan in place. I'm thinking of adding a spot per shift since it's been so busy lately. And that would mean you and I can skip out on work more often." She chuckled before pushing her way to her feet with a popping of her knees.

"I already feel like I'm not around here enough," I said. "But I do have news that might change that."

"Oh?" Vicki asked. "Good news, I hope."

"Well . . ." I proceeded to tell her about Valerie's call and her wanting to sell Death by Java. "I know it's clear across the country, but . . ."

"But it might work," Vicki said, a faraway look in her eye.

"Do you really think so?" I asked, not quite able to hide my skepticism. "When I left there last, the place was a mess, even after I'd tried to help. And with it all the way across the country, it'll be hard to monitor."

"I'm not saying it would be easy," Vicki said. "And it would probably require one of us flying out there every week or two until things got settled, but that's not a big deal. Both our families live there, so it would almost be nice in a way."

I thought about Dad and his broken hip and how much it would take off my mind to be able to see him more often. "We could always rename the place Death by Coffee," I said.

"Make it a franchise." Vicki nodded and smiled. "I like it. I'll need to talk to Mason, look over our finances to make sure it won't stretch us too thin in the short term. I should call Valerie and see what she's asking. Knowing her, she'll probably try to squeeze as much money out of us as she can."

"I don't know," I said. "She seemed pretty eager to be done with the place."

Vicki retrieved the schedule from the floor, then we headed back downstairs, leaving Trouble to nap on what I assumed was a blank page brought up for that very purpose.

Pooky was back behind the counter, having finished with the dining room, as we descended the stairs. She was busy making fresh coffee, and she would glance toward the door every few moments, as if she was expecting someone. It could have been Eugene, but I also wondered if Donnie planned on making an appearance.

"I was thinking we should get together for dinner

soon," I said to Vicki as we reached the counter. "All four of us. I'll just need to check with Paul about his schedule, but I'm pretty sure he could make any time work." Unless whatever was going on with his mom was a big deal. I tried not to think too hard about *that*.

"I'd love to," Vicki said. "Just shoot me a text, and Mason and I will be there."

"Great. I'll let you know as soon as I do."

"Looking forward to it." She sighed. "I'm going to call Jo and Justin and let them know they're good to go. Here's hoping they don't have any major schedule requests that will force me to rethink my hard work."

"Good luck with that," I said as she headed to the back to make those calls.

I wasn't ready to go home yet, so I sat down at one of the recently cleaned tables to sip my coffee and think. I placed my phone on the table in front of me and stared at it, willing it to ring. I was curious about what Paul had found out about his mom's retirement. I wanted to talk to Dad and see how he was doing. Heck, right then, I would have been thrilled with a call from Rita, even if she had little new to say.

But my phone remained stubbornly silent. I considered calling someone—*anyone*—but the idea of bothering Paul about Chief Dalton or Dad about his hip made me feel like a pest.

I need to find a hobby.

One that preferably didn't consist of me running around town, interfering with police investigations, would be best, but as they say, beggars can't be choosers.

I drummed my fingers on the table as I mentally replayed everything I'd learned about Bucky and who might have had reason to hurt him. There was Geno and Jaqueline, of course. Dwayne and Ivan. I'd still even throw Ruth Camden in there, despite her assurances that she and Bucky had had an understanding.

Then there were the people who worked for him. Kandice, whom he'd also been dating. Grant, who had given him a coffee before he'd started going downhill, and who had talked about how owning a bar might help him earn back his family. I supposed I should throw Jazz in there, though I hadn't seen him do or say anything that made me think he had a problem with Bucky, other than his demonstration with the sugar cubes.

I felt like I was missing someone.

Skinny?

I found it hard to believe that Skinny Jefferson would have wanted to kill Bucky over a broken camera, especially since their argument had happened *after* Bucky had already gotten sick, but that didn't mean talking to him would be a waste of time. From what I knew about Bucky Sweeny, he wasn't a man who flew off the handle easily. Skinny must have caught something on his camera that upset him.

And that something could very well give some insights into Bucky's death.

I picked up my phone and scrolled through my contacts until I found Skinny's number. I barely knew the guy, having only talked to him a couple times before, yet I'd saved his contact information out of habit. I dialed, hoping that I wasn't wasting my time—or putting myself in a situation I'd rather avoid. Skinny's tastes were less than savory, and while I didn't begrudge him for his choices, I wanted no part of them.

There was a rustle as the phone was answered and then a breathy, "Yo."

I paused, not quite sure I recognized the voice, even though the greeting was typical of him. "Skinny?"

"Yeah." A brief pause. "Ms. Hancock?"

I was surprised he not only recognized my voice, but my name as well. "That's me," I said. "I have a strange question for you."

"Sure." Now that he was breathing easier, he was starting to sound more like himself. "Hit me with it."

"Were you at Bucky's Tavern after the St. Patrick's Day parade?"

There was a beat of silence before he said, "Yeah, man, that was me. I kind of wish it wasn't, though. I had a golden opportunity get ruined because I was there."

"Bucky threw you out," I said. "Broke your camera. Why?"

"Yeah, he did." Anger simmered just under the surface. "Cost me—not just a job, but a lot of money. Those things aren't easy to replace." He took a deep breath, and when he next spoke, some of the anger was gone. "As for the why, it might be easier if I showed you. Do you think you could stop by my place? I'm here now."

I didn't hesitate. "I'm on the way."

Skinny Jefferson lived in a log cabin that had been updated to look more modern. The property was secluded, surrounded by trees, and pulling up in front of it a short time after we'd disconnected, I was hit by the same old sense of unease that I'd had the last time I'd been there. Skinny had a reputation for taking what many would consider "inappropriate" photographs, and he had no qualms about asking any woman he saw to pose for them.

Like, I assumed, many other women before me, I had declined.

Skinny was waiting for me outside the front door of his house. He had a scrape on his cheek, likely from being tossed from Bucky's, but I couldn't be sure. He was dressed in a T-shirt with a neck that had been stretched out to the point that it sagged halfway down his barrel-shaped chest. Ratty jeans covered his scrawny legs while socks with sandals completed his relaxed attire.

"Been a while," he said with a chagrined smile as I approached him. "Come on in."

I entered Skinny's home and was immediately struck by how *different* it was. The photography equipment was still where I remembered it, but everything else had been changed to look more like an official portrait studio and less like one that you'd see tucked away in some dirty apartment with bad lighting and questionable props.

Skinny noted my surprised expression and laughed. "I've given all that old stuff up," he said. "I want to go legit, you know?" He motioned toward where a pirate chest had once sat, filled to the brim with see-through clothing and other items that were best not discussed. "I don't really miss that stuff. It took me a while, but I realized how it made me look, and I wanted to change everyone's perception of me."

"That's . . . good?"

"It is," he said. "I've even started filming video, though it's not my passion." He led me to a small couch, where I sat. Skinny chose to stand as he continued. "I've been trying to land weddings and other ceremonies, but my reputation has caused me some troubles in that regard. It's why I decided to film the parade and the whole shebang. I was hoping I could put together a short film that really showed Pine Hills as a town united, you know?" He shrugged. "It was going fine until . . ."

"Until Bucky threw you out."

"And broke my camera." He clenched his fists, released them. "It was the only one I had. Smashed it to bits and then kicked me out to boot. Didn't even offer to pay me back or anything afterward."

"You said you could show me what might have upset Bucky," I said with a frown. "But if he broke your camera . . ."

Skinny wagged his finger and smiled. "Ah, that's the beauty of modern filming." He turned to a computer he'd set up since the last time I was there. The monitor was the size of a rather large television, while the PC itself looked like it might slide into a laptop case. "Everything is saved to the cloud these days," he explained as he clicked. "While the camera is toast, the storage was fine. I uploaded everything as soon as I got home, just in case nothing was saved on-site." A final *click*, and the TV-sized monitor sprang to life.

The footage was of the parade. I was surprised by how steady Skinny's hand was as he followed the acts, while also managing to capture the enjoyment on the faces of the crowd. I was no expert, but there was a skill to the way he filmed that he couldn't have mastered without significant knowledge of lighting and framing.

"Do you have the footage from Bucky's?" I asked as Robert appeared on-screen in his leprechaun outfit. He tossed some candy toward the crowd, paused to wave at what I thought were his wife and son—I couldn't be sure since they were behind a tall couple—and then moved on, appearing as if he was having the time of his life.

"One sec." Skinny didn't fast-forward the footage, but instead, he advanced in jumps. More of the parade. A lingering shot on a trio of college-aged girls in green skirts that were too short, though their shamrock-adorned leggings kept them from being indecent.

And then, Bucky's.

"That's it!" I said, sitting forward, eyes riveted to the scene playing out before me.

Kandice was working behind the bar, which was full of patrons, including Robert, who'd clearly had too much to drink by then. He was slouched forward, saying something to Kandice, who was doing her best to ignore him while she continued to serve drinks to the other customers situated around the bar. Both Jazz and Grant were hard at work behind her, making Irish coffees and handing them out as if they were candy.

The camera swung around, giving a good look of the packed tavern. There were families seated at the tables, enjoying meals. A handful of guys stood near the fire, drinks in hand, cheeks ruddy, as if, like Robert, they'd been at it already for hours. There was a lot of green. A lot of friendly banter. And briefly, a spurt of off-key singing that devolved into inebriated laughter.

But where was Bucky?

The camera panned around the room a couple of

times, lingering on the prettier girls. While Skinny might claim he wanted to change, some of his old habits were still present in his choice of subjects. After one pass, I caught a glimpse of someone who looked like Bucky walking briskly toward the short hallway that led to the restrooms, but it had happened so fast, I couldn't be sure.

I desperately wished I could pan the camera myself, but I was forced to watch as Skinny made the rounds once more, before heading in the direction where the maybe-Bucky had gone.

And then he entered the hallway.

I couldn't hear what was being said because the background erupted with laughter, but I could see a conversation was taking place. Bucky had his hand on the wall and was leaning down over someone shorter than him, though I couldn't see them to be able to tell if I knew them. A hand rose and touched his arm. It was feminine, nails painted green. She squeezed his bicep, then shifted, which caused her to look past him, directly into the camera.

The woman had light brown hair that went down to her chin, dark blue eyes, which were wide with surprise. I'd put her age at somewhere in her early twenties, with a face that was both pleasant, yet oddly familiar, despite me not knowing who she was.

She gasped when she saw Skinny, then said something to Bucky, who whirled around, not quite in panic, but in something close enough to it that it caused my heart to leap. I was shocked by how awful he looked. His eyes were bloodshot, nose fiery red, as were his lips. He took a step toward Skinny, pointing at him with a finger that trembled. I couldn't tell if it was anger, or if he was just that sick.

"Turn that off," he demanded. Bucky sounded as bad as he looked.

"I'm allowed to film here," Skinny replied, holding the camera steady.

"I said off!" That's when Bucky lunged. The world did a few loops, then the floor came rushing upward before . . . black.

"That's it," Skinny said, stopping the playback. "I got tossed out after that. I'm just glad that chick brought me my camera, or else I would have lost everything."

"Do you know who she was?" I asked, still staring at the screen as if willing something new to appear, something more definitive.

"Didn't ask, and she didn't say." Skinny turned and leaned against his desk. "I just know that whatever was going on between those two, it was almost intimate. Just before I got it on film, I saw the guy lean forward. I can't be certain, but I'm almost positive that I walked in on him kissing her."

"Are you sure?" I asked. "That they were kissing?" Because if so, then I might have found one of the secrets Ruth Camden had said Bucky had.

"No," he admitted. "But what else could they have been doing? I mean, it's one thing to not want to be filmed, but it's another entirely to go and break my camera because you were talking with a pretty girl if that conversation was innocent, you know?"

I agreed. "Can I see it again?"

"Sure."

Skinny ran the video back, and I watched the scene

play out once more, but I saw nothing new. The woman was familiar, yet I had no idea who she was. Bucky appeared both sick and angry, and nothing he said or did explained why he was so upset about being filmed.

But if Skinny was right and Bucky and the mysterious woman *had* been kissing, I had a pretty good guess as to why someone had wanted him dead.

15

"Krissy! Hold up a sec."

I shifted my bags from one hand to the other so I could more easily unlock my front door as I waited for Jules to trot across the yard to join me. I'd spent a few hours after my visit with Skinny trying to forget about my visit with Skinny. I didn't like thinking that Bucky could have been cheating on Kandice with someone who looked so young.

My first thought was that it had been Jaqueline, but that wouldn't have worked. The girl in the video was in her twenties. Kandice had said that Bucky and Jaqueline had dated some fifteen years ago, as far back as high school. There was no way this woman was that old.

Could it have been a secret child between them?

It was possible, but I found it unlikely. The age didn't

quite mesh up properly, but I could have misjudged her age, and just because Jaqueline and Bucky had started dating in high school, that didn't mean they weren't *together* before then.

"I'm glad I caught you," Jules said. Maestro, his white Maltese, was squirming in his arms, desperate to be set down.

"Hey, boy," I said, ruffling the energetic dog behind the ears, careful not to poke him with my keys. "What's up?" I asked Jules when I was done. He didn't get ear scratches.

"Lance and I were wondering if you might be interested in joining us for dinner this evening," he said, shifting Maestro in his arms to better keep him from squirming free. "Lance wanted to experiment with a few Irish dishes this week, and he managed to overdo it tonight."

"Like you two did with the drinks?" I asked, smiling.

Jules gave an exaggerated eye roll. "Don't remind me. Though I'm sure we'll be having a few of those this evening as well." He chuckled. "We have enough food to feed an army. And while you aren't an army, you'd do us a massive favor by coming over and taking some of it off our hands. Paul too, if he's coming over tonight?"

"Actually, I'm not sure," I said, only slightly miffed that I hadn't heard from him. I was dying to know what was going on with his mom. And I, of course, wanted to ask him if there'd been any developments in Bucky's case. "Once I get these inside, I'll text him and find out." I raised the bags, as if he couldn't already see them.

"And then you'll be over?" He sounded so hopeful, how could I refuse?

"I will."

"Fantastic." Maestro barked his agreement. "I'll let Lance know. You can come over any time within the next fifteen, twenty minutes. We won't start until you're there. If Paul is coming and will be later than that, I'm sure we can delay serving until he arrives."

"Sounds good." My stomach grumbled. "I haven't had much to eat today."

"Even better."

Jules trotted back home to give Lance the news as I unlocked my door and headed inside. I deposited the bags onto the table and then shot Paul a quick text, asking about tonight. Then, while I was at it, I asked him about dinner with Mason and Vicki. That done, I spent the next few minutes putting my purchases away, making sure to move the treats so they didn't make a sound, or else Misfit would be relentless until I gave him some.

My phone rang as I finished up, and thinking it was Paul, I snatched it up, only to be met with a name that caused my anxiety to spike. I answered with a tense, "Tell me you're doing okay."

"Would you believe me if I said I was?" Dad asked with a pained laugh.

"No. Are you out of the hospital yet?"

"Would you believe me—"

"Dad," I warned.

"Tomorrow morning," he said, sounding resigned. "I don't know why they're making such a fuss over this. I'm fine, Buttercup."

"You're not fine. I could always fly—"

"No." Firm. "I will not allow it. And if you do, I'll bar you from seeing me. I know people at the police station who will back me up on this."

"But—"

"How are things in Pine Hills?" he cut in, clearly done with the topic of his health.

I sighed, frustrated, but fighting with him over this would only upset the both of us. "Fine. I'm stressed about the wedding." And the murder, but I wasn't about to tell him about that, not with him sitting in a hospital bed with a broken hip. "I don't know where we're going to move or how Misfit is going to handle having dogs around."

"It'll work out, Buttercup. These things always do."

I wished I could be so confident. "I did get a call from Valerie Kemp." I told him about her wanting to sell Death by Java and her suggestion that I take the bookstore café off her hands.

"That . . . could be interesting," Dad said. "You know, Laura's been talking about finding a job, something to keep her busy when I'm locked away working on one of my novels. Nothing strenuous, mind you, but I bet she could handle managing a bookstore café for you. I'd have to bring it up to her, of course, and I know nothing's final, but it is something to think about. And, honestly, it would be nice to see you a little more often."

"Yeah, it would," I said. I didn't know what kind of experience Laura had with managing anything since I didn't even know what kind of job—or jobs, for that matter—she'd once held. But I *did* trust her. If nothing else, she could keep a close eye on the place and let me or Vicki know if something went wrong.

"I'll float the idea by her, see what she says," Dad said as my phone *ping*ed with an incoming text.

I peeked, saw it was from Paul, and decided I needed to cut the call short, as much as I wanted to keep talking. "I'm sorry, Dad, but I need to go. I'm having dinner with Jules and Lance next door and—"

"Say no more," he said. "I think the pain meds are kicking in anyway. I'll be out like a light in minutes." When he laughed, I could hear the pain and exhaustion in his voice. The medication might be kicking in, but he was still hurting.

"Get some rest," I told him.

"I will, Buttercup. And please, don't worry about me. You have enough on your plate as it is."

We disconnected, and then I checked Paul's response.

Can't tonight. Going to be working late. Send them my best, though. But dinner with V and M sounds great. Tomorrow? Let me know when you want to do it, and I'll pick you up. Any time works.

I was disappointed, but not surprised. I shot him a thumbs-up emoji, sent a quick text to Vicki, and then gave Misfit his dinner, before I crossed the yard for my dinner date with Jules and Lance.

"Hi, Krissy!" Lance bussed my cheek when he answered the door. "I'm so glad you could make it."

"Thanks for inviting me," I said, entering the house. As always, the place was pristine, with only a few stray tufts of Maestro's fur marring the perfection. "It smells fantastic in here."

Lance laughed as he led the way to the kitchen. Tall, blond, and built like a swimmer, it was impossible not to admire Lance Darby as he walked in front of me. No, I had no romantic interest in him, and he definitely didn't have any for me, but that didn't mean I couldn't appreciate his good looks.

"There you are," Jules said, handing me a drink without asking. "I was beginning to wonder if you were going to stand us up."

"Dad called," I said, sipping the drink. I had no idea what it was, only that it was very good and very alcoholic. My eyes instantly started watering as I explained about Dad's fall.

"Oh no!" Jules said. "Is he doing okay?"

"He says he is, but who knows?" Another sip, and then I set my glass aside before it knocked me out. "Dad doesn't want me to worry, so he'd never tell me if he was hurting. But he sounded well enough, so I'm willing to take his word for it."

"I take it Paul can't make it tonight?" Lance asked as he checked the oven.

"He's working, or he would. He sends his best." I took a deep breath, savoring the heavenly smells that permeated the kitchen. "What are we having?"

"Irish stew along with some soda bread," Lance said. "I also made some barmbrack for dessert. I'm sure we could all use the good luck, though I didn't include anything inedible inside it, as is sometimes tradition. Besides"—he smiled—"I feel as if the ring would go to waste with this group."

I had no idea what barmbrack was, or how a ring fit in with anything, but I didn't ask. "Sounds great." Though

I did note that there didn't appear to be enough food for an army like Jules had indicated, let alone much more than what would feed four people. I turned to Jules. "I take it you had ulterior motives in inviting me over?" Said lightly, so as not to imply I was unhappy about the invite.

He met Lance's eye briefly, before giving me a chagrined smile. "I suppose I did. We *do* have enough food to feed you, of course. I might have exaggerated on the amount."

"I can see that."

"Jules told me about what happened," Lance said. I didn't have to ask to know what he was referring to.

"Have you heard anything more about it?" Jules asked, leaning against the counter. "Do the police know what happened to him?"

"They think Bucky was poisoned," I said, causing both Jules and Lance to turn wide eyes on me.

"Poisoned?" Jules said. "Like something out of a mystery novel?"

"It's hard to say," I said. "They never told me what kind of poison was used or how he'd come into contact with it. As far as I know, it was an allergic reaction, like what happened to Mason's brother." I inwardly winced at the memory. It had happened so long ago, I often forgot that Mason's brother, Brendon, had been murdered just about the same time Death by Coffee opened. It made me wonder how Mason had managed to come in and work with Vicki with that memory always staring him in the face.

"Wow," Jules said with a shake of his head. "Do you think Ivan might have been involved in Bucky's death?"

Lance opened the oven and pulled out a loaf of bread that smelled so good, my mouth instantly started watering. His soda bread, I assumed.

"I'm not sure," I said, trying my hardest not to drool. "There's . . . a lot going on."

"And we can talk about it while we eat," Lance said, removing the lid from the stew.

We spent the next few minutes scooping the stew into bowls and splitting up the bread between us. By the time we sat down, my stomach was growling nearly nonstop, and my mouth watering so badly, I kept smacking my lips together in anticipation of the first bite.

"The stew is made with lamb," Lance said as I spooned the first bite into my mouth. "I hope that's okay."

I chewed and fought the urge to let my eyes roll into the back of my head in pleasure. "It's more than okay. This is amazing."

"Thank you." Lance dipped a chunk of his bread into his bowl and swirled it around briefly before taking a bite. "It's a rather simple recipe if you want it."

I nodded, mouth too full to speak. The next five minutes were filled with pleasured eating sounds as I devoured my first bowl, along with the bread. It wasn't until Lance served me seconds—without me having to ask, of course—that we continued our discussion. It was Jules who spoke first.

"Did you know that many people consider poison a woman's weapon?" He waved his spoon at me. "Not that I totally buy in to that, but it is something to consider."

"Bucky was dating his bartender, Kandice Vaughn," I said. "And there was a rumor that he was seeing his ex, Jaqueline Lyon, behind her back."

Lance's brow furrowed. "That seems dangerous. And I don't just mean that because he was poisoned. Being seen with your ex, no matter how innocent it may be, always causes people to talk, especially around here."

I knew from experience how true that was. It *still* sometimes caused rumors to swirl whenever Robert showed up unannounced on my doorstep. He was married and I was soon to be, and yet those rumors persisted.

"It's just . . ." I frowned as I regarded my now-empty second bowl. I didn't even recall emptying it. "I'm not sure what to believe at this point." As quickly and as concisely as I could, I explained everything I'd seen and been told. About Ruth. About Skinny's video. About everything Kandice and Jazz and Grant had said. "It's as if everyone wants to point fingers at everyone else, and I'm not even sure they have any proof, just that they *hope* that the police believe the others are responsible."

"And none of it is confirmation of anything," Jules said. "The video only proves that Bucky was talking to someone. It might have been a relative or someone's daughter asking for money for all we know."

"Though it does seem strange that he was angry about being seen with her," Lance pointed out.

"It might not have been about the woman," Jules said. "They may have been discussing something Bucky didn't want to get out."

"Like what?" I asked.

Jules considered it a moment before saying, "You said he worked out a deal with Ruth? Maybe it included pushing one of the other bars out of town? Could the woman on the video work at Bar? A sort of go-between for Bucky and Ruth?"

"I don't know," I admitted. "I swear I've never seen her before, yet she seemed familiar."

"Perhaps you saw her at Bar once," Jules said. "Or at Bucky's. Or maybe she works for Ivan. You did say she was young."

"Yeah." I frowned as I thought about it. I never paid much attention to Ivan's bar, Beers and Rears, but it was possible I'd seen her outside once when I'd driven past. "Ruth implied Bucky had secrets," I said. "What if the girl was his daughter? He could have had her with Jaqueline, but kept it a secret all these years. Do either of you know her? Jaqueline Lyon, I mean?"

They both shook their heads.

"Honestly, you might be on to something with the daughter thing," Lance said. "Although that seems like something the rumor mill would have run with before now if it were true."

I agreed. I hated thinking that Bucky might have kept such a secret from, not just me, but Kandice as well. It made me wonder why he and Jaqueline had broken up, and if the young woman was somehow the reason. *Like maybe he'd cheated on Jaqueline and gotten his mistress pregnant.*

But if that were the case, who was this other woman? And could *she* have been his poisoner?

"What you need to do is find that young woman," Jules said, pointing his spoon at me. "If you can discover who she is, and what connection she has to Bucky, it might go a long way in unraveling this whole mess."

"It's sad," Lance said with a shake of his head. "If she's his long-lost daughter or something, then she might have lost him as soon as she found him."

"But what if she's connected to his death?" Jules asked.

We ruminated on the question as Lance cleared the table. He returned with something that looked like a cross between a cake and bread, speckled with dried fruit. The barmbrack, I assumed.

"Have you talked to his ex, Jaqueline, yet?" he asked, cutting the barmbrack and serving each of us a slice. "Perhaps she could shed some light on her relationship with Bucky. She might even know who this video woman is."

"I haven't," I admitted, taking a bite. Somehow, despite being full to bursting, I found myself eating the barmbrack like candy. "I'm not sure what to say. 'Hey, were you cheating on your husband with your ex, who just so happened to have been murdered?' seems like an awfully bad way to introduce myself."

Jules laughed. "You wouldn't have to phrase it like that. But yeah, it would be good to get her take on things. He *was* found in the bed of her truck, after all. You'd think she might have some idea why that was."

"I'll think about it," I said, though I'd already made up my mind. Merely *seeing* Jaqueline might tell me everything I needed to know. If she looked like an older version of the girl in the video, for example, it would tell me something.

Conversation soon moved on to other topics, which was something of a relief. I was becoming fatigued from thinking about murder—the whos and whys and all that—and needed to take some time to get away from it all.

Jules served coffee—thankfully, alcohol-free—and we headed into the living room to talk. I relaxed and forgot about Bucky and everything that had been happening of late. It was nice, even when a pang of regret shot through me when I realized that once I moved, I wouldn't be able to walk across the yard to have a dinner with my friends like this anymore. It would take planning, and I am admittedly bad at planning.

Later, after our coffees were empty and the yawns became frequent, Jules walked me to the door, while Lance remained on the couch, Maestro curled up next to him. We said our goodnights, and I stepped out under the clear night's sky, refreshed. I was glad I'd done this, glad that I'd managed to talk through things, though I was no closer to figuring out who might have killed Bucky.

I returned home, mind as full as my stomach. When I lay down in bed a short time later, I did so with a contented smile. I'd just closed my eyes and was about to zonk out when the coffee caught up to me, and I trudged my way, half-asleep, into the bathroom to relieve my near-bursting bladder. Once that was done, I returned to the bedroom, eyes slowly adjusting to the dark.

I reached for the covers just as something moved

across the room. I looked up toward the window, thinking I'd caught my reflection out of the corner of my eye, which sometimes happened, especially when I was dead on my feet.

There was, indeed, a face in the window.

But it wasn't my face I saw staring back at me.

16

Everything happened at once.

I screamed, recoiling back toward the bathroom in my surprise. The noise caused Misfit, who'd been snoozing at the foot of the bed, to shoot straight up into the air, as if he'd been sleeping on a spring-loaded trap. His legs pinwheeled, and when he hit the floor, he shot straight into the hall and out of sight. I slapped my hand against the light switch, just barely missing getting run over by the fleeing feline on his way out the door. The bright light immediately blinded me, forcing me to squint as I scanned the window for the face, which had been glowing with a bluish light.

Of course, no one was there now.

I gave my heart a few moments to calm as I reassessed. I was tired, yes, but there was no mistaking the fact that I'd seen a glowing face peering in at me. I might be tired, might have had Lance's alcohol-laced beverage still muddying my thoughts, but I was positive I'd seen someone looking through my bedroom window at me.

Watching by the light of a phone, I realized. Recording me? Talking to someone? I didn't know.

And if I continued to stand around, doing nothing, I might never know.

I snatched my phone from the wireless charger I kept on my nightstand and ran for the front door. I made a quick detour to grab a knife from the kitchen along the way, and then brought up the number for the police as I quickly unlocked the door and burst outside, knife held up at the ready, just in case the Peeping Tom was waiting for me.

Only the sound of insects met me as I stepped outside in my bare feet. The night was cold and bit right through my nightclothes, which consisted of a pair of old cotton shorts and a too-long tee. I scanned the yard around my house, not willing to move from the safety of my doorway quite yet.

At first, I saw nothing out of place. No one was creeping around the house—or worse, toward me. Nothing was in my driveway or anywhere in the immediate area. No cars. No stalkers. Nothing.

But then I saw it: a car parked down the street so that it wasn't sitting directly in front of my home.

It was hard to know for sure with it being so late at night, and with my head buzzing with adrenaline, but I was pretty sure the car was red with a rusty driver's-side door—the same car that had been idling out in front of my house just the other day.

Anger shot through me then. No, I wasn't positive I

knew the car's owner, but I suspected. And right then, that anger—and suspicion—was all the courage I needed.

"Sabrina?" I shouted. I was proud to note there was little to no tremble to my voice. "I know you're out there."

I was met with crickets. Both literally *and* figuratively.

"I'll call the police," I said, raising my phone above my head and shaking it slightly. I didn't know if Sabrina—or whoever was there—was watching, but I suspected they were. "I doubt that getting arrested would make your bosses at the *Herald* very happy. Not all press is good press, no matter what they say." Whoever *they* were.

I waited, but there was still no response. Doubt started to creep in. Yes, Sabrina Mayfield *had* once peeped into my window while I wasn't home, but she'd also wanted to interview me. She was writing a story back then and had wanted me to comment on it, something for which she'd needed my cooperation.

But that face in the window . . . that didn't seem like something a reporter chasing a story would do. You didn't ask for an interview while staring in at someone who was trying to sleep. Not this late at night. Not *ever*.

A killer, however, might stalk their intended victim that way.

I mentally rewound and tried to conjure the image of what I'd seen, but I'd been half-asleep, and admittedly, slightly buzzed from Lance's drink. I vaguely recalled seeing eyes and a nose, all lit from beneath by a blue glow that I assumed came from a phone's screen. But details? I couldn't recall if the eyes were blue or brown or some other shade in between. Was the nose round or beaked? No clue. I couldn't even recall whether the face had been framed by a head of curly blond hair, or if the Peeping Tom was bald.

Nerves had me unlocking my phone's screen, hand shaking ever so slightly.

"All right," I said, voice dropping, as I no longer was interested in coming face-to-face with the intruder. "I'm calling the police."

"Don't."

The voice coming from the darkness caused me to jump and let out a little squeak. Me being me, of course, I fumbled my phone in the process. It hit the ground— on the grass, thankfully—and bounced away as I spun, knife upraised toward, well, the darkness surrounding my house.

A shadow moved. I could just make out a silhouette. From that, and the single spoken word, I knew my Peeping Tom was female.

"Who are you?" I asked, desperately trying to make out features in the dark. She was standing at the corner of the house, having stepped around it when she'd spoken, as if she'd been on the way to her car from the backyard when I'd rushed outside.

A couple of seconds passed before she retorted with, "Who are *you*?"

We stared at each other with her in the darkness, and me backlit from the light coming from inside my house.

I could make out a few features now, none of which I recognized as familiar. Short-cropped hair. A glint under the nose that I took for a nose ring, but I couldn't be sure.

"Why were you looking through my bedroom window?" I asked, voice growing firmer. Nothing in the woman's demeanor indicated that she had any intention of attacking me. That didn't mean I was going to put my knife away or relax.

"That's not your bedroom." She spoke with a firm, confident tone.

What?

"This is my house," I said. "Which kinda does make that my bedroom."

"No." A shake of the head. "You don't belong here."

Was she . . . *crying*?

"All right," I said, doing my best to project confidence. "Stay there. I want to see you."

I waited a beat to see if she might respond, then I crouched down and blindly reached for my phone, not wanting to take my eyes from her. I patted the ground, felt nothing but grass, so I glanced away so I could search for my phone.

The moment my gaze left her, the woman bolted toward the car parked on the street.

"Hey! Stop!" Cursing under my breath—and leaving my phone lying somewhere in the yard—I ran after her.

The car's location on the street meant the woman ran through Caitlin's yard next door, which meant she was running *away* from me. If she'd parked in front of

Jules and Lance's place, she'd have had to have gone through my yard, which would have made it easier to intercept her.

As it was, I had to put everything I had into running to gain ground. My shin throbbed from the excursion, but that didn't hamper me as I tossed my knife away, not wanting to trip over my two feet and end up impaling myself. I might have done a lot of dumb things in my time, but running with knives wasn't going to be one of them.

I was surprised how quickly I caught up with the fleeing woman, though I suppose I shouldn't have been. I'd gotten in much better shape ever since I'd started exercising with Cassie. No, I wasn't a world-class runner or even a mildly average runner, but I *was* much better than I had been, with far better endurance than I ever recalled having.

The woman must have realized I was going to catch her because about halfway across Caitlin's yard, she abruptly stopped.

I didn't have time to react. I slammed into her back with an, *"Oof!"* that pushed all the air from my lungs. I grabbed her out of reflex, wrapping my arms around her chest, as I lost my balance. The woman staggered forward two steps, and then, with my weight on her back, she pitched face-first into the grass, with me landing heavily on her back.

"Get off!" the woman gasped as she tried to push her way back to her feet, but I didn't budge, both because I didn't want her to escape, and because I couldn't, at least until I got my wind back. "Leave me alone!"

She wriggled beneath me for a few seconds more, but when she realized she couldn't shake me, she collapsed in a huff.

Thinking she'd given up, I eased my weight off her ever so slightly, and now that I could breathe somewhat, I asked her again, "Who are you?" just before her elbow shot back and connected solidly with my gut.

I grunted and almost fell from her back, but I tightened my grip on her just before I did. She made a frustrated sound and once more went limp. This time, I didn't relax, not even a little.

"Why were you at my house?" I demanded through gasps for air. She'd nailed me good, and I expected to have an elbow-shaped bruise on my stomach to join the one on my arm and the one growing on my shin.

"That's not your house!" she shouted. "You don't live there. You can't!"

A light clicked on, illuminating the yard where the woman and I lay. Then the door to Caitlin Blevins's house opened, and Caitlin stepped outside, dressed for bed in loose-fitting, all-black clothes. Her arms were crossed over her chest as she regarded us. There was a deep, eerie silence before she finally spoke a single, harsh word: "Dee."

The woman beneath me sucked in a breath, then deflated beneath me, the fight going completely out of her. "Caitlin."

Caitlin sighed, let her arms drop to her sides. It sounded as if the entire weight of the world had just come to rest on her shoulders. "You can get off of her now, Krissy. She won't run."

It took some doing, considering my hands were trapped underneath the woman—Dee, apparently— but I soon worked my way to my feet. Dee rose a moment later, head lowered, and in the light of Caitlin's front stoop, I could see her flushed cheeks. I suspected the flush wasn't from our run or subsequent scuffle.

"Why are you here, Dee?" Caitlin asked, before saying, "No, I know why. How did you find me?"

And just like that, it clicked.

Caitlin had once told me that she'd had a friend who used to stand over her while she slept, who would peek through the windows of her old place and watch her. It had gotten so bad, Caitlin had been afraid to go out because the woman would follow her. It was why she had moved next to me in the first place—to get away from the woman. It was also why she kept security cameras in her windows.

My gaze flickered to the window where the camera must have triggered when Dee and I tumbled into Caitlin's yard.

Dee stared ahead before her gaze moved from Caitlin, to the house behind her. "So, *this* is your house?" She laughed, though it sounded as if she were close to tears. "I thought—"

"Dee." Snapped. "Why are you here?"

"I . . ." A deep breath, and then, all at once, "I wanted to see you one last time."

A beat of silence before Caitlin asked, "What are you talking about?"

"I'm moving," Dee said. "Out of Ohio. Away from . . ." She waved her hand vaguely in the air behind her. "All of this. I wanted to see you before I left."

"So you peeked in through *my* window?" I asked, unable to hold back.

"I thought it was Caitlin's house." Dee scuffed the toe of her Converse into the grass. "I was given the wrong house number."

The obvious question was, *"By whom?"* but that's not what Caitlin asked.

"Why didn't you just knock?"

Dee shook her head as if she didn't want to say, yet she responded anyway. "I didn't think you'd answer. After how things went before, you know? I mean, I was going to talk to you the other day, but things happened, and, well . . ." She shrugged a single shoulder. "I didn't."

"What things?"

More shoe scuffing. "I went to your show."

My brow furrowed. I knew Caitlin was in a band, but I didn't know she was playing anywhere or else I would have stopped by to listen. She didn't play my sort of music, but with friends, that sort of thing didn't matter. You supported them nonetheless. "Your band played somewhere?" I asked.

"At the Whistling Wet Weasel," Caitlin replied, eyes never leaving Dee. "On St. Patrick's Day."

"You covered a few Black 47 songs," Dee said, smiling. "I remember listening to them with you every year around this time. It's not your usual sort of music, which is why it stood out so much. Why I remembered it so well."

Caitlin didn't return the smile, or seem to soften in the slightest. "I didn't know you were there."

"I kept to the back," Dee said. "It was easy enough to blend in. If you glanced my way, I'd look away to make sure you didn't recognize me until I was ready for you to. When the accident happened, I realized the timing sucked, so I slipped out before you could spot me. I guess I chickened out."

"Wait," I said, still playing catch-up. "What accident?"

Caitlin stared at Dee a moment before finally turning to me. "We were in the middle of 'James Connolly' when some guy fell. He took out the mixer on the way down, breaking it, which effectively ended the show."

My heart did a solid *thump* in my chest. I didn't have to ask, but I did anyway, "Who was it that fell?"

Caitlin shook her head. "I didn't know the guy. Short hair. Beard. He was arguing with the owner of the Weasel, and then he suddenly went down. I saw it out of the corner of my eye, but I don't really know what was going on when it happened. All I know is that when he was being led away, the owner, Dwayne, told him that he was getting what he deserved. I assumed the dude was drunk and had started a fight or something, but like I said, I wasn't paying much attention."

My heart did one of those slow, heavy *thump*s as my mind whirled.

Bucky was at the Whistling Wet Weasel. While short hair with a beard could describe quite a lot of people, I *knew* Caitlin was talking about Bucky Sweeny. I also knew without having to ask that this had likely taken place sometime during the evening, well after the parade, and quite possibly after Skinny's video. He'd looked bad at the parade, and just as bad, if not worse, in Skinny's video, but not like he would fall over at any moment. If he'd collapsed from his illness—or, more likely, the poisoning—I assumed that he did so close to his time of death.

It made me wonder if Dwayne might have been the last person to see Bucky alive.

"Please, Dee," Caitlin said, pulling my attention back to the here and now. "Go. We've said everything that needs to be said to one another. I just want to be done with all of this." She gestured toward the flattened grass where Dee and I had fallen. "I can't go through this again."

Dee blinked rapidly, as if fighting back tears. "I know. I realize I made mistakes. Lots of them. And I suppose I haven't learned my lesson, but . . ." She took a deep, trembling breath, shook her head, and then turned and walked away without another word.

Caitlin watched her go. I noted her entire body was tense, though I couldn't tell if she was afraid that Dee might change her mind and not leave, or if she was fighting the urge to tell her to stop.

Either way, she let her go. Dee didn't look back as she climbed into her car, and in a puff of black exhaust, she drove away.

Silence fell as we both stared in the direction she had gone. Then, quietly, Caitlin said, "I'm sorry about that, Krissy. It should never happen again."

"It's all right," I said. "Are you okay?"

Caitlin remained silent for a few moments longer

before turning to me and smiling. "I think I am. For the first time in a long time, I feel . . . free."

I returned home a few minutes later, glad for Caitlin, but with my head full of questions.

Why had Bucky gone to the Whistling Wet Weasel that day? And what did Dwayne Morris know about Bucky Sweeny's death?

17

I stifled a yawn as I handed a vanilla latte to the last customer in line. Sleep hadn't come easily after my encounter with Dee, both because of her shocking first appearance and because of what Caitlin had told me about Bucky's collapse. I kept expecting to see a face appear at my bedroom window again. Sometimes it would be Bucky's face I'd imagine. Sometimes it would be Kandice's or Grant's or Jazz's. And then, just before sleep would finally overtake me, I'd start to imagine faces from my past, killers who were currently sitting behind bars because of me.

Needless to say, it was unsettling, and when I finally did fall asleep, I did so with the proverbial one eye open.

When morning came, I'd planned on staying in bed an extra hour or two, but my phone rang, tearing me out of that space between waking up and sleep. Pooky

Cooper, who was due to open with Beth that morning, had had an emergency crop up, though she didn't say what that emergency might be. She needed someone to fill in for her.

That someone turned out to be me.

"Well, that was fun," Beth said, wiping sweat from her brow. "I swear, we get busier by the day. Don't people make coffee at home anymore?"

"Not as good as ours," I said, slouching against the counter to watch the customers chatting and sipping their coffees in the dining area. There were a few people upstairs, browsing the books, but so far, no one had wandered over to buy one, which was good. I wasn't sure my legs could handle the trio of steps right then.

"Ain't that the truth," Beth said with a chuckle. "But I won't be sad when we have a few more hands around here." She glanced at me. "Vicki said something about new employees? Please tell me I didn't imagine that."

"You didn't imagine it," I said. "They should start next week."

"Good." She heaved a sigh. "You know, when you first opened the shop, I didn't think you'd last long. And I don't mean because of what happened to Brendon." She blinked a few times, moved on. "I suppose having Raymond grouching about you from the start didn't help my impression of you."

Raymond Lawyer, Mason and Brendon's dad, owned Lawyer Insurance across the street. He'd never liked me, which I supposed shouldn't have come as a surprise considering how I'd been snooping around his business after his son had died. Back then, Beth had worked for him, and I'd taken her for something of an airhead. She'd been Brendon's mistress, had acted the part of the flighty receptionist, so my view of her was somewhat justified at the time.

But then she'd left Lawyer's Insurance and applied at Death by Coffee. Ever since then, her true personality had come out, and I found I liked her far more than I thought I ever would.

"It's funny how things change," I said, thinking back to how much *had* changed since the day we'd opened. It was almost like another life.

Beth smiled and then snatched up a rag. "I'm going to get a head start out there. Yell if you need me."

"Will do."

As Beth headed out into the dining area, the door opened, and Paul Dalton walked in, dressed in his uniform. Maybe it was that brief reminiscence with Beth, but I suddenly flashed back to the first time I'd seen him. He'd waltzed into my life through that very same door, looking like an angel in uniform, to ask me questions about Brendon's death. My heart did a little *pitter-patter*, and I flushed like I'd done all those years ago.

"What?" Paul asked, dimples flashing across his face as he smiled. "Did I miss something?"

"No. It's just you." I cleared my throat and fought back my own smile. "Can I get you something, Officer?"

"A coffee would be great," he said. "I saw your car out front and figured I might as well stop in to get one. And I wanted to make sure we were still on for tonight?"

I turned to pour his coffee. "We are. At least I think

we are. I'll double-check with Vicki." I handed him his coffee.

Paul took a sip, then groaned in pleasure. "I really needed that." He saluted me with the to-go cup. "I'm glad to see you're keeping yourself out of trouble. I don't think John's said one foul thing about you yet in this investigation."

"Give it time," I said. "Though I suppose it *is* progress."

"For which one of you?"

"Both?" I laughed.

Paul joined me, then sighed. "I'd best get back to it. See you later tonight." He started for the door, then hesitated. I hoped he'd say something about his mom's retirement, but all he did was glance back, shoot me another smile, and then walk away.

Before the door could swing closed, Cassie Wise slipped in, dressed in a rather nice skirt and blouse. Her cheeks were flushed, and she looked like she was in a hurry.

"Hi, Krissy," she said, hurrying over. "Can I get a coffee? Black is fine."

"Sure." I poured, then rang her up. "You look nice."

"Thanks." She sighed, as if the compliment had added weight to already overburdened shoulders. "Some things have come up. Not bad, just . . . things."

I nodded. I'd been there. "Keeping you busy, I take it?"

"Too busy." She took the coffee, then closed her eyes in bliss as she sipped. "I'm going to have to cancel our walk, not that we had a definite date planned. I'm just not sure if I'll have the time, and I don't want to leave you hanging."

"That's all right. I'm pretty busy right now myself." With Bucky's murder. With Dad's hip. With, well, *everything*.

"Next week?" she asked.

"Next week," I agreed.

The door opened again, and Caitlin Blevins entered. Cassie waved as she slipped past her and out the door. Caitlin was dressed in jeans and a long-sleeved shirt with some sort of band name scrawled across the front. I didn't know whether it was the name of her own band or one of her favorites. Either way, I couldn't make heads or tails of it, but that was okay. I didn't need to be able to read it to appreciate that it mattered to her.

"Hey, Krissy," she said, stuffing her hands into her pockets and hunching her shoulders.

"Hi, Caitlin. Can I get you something?"

"Sure." She paused, then seemed to realize I'd need to know what to get her. "Just black."

Suits her. I poured and then handed over the coffee. "Last night was . . . interesting."

"Yeah." She ran her hand over the back of her neck. "I'm really sorry about that. I'm not surprised Dee came looking for me, but I expected her to . . ." She frowned. "Actually, I don't know what I expected."

"Do you believe her when she says she's leaving the state?"

"Yeah, actually I do." She took a big gulp of coffee and didn't seem affected by the heat. "She might have caused me no end of trouble in the past, but she's always been honest. I know that sounds strange, but it's true."

I had questions, but I refrained from asking them.

How close had Dee and Caitlin been? I knew they were once friends, possibly *best* friends, but that could mean just about anything. I wondered if Caitlin would miss her when Dee was gone. Yes, I knew that Caitlin had been hiding from her, but I knew from experience that sometimes, when the past shows up on your doorstep, old memories resurfaced, along with old feelings that were often better forgotten.

"I'm glad it's over with," Caitlin went on, though I noted a twinge of melancholy in her tone. "I've been living my life afraid that she'd pop up at any moment and that the nightmare would start all over again. Last night, when I saw the two of you rolling around on my camera, I thought that it had, that I'd wake up the next day and find her standing over me again."

"She was peeping into my window when I saw her," I said. "My *bedroom* window."

"She does that. Did that. I really hope that's the last time." Caitlin ruminated on that a moment before going on. "I took down all my cameras. Well, at least the ones facing out the window. No reason not to keep a security system going, just in case someone else gets any funny ideas about breaking in."

Which made me think that perhaps it was time I invested in a security system of my own. I'd been attacked by killers in my own home, had people snooping around the house at all hours of the night. Having some way to keep an eye on my place would be nice. Perhaps when Paul and I moved in together, it could be one of our first big purchases. And since he was a cop, he probably knew which security systems were the most effective.

"I'm glad to hear that things seem to be getting better now," I said. "No one should be afraid to spend time at home."

"Yeah." Her eyes went distant before she snapped back to herself. "Anyway, I just wanted to apologize."

"There's no need."

"Sure, there is. My crap ended up on your doorstep. Quite literally. I never wanted that. It's my business, and I hate that it spilled over onto you." She tipped her head back and drained the last of her coffee. The only indication that it was hot was how her cheeks flushed when she was done. "By the way, I almost forgot to mention something last night. It's about what happened at the show."

My chest clenched. "With Bucky? He's the guy who collapsed."

"Sort of. I think?" Her face scrunched up. "You know how I told you that the dude collapsed and the owner led him away, right?"

"Right."

"You seemed pretty interested in it, so I assume that you knew the guy. This . . . Bucky?"

"I did." I didn't tell her that he'd later died, because I didn't want to distract her from whatever she was about to tell me. Or make her feel guilty. I knew that sometimes people felt responsible for things they couldn't control. I was living proof of that.

"Well, while we were trying to get the mixer working again, I noticed someone lurking near the door. He was staring after where Dwayne had taken the guy who'd fallen, real intense-like."

"Do you know who it was?"

"No clue," Caitlin said. "It was just some guy, that's all I know. Mid-forties, maybe? I only saw him for a moment before he turned and walked away."

"Did this guy look angry?" I asked. "Or . . ." I fumbled for a word and ended up with, "satisfied? Like he was happy about Bucky's collapse? Or worried? Or, I don't know, *anything*?"

Caitlin shrugged. "Hard to say. The dude was clear across the room, and I was more concerned about the mixer and continuing the show. If I'd known it might be important, I would have paid better attention. I'm not even sure why it stuck in my head. I suppose the guy gave me weird vibes. It was like he didn't belong, you know? Like he was out of place, that the Weasel wasn't his vibe or something."

Caitlin left a few minutes later, and I went back to work, mind churning over what she'd told me. A strange man was lurking at the Whistling Wet Weasel right when Bucky Sweeny collapsed, likely because of whatever poison was coursing through him. Why was Bucky even there in the first place? And who was the man who was watching him? Could he have had something to do with Bucky's death?

I needed to talk to Dwayne Morris. If anyone would know the details about what had happened that night, he might.

The tables were clean, and Beth was busy cleaning one of the coffee machines a short time later, when the door burst open and Pooky Cooper entered at a near run, looking half-frantic.

"I'm so sorry," she said. "Donnie was having an anxiety attack, and I wasn't sure what to do and—"

"Pooky," I said, cutting her off before she could hyperventilate. "It's okay."

"It's not," she said. "I didn't want to leave you hanging like that, and I hate having to call off, even for a little while, but I didn't know what else to do." She pushed her hair out of her face with both hands, eyes practically bugging out of her head. "I'll make up for it. I'll—"

I took her by the arm and led her behind the counter while she continued making promises. Everyone in Death by Coffee was watching, which only seemed to make her that much more upset.

"Is Donnie okay now?" I asked.

Her nod was jerky.

"Good. And you're okay too. We got through it. Everyone is fine. There's no reason for you to worry about any of it."

"Yeah, but—"

"No," I said. "No buts."

She took a deep breath and let it out in a relieved huff. "I didn't mean to barge in here like that," she said after a moment. "When he called, it rattled me, and I kept expecting the worst. I've been running around with my hair on fire for the last few hours, and I guess I hadn't quite calmed down from the excitement."

"Are you calm now?"

She considered it and then gave me a shaky smile. "I am."

I patted her on the shoulder. "Then clock in, and we can move on like nothing happened."

Pooky gave me a grateful smile and started her workday.

With Pooky there, I was no longer needed, so I grabbed my things and headed for the door, thinking I could talk to Dwayne Morris about Bucky, but the door opened, and yet another of my friends walked in, already talking.

"Oh my Lordy Lou!" Rita said, spotting me immediately. "What a fantastic day. When I woke up, I swear I heard the angels singing outside my window, and I *knew* that everything was going to be just fine."

"It sounds like you had a good morning," I said.

"And an evening." She grinned from ear to ear. "I even had to put James in the closet, if you can believe it?"

Rita had a life-sized cardboard cutout of my dad that she often kept in her bedroom. Don't ask.

I took her in, how her cheeks were aglow, her eyes bright. She was dressed like always, though there was something . . . freer to her. I wasn't sure if that was the right word, but she moved with a grace I wasn't used to seeing on Rita. The last time she'd acted like this, she'd met someone, but that someone had left town after a criminal connection of his came to light.

"Johan?" I asked, wondering if he might be back in town. That would make for an interesting situation, considering the police still wanted to talk to him—and would likely stick him behind bars when they found him.

Rita waved off the suggestion. "Pah, Johan Morrison is well behind me now. We parted on good terms and remain that way, but there's no future there."

"Then . . . ?" I raised my eyebrows, urging her to spill.

Rita surprised me, however. "Now, I'm not one to kiss and tell." She winked. "And, to be frank, I'm not admitting to any kissing or contact of any kind." She paused, looked me up and down. "Though you look like someone kept you up all night. Do you have a story to share about you and that fiancé of yours?"

"Nope. I spent the night alone with my cat."

"That's too bad." She *tsk*ed. "Of course, it's not all that surprising."

I opened my mouth to object, but she plowed on right over me.

"Georgina called me twice this morning to talk about what happened to Bucky Sweeny. The first time, I was preoccupied, so I didn't have time to chat, but the second . . ." She *cluck*ed her tongue as she shook her head. "Sometimes Georgina McCully can really be long-winded."

I didn't point out that Rita was often just as long-winded when I asked, "Has she learned anything?"

"Well, you'd have to ask her that," Rita said. "I was a smidge distracted at the time, even though I did my best to listen to her. Mentally distracted, mind you. Nothing physical." There was that flush again. "I do re-call her saying that she remembered something about that night before the body was found. Or was it the day of? I'm not sure, but it did have something to do with all of that." She fluttered her hand.

I wanted to scream, but I kept my voice calm when I asked, "Could you call her and ask her about it?"

"Well, I suppose I could," Rita said thoughtfully, though she made no move to reach for her phone. "But you look as if you are done here for the day?"

"I was just leaving, yes."

"Then why don't we head on over to Georgina's together, and we could both have a little chat with her? I was thinking of heading over there anyway. I'm sure Georgina would love to have the company, yours included. She's getting up there in years, and many of her friends are gone, you know? It would be good for her to have a couple of visitors."

Georgina lived in the opposite direction from where I'd been heading, but was going to see her really such a bad idea? She lived only a few houses down from Geno and Jaqueline Lyon. She'd seen the police arrive when they'd found Bucky's body. She could have insights into the Lyons' relationship, not just with each other, but with Bucky. If he'd been coming around, whether it be to argue with Geno, or to have secret liaisons with Jaqueline, there was a good chance Georgina might have noticed.

And who knew? Maybe it would give me more ammunition for when I talked to Dwayne about what happened that night at his bar. What she could possibly know about that? I had no idea. But when one of Rita's gossip pals was involved, anything could happen.

I fished my keys from my purse and held them up. "I'll drive."

With a grin and a familiar sparkle in her eye, Rita spun and led the way out the door.

18

Georgina McCully lived in a tree-lined neighborhood perched on a slight incline amid a smattering of gently rolling hills. Every yard sloped just enough that I was pretty sure no one used push mowers during the summer. A riding mower would have given me an anxiety attack on some of the more angled yards, but the thought of trying to hold on to a push mower was even worse. Most of the houses were older, but they were all well-maintained. It was quiet, peaceful, and just the sort of place I might like to live—sloped yards aside.

"That's the Lyon place," Rita said, pointing to the white house as we passed. "I suppose that truck in the driveway belongs to Jaqueline. I'm surprised the police didn't impound it. I recently read a book where the key evidence was tucked down beside the passenger's seat, and the police missed it the first time they went through the vehicle. Sometimes it takes more than one look-see to find something that doesn't want to be found."

Since I was driving, I couldn't look too long, but I did sneak a glance at the truck and the house it sat in front of. It all appeared, well, normal. I didn't know what I expected to find, considering Bucky had been poisoned. There'd be no gunshot holes or chalk outline or anything that would indicate that something bad had happened there. Just a house and a truck that looked like every other house and truck in the neighborhood.

"Georgina's there," Rita said as we continued down the street. "Two houses down from that green monstrosity up ahead." She shook her head and clucked her tongue. "Why someone would choose that color, I don't know. But from what Georgina says, the person who lives there doesn't often think things through. That house is proof enough of that, let me tell you."

I didn't think the house she was indicating was *that* bad, but then again, I wasn't a fan of green in most cases, so I wasn't the best judge. I thought them all ugly. I drove past, the road curving so that by the time we were pulling up in front of Georgina McCully's house, we'd made a near-inverted *J*.

Georgina watched us from a low-set window inside her house. She was seated in a rocking chair, her white hair fluffed around her head. She wasn't wearing her reading glasses, though what appeared to be a book sat in the windowsill next to her. She didn't get up to greet as us we approached the door. Since Rita pushed her way in without knocking, I assumed that was typical.

"We're here," Rita called, leading the way into the living room. "I know I didn't call ahead, but I figured you'd be home anyway. I brought Krissy."

"I see that," Georgina said. She didn't rise as we entered the room, though she gestured to the love seat and chairs spaced around a well-worn rug that looked to be as antique as everything else in the room. "Don't mind me. My arthritis is acting up."

I sat. "We won't keep you."

"Keep me as long as you'd like," she said. "I don't get much in the way of visitors these days." Her tone told me the last was aimed at Rita more than me. "And I don't get out as much as I used to."

Rita huffed as she sat. "I'm here as often as I can manage. You know I've been busy of late."

"Busy with that old hanky-panky." Georgina tapped the side of her nose and chuckled. "Acting like a teenager all over again is what I hear."

"I am not!" Rita's hand fluttered to her chest.

"I'm just reporting what I've heard." Georgina settled back in her chair, smug as could be.

"Well, you heard wrong."

I looked between them, painfully curious as to what they were talking about, but that appeared to be the end of that line of discussion.

"I assume you're here because of what happened?" Georgina asked, nodding toward the window. The view was near-unimpeded, and since we were up the slope, it looked down almost directly to Jaqueline and Geno's home. I could see the truck in the drive, as well as the front door. If anyone came or went, Georgina would have a clear view of them.

"We are," I said. "Rita told me that you remembered something? Was it from St. Patrick's Day? The night before?"

Georgina nodded, then started rocking as she did. "It's a real shame what happened. I can't say I ever much cared for Jaqueline and Geno Lyon, but I never imagined them finding a *body* on their property. Out here? It's simply unheard of."

Rita leaned toward me and whispered, "Here we go," as if she'd never rambled in her life.

I ignored her and politely listened as Geogina continued.

"Did you know that Jaqueline poisoned Geno?" she said. "This was years ago. I've lost count how long ago it was, since my years tend to blend together these days, only that it was such a scandal, I was positive Carter was going to ask them to move. Carter lives three houses that way." She motioned out the window, farther up the hill. "He likes to pretend he's some sort of . . . what do you call it when someone wants to run a neighborhood and make choices for everyone else?"

"Like a homeowners association?" I guessed.

"Close enough." Georgina stared out the window. "Jaqueline denies the allegations, of course. Why wouldn't she? If it was proven that she'd tried to kill her husband, then she'd not only have served time, but she would have been ostracized from the community. Not that she's been much of a neighbor as it is. They keep to themselves, never show up to neighborhood events or welcome new additions like a normal person would."

"But you think she did it?" I asked. "Poisoned him, I mean?"

"Oh, I'm almost positive she did. Who else would have tried to kill him in such a way? An enemy of his would have gone at him physically. But poison?" She shook her head. "That's the weapon of someone close to you, someone who doesn't want to get caught."

I was pretty sure nearly every murderer didn't want to get caught, but I let that last go. I understood what she meant.

It *did* make me wonder, though. Jazz had said Bucky was the one who'd poisoned Geno. That seemed to be the sort of thing that someone like Georgina would love to gossip about if it were true.

"What does any of this have to do with what happened on St. Patrick's Day?" Rita asked.

"I'm getting to that." Georgina scowled, continued rocking. "I'm simply setting the stage. Context is important, you know? I'd figure that you'd know that, considering we were once writers." She stared off wistfully for a moment, making me wonder if she'd given up writing. I hadn't heard much about the writers group they were both a part of as of late and wondered if they met much anymore.

Georgina continued to rock silently a few moments, as if punishing Rita for interrupting, before she started speaking again. "As I was saying, Jaqueline poisoned her husband once before. The two of them haven't gotten along for quite some time. You can see how far away they live from me, yet I've been awakened more than once by the two of them howling like cats and dogs." A pause. "Though I suppose cats don't howl. Howling and yowling, then." A sharp nod.

"Has it ever gone beyond yelling?" I asked. "Have they ever fought physically?"

"That, I can't say," Geogina replied. "If there's been any violence beyond that previous poisoning I mentioned, they kept *that* quiet. Most of the ruckus I hear around here comes from some of the younger folks who've moved into the neighborhood recently. I'm sure you've noticed that a lot of the houses out this way are of the older sort. Wiring often needs to be replaced. Water lines are all copper or what have you. Makes it cheaper to buy, but more expensive in the long run."

"Tell me about it," Rita said. "It costs near an arm and a leg these days to get anything fixed."

"It's why I take good care of my place. A gentle hand does wonders, you know?" She nodded to herself, then went on. "I got to thinking about things last night while in my bath. There's not much more I can do there but think. I told Rita I was woken up the morning after the St. Patrick's Day hubbub by the noise down the street, but it didn't hit me until now that I'd seen something earlier. You know, the night before?"

I leaned forward, anxious, but kept myself from prodding her with questions.

"I'm not sure what time it was," Georgina said. "I go to bed early these days, but with all the excitement, I might have been up later than usual. Hard to say, to be honest. I never look at the clock, because if I do and I find I'm up past my normal bedtime, I get suddenly tired, even if I wasn't before, and I hate it."

"I do that when it comes around to dinnertime," Rita said. "If I realize it's past time I ate, I suddenly become hungry."

Georgina nodded. "All I know is that it was dark, and I was sitting right here, a book in my lap. I'd given up on reading since my eyes were growing tired, and I suppose I'd dozed off when I noticed headlights coming from down the street. Curious, I looked out the window, and that's when I saw the truck."

"The Lyons' truck?" I asked.

"It was," she said. "I thought it was the two of them coming home, but that wasn't it. I realized I recalled seeing the truck there an hour before, when I'd first sat down. And I'm certain no one left again, though I suppose it was possible when I'd closed my eyes that someone had. Like I said, I wasn't sure what time it was by then."

Her gaze drifted to the window, and her rocking ceased. "I would have gathered myself and gone back to bed then, but that's when I noted there was another light. Not headlights like before, but smaller."

"Like a flashlight?" I asked.

"That or the light from a phone," she said. "It was hard to tell, especially with how my vision is going. All I know is that it was bobbing this way and that, like someone was moving around a lot, but it was centered around where Jaqueline Lyon's truck was parked. I watched for a moment, but I couldn't see anything else, so I went to bed."

I blinked at her. "You don't know who it was or what they were doing?"

"No, I'm not some sort of lookie-loo." She scoffed.

"At the time, I assumed it was Jaqueline or Geno, and that one of them had forgotten something in the truck. But now that I've had time to reflect, I realize that those headlights weren't from them, but from someone else, someone who'd been lurking around their vehicle well past the time when any good person should be out."

I desperately wanted to ask her if it was Bucky or someone else that she'd seen, but I knew it was pointless. She'd already established that she hadn't been able to see who it was.

But her story *did* tell me something. Someone was lurking around the truck where Bucky's body was found. If Bucky had climbed into the truck before they'd gotten home, wouldn't the person who'd been poking around have found him?

No, I found it more likely that Bucky ended up in the truck *after* the Lyons had gotten home. And if I didn't miss my guess, I was pretty sure that someone else had put him there, because if he had driven himself all the way out here before succumbing to the poison, his car would have still been sitting outside their house.

Rita and I left a short time later, when Georgina said she needed to take a nap. I was convinced that Bucky hadn't driven out here on his own. I was also positive he hadn't hitched a ride with the Lyons and died sometime during the night, because, well, why would he?

That meant that sometime after Bucky had left the Whistling Wet Weasel, he'd ended up at the Lyons' house. How did he get there? When exactly did he die? Before he'd arrived? After?

And if so, who had brought him there?

He could have called a cab or an Uber, I realized. Bucky could have driven home after collapsing at the Weasel. From there, he could have called someone to take him to the Lyons' place, and . . .

That's where I drew a blank. He may have wanted to confront Geno. Or maybe see Jaqueline, especially if he thought he might be dying.

But if that was the case, why not go to a doctor?

"What are you doing, dear?" Rita asked when I slowed, and then pulled into the Lyons' driveway, next to the truck where Bucky was found.

"I'm going to talk to whoever is here," I said.

"You mean, you want to talk face-to-face with a possible killer?" Rita didn't sound as if she disapproved. She sounded impressed, in fact.

"Or someone who might know one."

We got out of the car, but before we could approach the door, it opened, and a woman stepped out. She was in her mid- to late-forties, with sharp features and dark, curly hair. Nothing like the woman I'd seen on Skinny's video.

"No comment," she said, not breaking stride as she headed for the truck.

"Jaqueline Lyon?" I asked.

"No comment."

"We're not reporters."

She hesitated, hand on the handle of her truck. "Then, who are you?"

"Krissy Hancock," I said. "And my friend Rita Jablonski. I was friends with Bucky Sweeny."

Jaqueline flinched ever so slightly. "I'm sorry for your loss, but I have nothing to tell you."

"You once dated Bucky," I said, opting for blunt.

Jaqueline didn't show any sort of reaction other than irritation. "I did. A long, long time ago."

"Were you seeing him again?" Rita asked, drawing Jaqueline's eye.

Her lips pressed into a fine line, and when she spoke, she barely moved them. "No."

"Even as friends?" I asked.

Anger started simmering behind her gaze as it swiveled back to me. "No."

"Who found him?" I asked. "Bucky, I mean. He was found in the back of your truck, wasn't he?"

Her jaw worked as her hand fell away from her truck's door handle so she could cross her arms. "I did. And I don't see why you should care. I had nothing to do with it, nor do I know who did. I came out here, found him, and called the police. Before that, I hadn't seen or talked to Bucky in any meaningful way in weeks, maybe months."

"What about Dwayne Morris?" I asked.

Anger turned to confusion. She looked from me to Rita and back again. "What does Dwayne have to do with anything?"

I noted she called him by his first name, in a rather familiar tone. "Have you seen him recently? Talked to him? About Bucky, perhaps?"

"Why would I talk to Dwayne about Bucky? Why would I talk to him about anyone?"

"You tell me."

Jaqueline stared at me like I'd grown a second head before she checked her watch. "I don't know who you've been talking to, or why you're out here hounding me, but I know nothing about what happened. I found him, and that's it. So, please, if you would, I have somewhere I need to be." She motioned toward where I'd parked.

"They think Bucky was poisoned," I said, hoping for a reaction.

"And?" Jaqueline's eyes narrowed. "You think I did it, don't you?" She laughed. It was as bitter of a sound as I've ever heard. "Of course you do. Haven't I already been through enough? Poison? Unfounded accusations?" She shook her head, then leveled a finger at me. "I've never poisoned anyone in my life. Not Bucky. Not *Geno*. No one. And I'd appreciate it if you never came back here."

And with that, she jerked her door open, climbed inside her truck, and sped off.

"Well," Rita said, hands on her hips, as she watched her go, "that wasn't the least bit suspicious, now, was it, dear?"

19

"I don't see how you can eat that," Rita said from across the table at Death by Coffee. After our chats with Georgina and Jaqueline, we'd come back to the bookstore café to regroup.

"It's good," I said, spooning a chunk of soggy cookie into my mouth. "Comforting."

"It looks terrible."

I shrugged, took another bite from my cookie. My coffee was long gone, which meant it was time for my favorite part: the gooey cookie-dregs. "I like it."

Rita made a face, then gathered herself as she stood. "I'd best be going, I suppose. You'll tell me if you hear anything more, right? I don't want to be left out of the loop, especially since I've been so vital to you."

"I'll call you if I learn anything." Though I did cross my mental fingers. It was one thing to put myself into dangerous situations by poking around in murder investigations. It was another thing entirely to drag my friends into it.

She eyed me a moment longer before nodding to herself. "I'll be at home. If I don't answer your call . . ." The smile that followed was full of mischief. "Well, don't expect a return call if that's the case. Not right away, anyway."

I was dying to know what—or, more likely, *who*— would be keeping her so busy, but I decided to leave her with her secrets. For now.

As Rita left, I went back to my cookie. I had hours yet before Paul and I were due to meet with Vicki and Mason for dinner, so I had some time to follow up on what little we'd learned. And yeah, I could go home and try to put it all behind me, but that wasn't going to happen. I'd drive myself crazy if I tried.

I grabbed my phone, and after a moment's debate, I found a number and called, fully expecting it to ring unanswered. Instead, it was picked up almost immediately.

"Hello?"

"Kandice?" I asked, though I recognized her voice. "It's Krissy Hancock."

There was a beat before, "Hi, Krissy. I can't really talk right now."

"That's okay. I only have one question." More than that, really, but there was one thing that had been bugging me since I'd come across it. "On St. Patrick's Day. You remember when Bucky threw someone out of the bar?"

"Yeah? We've already talked about this."

"I know, but I'm curious . . ." I considered how best

to phrase it. "The guy he threw out was a man named Skinny Jefferson. He was recording video of the town and the St. Patrick's Day celebrations."

A pause, and then, "Okay?"

"I saw the video." I waited to see if she'd react, but all I was met with was silence, so I continued. "Bucky was talking to a young woman. Privately. She's somewhere in her early to mid-twenties, so too young to be Jaqueline?"

Silence.

"She has chin-length hair. Blue eyes." After more silence, I asked, "Does she sound familiar to you? Does she frequent Bucky's Tavern? Work there?"

"I'm sorry. I didn't see anything that day, so I can't help you." There was a slight hitch to Kandice's voice. "I'll talk to you later, all right?"

"I'm trying to find out who she was," I hurriedly said before she could hang up. "This woman might know something about Bucky's death. We both want to know what happened to him, and this might be the way we find out."

Kandice blew out a breath, then said, "I'm truly sorry, Krissy. I can't help you."

"Please, Kandice, just a name."

"I—" There was a long pause, and I imagined her weighing her options. And then, spoken quickly, as if she was indeed in a hurry, "We're meeting at five tonight at Bucky's Tavern to discuss the future of the place. If you really want to talk about this, we can do so after that's done. But for now, I really do have to go."

And this time, she clicked off before I could respond.

I frowned as I considered the timing. Depending on how long the meeting ran, I'd be cutting it close for dinner tonight, but I thought I had to at least try to get Kandice to talk about the mysterious woman. Something told me that Kandice knew who she was and that her identity might be important to the case. How? I wasn't sure. But there had to be a reason as to why Bucky had gotten angry when he'd caught Skinny filming them, just as there had to be a reason as to why Kandice didn't want to talk about it.

While my schedule was quickly becoming cramped later, for now, I had little else to do but keep poking the hornets' nest, so I checked the tables around me to make sure I wasn't bothering anyone before doing a quick search and putting in another call. This time, the phone rang for long enough, I was about to hang up before a breathy, "Hey, yeah, sorry. This is the Weasel. What can I do for you?"

"Hi. I'm looking for Dwayne Morris? Is he in?"

"What? Dwayne? No, sorry." Then, a muffled, "Be right there." And then, back to me. "Sorry, ma'am, I've got to go. He should be in sometime within the hour."

"Thanks—" but he was gone.

I drummed my fingers on the table and considered what to do next. Kandice was too busy to talk, but Dwayne . . . Did I really want to talk to him face-to-face? It was just the sort of thing that would annoy Detective Buchannan and make Paul give me one of those semi-disappointed, worried looks of his.

But Dwayne Morris's name kept coming up in conversation with others about Bucky. And if he and Jaqueline were as *familiar* with one another as it had sounded, there could be something there. What? No clue. But I might as well find out, just in case it had to do with what happened on St. Patrick's Day.

I finished off my coffee-soaked cookie, tossed the empty cup into the trash, and then was on my way to the Whistling Wet Weasel.

The bar looked lonely from the outside, with only a couple of cars parked out front. The windows were decorated with beer signs and posters, and muffled country music oozed out from a door that wasn't quite square with the frame. When I entered, there were only two other people seated around the place. Both were men, and both looked as if they were permanent fixtures.

A man with long gray hair stood behind the bar. Sweat ran down his face from the heat of the place. Apparently, the AC was down, and the couple of slowly spinning ceiling fans only seemed to move the overly warm air around rather than cooling anything off. It was strangely far cooler outside, so much so that I wondered if the heat was permanently running because there was no way that it should be this warm.

As I crossed the room, all three sets of eyes followed me with mild disinterest. The closer I got to the bar, the heavier the smell of stale beer and sweat became.

"Hi, I'm Krissy Hancock," I said to the bartender, who I assumed had answered the phone earlier. "I called about Dwayne."

"He's not in." Yep, same voice, though less breathy this time. "Could get you something to drink if you want. Shouldn't be too much longer." He held up a glass with spots on it that were of a shade that didn't look healthy.

"No, thank you." I flashed him a smile. "I'll wait."

"Suit yourself." The bartender moved down the bar, leaving me to my own devices.

I didn't sit, but I leaned against one of the stools as I turned to take in the room. There was no stage from which Caitlin and her band could have played, but there was a large, open space on the far side of the room near the restrooms where I could imagine them setting up. There wasn't a ton of seating inside, so the crowd wouldn't have been too terribly large. And if enough people *had* come in for post-parade celebrations, it would have been easy enough for someone like Dee—and the mystery man Caitlin had seen—to mingle unseen.

Near the restrooms, a hallway led to another small room. There was more seating in there, but not a lot. I wondered if it had served as a backstage area, or if, during the show, people could choose to drink there for a little more privacy, though it still would have been loud.

The door opened, and one of the men I'd seen talking to Kandice outside of Bucky's Tavern stepped inside. He was a bulky, bald man with hairy arms and thick eyebrows. He looked both physically and mentally exhausted, and I noted that the knuckles on both his hands were healing from what I suspected was a physical confrontation with something—or, more likely, someone.

Dwayne Morris, I assumed.

He glanced at the bartender, who tipped his head my way. The man I took for Dwayne immediately headed my way.

"You called for me?" he asked in a voice that was

rough and gritty, like he'd smoked most of his life. Up close, he was imposing, but not so much that it made me want to run.

"I did." I stuck out a hand and smiled. "Krissy Hancock. I knew Bucky."

Dwayne took my hand and shook. His palms were calloused, and his grip was firm enough that it hurt. "Shame what happened to him." He let me go and shoved both hands into his back pockets as he regarded me. "Though I can't figure out why you'd come here to talk to me of all people. Especially if it has to do with Bucky. I had nothing to do with him."

"I was told you went to his tavern, looking for a fight," I said. "Is that not true?"

Dwayne stared at me a moment, then a slow smile found his face. "Well, you got me there. I suppose I did pay him a visit, hoping to knock some sense into him, but that's all I was planning on doing, you hear? I didn't kill him, and I had no plans of doing so."

"Why did you want to fight him?"

"Why else?" Dwayne retorted. "He opened his place, despite my objections. It's not like I don't have enough issues without him stealing my customers. As you see"— he motioned around the room—"I try to keep a decent place. But a new bar in town? It would inevitably eat at my base, no matter what kind of clientele he was looking to attract."

Admittedly, the Weasel wasn't *that* bad. Small? Yes. In need of some updates? Of course. But it wasn't falling apart, and the tables did look relatively clean, as did the floor.

And I could see where Dwayne was coming from. When I'd opened Death by Coffee with Vicki, the owners of J&E's Banyon Tree, Judith and Eddie Banyon, weren't happy about it. Before our bookstore café, they were the town's best source of out-of-the-home coffee, and to their eyes, we were ruining that.

"Bucky came here sometime after the parade, didn't he?" I asked. "A band was playing, and he collapsed, taking out the mixer. Is that correct?"

Dwayne paled. "Yeah. It was the darndest thing. Caught me completely off guard, to tell you the truth."

"Do you know what happened?"

He pulled a hand from his pocket so he could wipe sweat from his face. "I wish I knew. Bucky came in here, angry about . . ." He shook his head. "Can't really say what it was about, truth be told. He was practically incoherent, yelling one minute, muttering to himself the next. He was saying something about being upset that I put 'her' up to it, though I have no idea who or what he was talking about."

"You said he was getting what he deserved. This was after he fell."

Dwayne barked a laugh. "I did, didn't I? But it wasn't about him being sick or that I thought he was going to up and die on us. I was just angry he was coming here, acting like a drunk who'd had twice his usual intake. Heck, I thought that was the problem—that he'd drunk himself into a stupor and come looking for a fight. Figured that's what killed him, you know? Can't say I've never been there myself, so I suppose a part of me felt for him."

"So, you have no idea why he came here?" I asked.

"None," Dwayne said. "I suppose he was accusing me of something, though I don't know for sure that he even understood what he was accusing me of himself. I'd never seen Bucky that out of it before. Even though I wanted to knock him down more than once, I ended up helping the guy up when he did hit the deck. He was just so pathetic, I couldn't do anything else. I'm not such a good guy as to not give him an earful as I led him out of my place. I told him to call a cab, sober up, what have you. But, of course, he ignored me and climbed into his car. I probably should have stopped him, but at that point, I just wanted to be rid of him."

I wondered if Bucky would still be alive if Dwayne *had* forced him to call a cab, but I dismissed the idea almost immediately. Bucky, by then, had been suffering from whatever poison had been coursing through him, not alcohol consumption. Yes, a bar owner who suspected someone of being overly inebriated *should* have prevented that same someone from driving anywhere. It was irresponsible and said a lot about the man, but I suspected it wouldn't have changed much of anything.

"I didn't kill him," Dwayne went on, voice firming. "I don't know who did. And I surely don't know why. Especially in such a strange manner."

"What about Jaqueline Lyon?" I asked.

Dwayne's face scrunched up in confusion. "What about her?"

"Could she have done it? Bucky was found in her truck." I paused for dramatic effect before taking a shot in the dark. "And from what I've heard, you two were getting pretty close to one another. Very . . . familiar."

Dwayne's confusion only increased. "From what you've heard? Who have you been talking to who would say something like that?"

"Are you saying you and Jaqueline don't know one another?"

"Of course we know each other," Dwanye said. "But we're not all that close. And we're definitely not doing whatever it is you're implying."

"She spoke of you in a rather familiar way," I said, feeling dumb, but pushing ahead nonetheless.

Dwayne gathered his thoughts before he responded. "I suppose she might have," he said. "Perchance we had occasion to discuss some things that pertained to the both of us before this whole Bucky business blew up in both of our faces. There was nothing romantic to it. It was, shall we say, two friends sharing concerns with one another."

"About?"

He scowled at me. "None of your business, that's what it was about."

Okay, that was fair. "You don't believe Jaqueline could have killed Bucky?" I asked instead.

Dwayne didn't immediately reject the idea, which I found telling. He thought about it, before shaking his head. "No, I don't. In fact, as much as I hate to admit it, over the last day or so, I've thought quite a lot about Bucky and what happened to him. We might not have gotten along, but it's still a shock when someone you know up and dies."

"You went to his place after his death," I said. "I saw you taking to Kandice with Ruth and Ivan."

Dwayne stared at me a long moment but said nothing.

"You were paying your condolences?" I prodded.

"Yeah. That's it."

Somehow I didn't believe him.

One of the customers rose and staggered past us, toward the bathrooms. His step wasn't quite steady, telling me he'd been there for a while already. Dwayne waited for him to pass before continuing.

"There were rumblings that Bucky didn't have a mind for business," he said before I could press him about why he'd been talking to Kandice. "That he was already running his tavern into the ground. He had good intentions. Even I could see that. But he didn't know what he was doing, and there were those close to him, people he worked with, who saw what he was doing and knew that if he remained in charge, things would go downhill fast."

"You think Bucky's Tavern would have closed?"

He spread his hands. "Can't say for sure, and I suppose none of us ever will know what would have happened if he hadn't died. But he came here complaining about something that had him tied up in all sorts of knots. Now, I know I'm not the brightest bulb, but I can put two and two together when it's staring me right in the face."

"Meaning?"

"Meaning, Bucky was upset. He came here talking about some woman. His place was struggling behind the scenes." He took a step toward me, leaned in close enough that I could smell the cabbage on his breath. "All I'm saying is that if you want to know who had reason to kill Bucky Sweeny, look no further than the one woman who was a part of both his personal and his professional life."

20

*K*andice Vaughn.

She stood in front of the bar, facing the employees of Bucky's Tavern, who were gathered around the room. Jazz and Grant were sitting next to one another at tables near the front, with the kitchen employees, whose names I didn't know, sitting at a table behind them. I was allowed in for the meeting, but was relegated to a back table where I'd be out of the way, which was perfectly fine by me.

"We all miss him," Kandice said, gesturing toward the bar. "Bucky didn't just give us all jobs. He—*we*—became family."

I watched her mannerisms, listened to her words, looking for deception of any kind. Kandice was the closest person any of us knew to Bucky. She'd started dating him sometime after she took the job as bartender, but what if there was a reason other than love as to why she'd gotten together with him? What if she'd always wanted the bar for herself? Would she have truly killed him for it?

She'd been talking for a few minutes now, and I had no idea.

"I've been on the phone these last few days," she went on. "I was stunned by what happened. We all were. I was mourning, yet I was expected to hold it together, not just for me, but for all of us. I tried. I really did. And then I got a call, one that had me questioning everything."

I leaned forward. Anticipation had my leg jiggling up and down as I waited for what would inevitably be the reason as to why she'd called everyone here for this meeting.

"The lawyers still have a mess to untangle," Kandice said, laying her hand on the bar and caressing it. "But it appears as if Bucky had recently made an amendment to his will. He . . ." She took a breath, closed her eyes, and then let it all out in one breath. "He left everything to me. His home. His valuables." Another pause. "This place was included."

A stunned silence filled the room. Even *I* found myself gaping at her.

"You?" Jazz said, sitting up straighter. "He left it to you?"

Kandice nodded, wiped at her eyes. "I never asked him for it, but yes, he named me as his sole beneficiary. It was as if he knew the end was coming, and he wanted to set his affairs in order. Somehow, some way, he chose *me*."

"You . . . you weren't with him for that long," Grant said, pointing out the obvious.

"I know." A smile flitted across her face, and she started blinking rapidly. "I don't know if he knew that someone was after him, or if it was because of his health problems, but Bucky made sure that we were all taken care of. He didn't want to leave anyone hanging, which is why there were instructions left for me to handle this very situation."

"Instructions?" one of the kitchen staff asked. "What kind of instructions?"

"I'll get to that. I—"

"How?" Grant asked. "He couldn't have known what was going to happen to him. Why would he have changed things now?"

"I don't know," Kandice admitted. "He never told me that he was even considering doing it. When the lawyers called me, I was positive it was some sort of joke, that someone was putting me on. But it's real. Once the kinks are worked out, I'll be the new owner of Bucky's Tavern."

"Kinks." This from Jazz, who looked as miffed as everyone else.

"I understand your frustrations," Kandice said. "I really do. But we all still have a place here, if you want it. Once some papers are signed, and yes, after those kinks are worked through, we can open again. I want all of you to stay. I'll likely have to hire a new bartender, or promote one of you and fill your current role with someone else, but none of you will go wanting for a job. Bucky wanted it that way, and I plan on following through with his wishes."

I studied her from my place in the back of the room, but saw nothing that told me she was lying. I didn't want to believe Dwayne in thinking that Kandice was Bucky's killer, but it was hard not to go there. She'd been dating him, had every opportunity to poison him. She knew of his health issues, knew his history with Jaqueline, including Geno's suspected poisoning.

And now she was the new owner of Bucky's Tavern.

"It's a lot to take in," Kandice said after a moment. "And there's no reason for you to commit to anything now. I'm going to make sure you all get paid for this week, even if we don't open. I'm not sure how much money is in the account, if any, but I promise, I'll do everything I can to make this work. Even if I have to take the money out of my own account or take out a loan, I'll do it."

The next few minutes were spent with Kandice fielding questions and giving the same answer to pretty much all of them. She didn't know why Bucky would suddenly change his will. She didn't know why she'd been chosen over someone like Jazz or Grant. She didn't know if he'd suspected someone was after him. She didn't know, she didn't know, she didn't know.

Once the meeting broke, she leaned against the bar, exhausted, while everyone else formed small groups to discuss the news.

I gave her a few moments to collect herself before I joined her, already with an excuse—and key—in hand.

Kandice glanced at the key to Bucky's house as I held it out to her. She sucked in a breath, then took it. "Thank you," she said, weighing it in her hand before pocketing it. "I can't believe any of this. Even the house is mine now. I . . . I'm not sure I want it, but I do need to go through some things. If nothing else, I should get my stuff."

"You didn't know this was coming?" I asked as gently as I could.

Kandice shook her head. "I had no idea. The lawyer called me the other day and laid it all out, but I barely heard him. I can't believe Bucky would do this to me." She laughed, then sniffed. "He'd made a joke a few days before he died that someday, we might end up running this place together. I didn't think . . . he couldn't have meant . . ." A tear slid down her cheek as she trailed off.

I wanted to feel sympathy for her, and perhaps a part of me did, but I kept thinking about what Dwayne had said, as well as my own doubts about her from before that. I didn't see deception in Kandice's demeanor, but that didn't mean it wasn't there. She could have gotten with Bucky for the sole purpose of taking his bar from him.

But to kill him for it? I was having a hard time seeing it.

"I'm sorry, Krissy," she said, taking a deep, calming breath. "I have some things to do. I know you wanted to talk, but it's going to have to wait."

I wanted to argue, to confront her with my suspicions, but I realized that if I was wrong, I would make things a whole lot worse for her. A few more days, and I might have a better grasp on what was true and what was pure, unsubstantiated rumor.

"Okay," I said, then let her go.

She went straight for the back kitchen area, her step

quick. Just before the door closed behind her, her shoulders hunched, and I saw her drop into a crouch. That brief glimpse showed me a woman full of grief, someone who was struggling to hold it together publicly. Did I really think she would act like that if she had indeed killed Bucky?

I turned and found the bar had mostly emptied while I'd been talking to Kandice. Jazz was standing at the table where he'd sat, arms still crossed, a perplexed expression on his face. I joined him.

"I can't believe it," he said before I could speak. "None of this feels right."

"I'm as surprised as you are."

He grunted. "I doubt it."

"Do you think you'll stay on?"

"I . . . I'm not sure. I think—" His phone rang, causing us both to jump. He checked the screen, then rolled his eyes. "It's my sister again. I should take this. I swear, she's been calling every day about this." He answered the phone as he walked away. "Allie. Slow down. I know what she's been saying, but it's not like you've helped—" His voice faded as he left the bar.

I remained standing there a moment longer, but everyone else had left. Bucky's had once felt full of life, even when it was just the handful of us standing around, talking about Irish coffee and our plans for the cross-promotion. Yet now it felt truly empty. It was as if Bucky's passing had sapped the very soul from the place. I didn't know what was going to happen, if Kandice would be able to open again or if questions surrounding Bucky's death would end up keeping the place closed for good, but I did know that no matter what, Bucky's Tavern would never be the same.

I headed for the door, doubts swirling in my head. Ruth had said I should be looking at the *why*, rather than the *who*, when it came to Bucky's death. Maybe the correct answer wasn't one or the other, but the combination of both. The why would be what caused the who to act. And, right then, I felt as if I'd been shown the why, which pointed directly at the who.

But just because Kandice had a reason to kill him, that didn't mean she went through with it. Nor did it mean she was the only one. I owed it to Bucky to keep looking.

I had stopped just outside the door when I noticed Grant pacing back and forth a few yards away. He was muttering to himself, hands clenching and unclenching.

"Is everything okay, Grant?" I asked, approaching him.

His laugh was harsh and half-crazed. "I don't know. Is it?"

He continued to pace. I watched him, concern building. "Grant? What's wrong?"

He glanced at me, then stopped. "I'll be okay. It's just . . ." He frowned, shook his head, as if to clear it. "I'm confused."

"About?"

"About all of this." He swung a hand wildly toward Bucky's, nearly clipping me as he did. "Bucky was . . . I wanted him to be . . ." He made a frustrated sound. "We were friends, and I had no idea that he was planning this. Or, I suppose, maybe not friends. Not like I thought we were."

"You served him coffee," I said. "On St. Patrick's Day."

Grant closed his eyes, jammed balled-up fists into them. "I know. I keep thinking about that. What if I poisoned him somehow? Accidentally." He dropped his hands. "But you had the same coffee, from the same pot, and you're okay. So, it couldn't have been me, right? *Right?*"

"I don't know," I said. "Did you put anything else into Bucky's coffee? Sugar? Cream? Or did he have something else to eat or drink earlier that day? Something prepared by someone else?" *Kandice, perhaps?*

Grant considered it, then made a frustrated sound. "I don't remember. Bucky usually takes his coffee black, so I'm pretty sure I didn't add anything to it. I recall thinking that I should add some Jameson, just to take the edge off for him, but since he never asked for it, I didn't. As far as I know, that was all he had. And if it was the coffee that killed him, does that make me an accessory? Will the police be coming for me?"

"No, Grant," I said. "If you served him poisoned coffee unknowingly, there's nothing for you to worry about." Other than *how* he'd managed to poison Bucky and not me. That'd be a question the police would want to know the answer to just as much as I would.

Grant didn't look like he believed me, but he nodded anyway.

"Do you recall Bucky acting strangely that day or any time before his death?" I asked. "Like he feared for his life? That he was afraid someone was after him?"

"No." Grant took a deep breath, then flexed his fingers, as he tried to center himself. "I guess he might have complained about his stomach some, but he did that often enough that it wasn't all that strange." He suddenly went still, met my eye. "I think I messed up."

"Messed up? How?" I braced myself for a confession of some sort. Grant had said he'd only be accepted by his family again if he was the owner of the bar, not just an employee. Had he poisoned—or hired someone to poison—Bucky to make it a reality?

"I told you about Bucky and Jaqueline, right? The day after he . . ." He blinked, pressed his lips into a fine line, as if he couldn't bring himself to say "died."

But I understood. "I remember."

"I figured Ivan had found out about the relationship, caused trouble. Ivan had called that day, which is probably why my mind went down that road. It made sense." He reached out, grabbed my hand. "It made sense, right?"

"It did," I said, a strange sense of foreboding coursing through me. I pulled my hand free without making it appear as if his touch had my alarm bells ringing.

Grant ran his fingers through his hair. "There've been whispers recently," he said, seemingly talking more to himself than to me. "People talk, spread rumors, gossip, whatever."

"You heard a rumor about Bucky?"

"It was the standard stuff, I guess. We all knew about him and Kandice. Then there were the rumors about him and Jaqueline, though those didn't really start up until recently, after he was found. And none of it was verified or felt . . . what's the word? True? Right?"

"I understand what you mean."

He nodded, paced away. "Then he was found in the back of Jaqueline's truck, and we all assumed he must have been cheating on Kandice with her. It made sense, you know? They were together once before, and Geno and Jaqueline weren't getting along, so why not?"

"But he left Kandice the bar."

Grant spun and pointed at me. "Exactly. Why would he do that if he was cheating on her? And then I started thinking, really thinking about it, and I remembered something I'd seen like a day or two before his death. It hadn't meant anything to me then, but now, after thinking about it some, I realize that it might be important."

The door to Bucky's opened, and Kandice stepped outside. She hesitated when she saw Grant and me together, waved, and then hurried over to her car. I noted that she gave us one last lingering look before driving off.

Grant watched her go, brow furrowed. He appeared not only to have aged in the last few days, but to have lost weight too. His face was gaunt, drawn, as if he hadn't been sleeping. Whatever had been going through his mind, it was weighing heavily upon him.

"I saw Ivan with Jaqueline," he said.

Now, *that* caught me by surprise. "You mean, *with* her?" I asked.

"No, I don't mean I caught them in bed with one another or anything like that, but . . ." He finally pulled his eyes away from the empty road down which Kan-

dice had gone, and looked at me. "But I saw them together. At the Banyon Tree. Do you know the place?"

"I do."

"They were just eating, I guess," Grant went on.
"Sitting there, talking. No holding hands or kissing or
anything that would make me think they were lovers or
whatnot. But something felt off about it. It was as if I
could feel the intensity radiating off them through the
window."

"Did you hear what they were talking about?" I
asked, mind whirling at the possibilities. First, I'd suspected Jaqueline and Dwayne were closer than they'd
seemed, and now this? It couldn't be a coincidence that
Bucky's ex was talking to other bar owners in town before his death. And then to have his body found in the
back of her truck?

"I didn't. I went in and ate, but I sat across the room.
And they didn't stay long once I got there. I . . . wait."
He frowned. "I suppose I *did* hear something."

I waited a beat, and when he didn't go on, I pressed
him with an impatient, "What?"

"I'm not sure of the exact nature of the conversation," Grant admitted. "But I'm pretty sure Jaqueline
was skeptical of something Ivan was saying. Maybe it
wasn't her words, but her expression that caught my attention." He shook his head. "I don't remember. I
didn't want to make it seem like I noticed them, but
what if they were talking about killing Bucky?" His
eyes widened. "What if they remember seeing me there
and think I overheard them plotting against him? Oh
man!"

Grant looked like he was about to run for the hills,

so I gently laid a hand on his wrist. "We don't know what they were talking about yet," I said. "And if they were going to come after you, I'm pretty sure they would have done so by now."

He didn't look convinced, and honestly, I couldn't blame him. It wasn't very reassuring. "I'm not sure I can do this," he said. "I like Kandice, and I liked my job here, but this is too much."

"It'll be okay," I said. "I'm going to talk to the police tonight." The police being Paul, but Grant didn't need to know that. "I'll tell them about what you told me, and if Ivan and Jaqueline were plotting against Bucky, they'll find out." And then, to ease his mind, "I won't bring your name into it."

"Yeah." His nod was jerky. "Okay."

"You'll be fine. Promise."

Grant left a few minutes later, still shaky, but calm enough that I didn't think he planned on making a run for it. Yet.

But if he was right and Ivan and Jaqueline *had* plotted against Bucky, it left me with a few unanswered questions, the biggest of which was Ruth's simple, *"Why?"*

And to find out that answer, it appeared as if I might have to go directly to the source, which meant talking to the one man I'd hoped to avoid: Ivan McGraw.

21

Social media had once been one of my favorite ways to do research. I used to be able to hop on, do a few searches, and get a decent idea of who someone was—or who they wanted others to think them to be. It was quick, convenient, and most importantly, *safe*.

But over the last few years, things had changed. More and more people kept their profiles private. And those who didn't often only posted memes or shared posts from questionable sources, to the point that very little could be gleaned about the person I was trying to understand. Sure, I might learn which way they leaned politically or what kind of music they hated, but of the person themselves, I got little of use.

Still, I tried. After getting home from the meeting at Bucky's Tavern, I sat down with my phone and looked up everyone involved with Bucky's Tavern, either directly or peripherally, in the hopes of finding something that would help me understand what had really happened. I started with the old standbys, Facebook and Twitter—or X, or whatever it was called these days—and then moved on to newer ones like Bluesky. No matter which platform I used, however, the results were the same.

I learned nothing.

Frustrated, I tossed my phone aside and slumped down onto the couch. Misfit was asleep next to me, and all I wanted to do was join him in a long, well-deserved nap. I didn't want to think that Kandice Vaughn might have seduced and then killed Bucky Sweeny so she could take over his bar. I didn't want to believe that *anyone* I knew could be responsible for his death.

Yet, here I was.

Paul was due to arrive at any moment, so the nap was out. I forced myself to stand and head into the bathroom to freshen up before our double date with Vicki and Mason. While we were going to the nicest restaurant in town, Geraldo's, that didn't mean I needed to dress up. I wasn't going to go as a total slob, mind you, but no dresses or fancy skirts or blouses were expected or required.

Once I'd freshened up and changed into something that didn't smell like stale coffee, I gathered my phone to wait at my dining room table for Paul to arrive. I puttered around online for a few, but I kept finding myself looking for something that would connect back to Bucky. I also considered calling Ivan McGraw to get his take on things, but decided against it. For one, I wasn't so sure I *wanted* to talk to him, not if his personality matched what others said about him. And second, if he did tell me something profound, I knew I'd skip out on Paul and Vicki so I could chase whatever lead he'd given me.

Would he even be honest about why he'd been talking with Jaqueline Lyon at the Banyon Tree? And was it any of my business?

Headlights lit up the front of my house as a car pulled into my driveway. I popped to my feet, grabbed my purse, and was out the door before Paul could shut off the engine. I slid in next to him, and after a brief exchange of pleasantries, and yes, a very welcome kiss, we were on our way to Geraldo's.

"How's your mom?" I asked as we left my driveway.

A beat. "Good. I was thinking . . . We didn't get much of a chance to look at the house. Perhaps we can set up a few visits next week?"

I frowned at his evasion, but let it slide. "Sure. Any new prospects?"

"I haven't looked. I've been busy with the investigation. How about you?" A subtle, quick glance my way. "You been keeping out of trouble?"

"Yes?" Despite my best efforts, it came out as a question.

Paul chuckled. "I assume you've spoken with the suspects in Bucky Sweeny's murder investigation?"

"Hey, I know most of those people," I said, a smidge defensive. "You can't fault me for making sure they're doing okay."

"No, I can't," Paul said. "And I won't. John won't

like it, of course, but he doesn't much care for your actions most of the time anyway."

"It's not like I'm *trying* to upset him," I said. "It's just . . ."

"You can't help yourself."

"What was I supposed to do?" I asked, not really looking for an answer, and Paul didn't give one. "Kandice gave me the key to Bucky's house—"

"She what?"

"—so I went and had a look around. The police had already been there, so it wasn't like I was messing up a crime scene."

Paul was silent a long moment before he asked, "Did you find anything?"

"Not really. There's a rumor going around that Bucky might have poisoned himself somehow, but if he did, there was nothing at his home that indicated he'd done so there. Although . . ."

Paul didn't prod, though he once more took his eyes off the road long enough to glance at me.

"There was an email."

"An email? From?"

"Ruth Camden."

"The owner of that bar near Hotel?"

"The same," I said. "There wasn't much to it, but it was strange. Everyone has been saying that Ruth and Bucky didn't get along, but the email implied the opposite. And when I talked to Ruth—"

"Of course you did." Spoken with a smile.

"—she indicated that she and Bucky had some sort of agreement. Like, a truce? I don't know. She didn't want it to get out that she wasn't against Bucky open-ing his tavern because the other bar owners in town wouldn't like it and might turn against her."

"When you say 'other bar owners,' I assume you mean Dwayne Morris and Ivan McGraw?"

"Yeah." I wondered if he knew their names because they were targets in the investigation or if he'd come across them in the ordinary course of his job. I couldn't recall whether we'd discussed the two men before now.

"Have you spoken to them?" Paul asked.

"Not Ivan, but I *have* talked to Dwayne," I said. "He implied that someone at Bucky's Tavern might have had motive to kill Bucky so they could take over the bar. The obvious suspect is—"

"Kandice Vaughn."

I fell silent, hating that I'd all but made her a target in the investigation, if she wasn't already. Often, it was the people closest to the victim who were the immediate suspects in a murder investigation, and Kandice fit that bill. Now that she'd inherited not just the bar but also Bucky's home and possessions, it made her seem that much more likely to have killed him, as horrible as that sounded.

"Does Buchannan have any other suspects?" I asked. "I don't need names. I guess I'm just hoping that he's on the trail of someone I don't have a personal or pro-fessional relationship with."

"There've been leads, yes," Paul said. "And John is chasing them down as quickly as he can, though man-power is limited, so . . ."

So, it was going slowly. Not the answer I wanted, but it was the one I'd expected.

We pulled into the lot at Geraldo's a short time later. Determined not to let Bucky's murder ruin dinner, I left my suspicions and concerns in the car as we headed inside. We were the first to arrive, but a table had been reserved for us by Vicki, so Paul and I were led to a semi-private corner, where we could speak without being overheard. Light jazz played over speakers hidden around a dimly lit room, which made each table feel semi-isolated from the rest.

My phone *ping*ed just as I sat down. I checked it to find a text from Vicki. Paul caught my frown.

"What is it?" he asked.

"Vicki and Mason are running late," I said, tucking my phone away. "Mason forgot his keys and wallet at Death by Coffee, and they have to swing by there to get them." Though I did wonder why he'd taken them out of his pocket in the first place.

Then again, maybe I didn't want to know.

The waiter arrived, depositing water, then took our drink order. Like the rest of the male staff, he was wearing a tuxedo, which should have been strange considering the diners were dressed so casually, yet somehow it worked. The female staff members had on form-fitting black dresses, though I did note one woman wearing black pants and a dark jacket, telling me that the dresses weren't required of everyone.

"Chief's retiring," Paul said.

The comment caught me by surprise, and I very

nearly choked on a sip of water. "I heard." Spoken carefully because, right then, I couldn't read his expression.

"It came out of nowhere," he said, fiddling with his silverware. "I was afraid she was sick or that something had happened that had forced her hand."

Which was the exact thing I'd wondered when I'd heard. "And?"

"And . . . nothing." He gave me an incredulous look. "She said that she'd merely decided it was time. I swore I'd have to drag her kicking and screaming from her office, and yet here she is, simply walking away, all on her own."

"That's good, isn't it?"

Paul sighed. "Yeah, you're probably right. It just feels so . . . wrong?" He shook his head in wonder.

The waiter returned and deposited our drinks. After assuring him that we'd wait to order until after our friends arrived, he left us to our conversation.

"I've got familial news of my own," I said.

"Oh boy." Paul, knowing my dad, smiled as he said it. "What's James done now?"

"He fell and broke his hip."

The smile vanished. "What happened? Is he okay?"

"He says he is. Laura told me that he tripped over his own slippers." I worried at my cloth napkin. "I know there's nothing I could have done about it, but it's made me wish I lived closer to him. What if he'd really been hurt? I'm so far away . . ."

Paul reached across the table to rest a hand on my own. "I get it. I'm not sure how I'd handle not being able to check in with Chief every now and again, see her with my own two eyes and reassure myself that she's okay."

I smiled. "You know, if she retires, you might actually have to start calling her 'Mom.'"

He laughed. "I suppose you're right."

"And maybe she'll call *you* 'Chief'?" I said, making it a question.

Paul turned strangely somber. "You know? I'm honestly not sure I'd want the job. There'd be more work, more hours to put in." He met my eye. "And since we are about to start our lives together, I don't think I want to do that."

I swallowed, looked away, embarrassed for a reason I couldn't pinpoint. "You'll get sick of me soon enough."

"I doubt that," he said. "Truly. I'd much rather be here than anywhere else."

"Keep it up, and I might recruit you to work with me at Death by Coffee." I grinned. "Or Death by Java. Did I tell you that Valerie wants to sell me the place?"

"No!" He shook his head. "Though I'm not surprised." He pushed back his chair and stood, hand on his tummy. "Hold that thought. I've been on the move all day, and—"

"Go," I said, waving him off. "I don't want you to burst."

He chuckled, then quick-stepped his way toward the restrooms, which were on the other side of the restaurant.

I sipped at my drink and scanned the room while I waited for him to return. I didn't recognize any of the other diners beyond possibly seeing them at Death by Coffee a time or two, which was something of a relief. I wanted this dinner to be between friends, and not have it turn into a big thing where seemingly half the town ended up seated around the table, which had happened before.

My phone *ping*ed with a text from Vicki.

On the way. Apologize to Paul for us. Mason is an idiot.

I chuckled and set my phone aside. I made a mental note to ask Vicki if she'd thought any more about buying Death by Java and whether we should turn it into a franchise. The more I thought about it, the more I liked the idea. And if it just so happened to allow me to see Dad a little more often . . . all the better.

And then, if we *did* buy it and—

Someone was staring at me from across the room.

I noticed it mid-thought and simply froze, eyes locked on the woman, who was quite clearly watching me. She was just inside the doorway of Geraldo's, huddled in a long-sleeved shirt that was a smidge too big for her smallish frame. She was in her twenties, with light brown hair and dark blue eyes. That old feeling of recognition shot through me, one that said I should know who she was.

It was the woman from Skinny Jefferson's video who'd been talking to—or kissing?—Bucky Sweeny the day that he'd died.

The hostess approached the woman, spoke to her briefly. The woman motioned toward where I was sitting, which caused the hostess to nod, then walk away.

And then the woman headed my way.

My pulse beat in my ears as I waited, perched on the edge of my chair. I desperately wanted to rise, to meet her halfway, but something warned me that would be a mistake. Maybe it was the way she kept her arms close to her body, shoulders hunched in her too-large shirt, as if waiting for a blow. Maybe it was how her eyes darted around the room, as if trying to take everything in all at once.

Whatever the reason, I didn't move, and when she reached me, she stopped a good couple of feet from the table.

"Krissy Hancock?" she asked in a voice that trembled ever so slightly.

"I am," I said, putting on a pleasant smile, even though I was a nervous wreck inside. "And you are?"

The woman fidgeted, didn't respond. She glanced left, stiffened, then relaxed, as if she'd briefly mistaken one of the diners for someone else.

"You came here to talk to me?" I asked, drawing her eye back to me. "Does it have to do with Bucky?"

Her nod was jerky. "You knew him. I saw you with him a few times."

I filed that away. The only place Bucky and I met semi-regularly was at Bucky's Tavern. That meant the woman had some connection to the place, though I didn't know what that connection might be. She hadn't been at the meeting, so I didn't think she worked there.

"I did," I said. "I'd like to think we were becoming friends." I let that simmer a moment before asking, "Did you know him?"

Another jerky nod. More nervous glances around the room. More fidgeting. "I . . . You . . ." She took a deep, trembling breath. "Someone said you might be able to help, that you're looking for his killer?"

"I suppose I am," I said, speaking carefully. "Do you know something about what happened to him?"

"I . . ." She swallowed, fell silent.

"If you know who killed him, you should talk to someone," I pressed. "The police would—"

"No police!" The terror in her voice had eyes shifting our way. "Please." Whispered. "No police."

"Okay," I said, voice gentle. "No police. But if you tell me what you know, perhaps I can pass on the pertinent information to them . . . if that's okay?"

The woman pulled her hands into her sleeves and hugged herself before nodding.

"Okay. Good." I glanced toward the restrooms, willing Paul to take his time. "Do you know what happened to Bucky?"

She nodded, then shook her head, before frowning in a way that told me she was at war with herself. "I don't want . . . If it gets back . . ."

"It won't," I promised, though I wasn't entirely sure what she was afraid of. The killer, most likely.

"I tried," she said at a near-whisper. "I tried to tell him, but he wouldn't listen. No one would."

"Tell him what? I assume you mean Bucky?"

Another jerky nod. "I—" Her eyes went wide as she glanced to the side to see Paul approaching the table. "I'm sorry. I've got to go."

And before I could stop her, the woman spun and fled from Geraldo's.

"Who was that?" Paul asked, sitting.

My heart thumped in my chest as I stared after the fleeing woman. She *knew*. Whoever that woman was, she knew who had killed Bucky, and if I didn't miss my guess, she also knew *why* he'd been murdered.

"I don't know," I admitted, tearing my gaze away from the door to smile at Paul. I wasn't going to let the interruption ruin my dinner. "So . . . where were we?"

22

Death by Coffee sat prominently displayed at the center of the bookshelf in Death by Coffee. Dad's name, James Hancock, wasn't stylized on the cover of the older novel like it was on his newer ones. It wasn't embossed, either. It just . . . was.

Yet, like on the shelf, the book held a special place in my heart. When Vicki had wanted to name our bookstore café after one of my dad's most popular early books, I'd resisted. I couldn't see the potential, and after someone had died after drinking one of our coffees, it had seemed like an even worse idea.

Now, looking at the old, relatively plain cover, it felt right. The novel was surrounded on the shelf by Dad's other books—at least the ones we had in stock, since some of his older, less-popular titles were out of print. I sometimes took for granted that he was such a big deal, that these books had helped to keep me comfortable and relatively happy when I was younger. They'd even provided the funds to make sure I was able to move to Ohio and live in the house I lived in today.

I patted the book and stepped back, mildly overcome with emotion. My foot hit something soft and fluffy, and I very nearly pitched over backward. Thankfully, I caught my balance before I fell.

Trouble glared at me, tail swishing in annoyance, before he turned and sauntered off, exuding attitude.

He's so much like Misfit.

I was still jazzed from last night's dinner. Not only had I spoken with someone who might know something about what happened to Bucky, I'd also talked to Vicki and Mason about Death by Java. No, we hadn't made a final decision as of yet, but I felt we were close to one. Valerie wasn't asking for much for the California bookstore café, so all that really needed to be decided were the logistics. Who would do what and when and how often. Stuff like that.

Then, after dinner, I'd spent the rest of the night with Paul. The good feelings had carried me through the morning rush, into the subsequent lull, which, these days, wasn't as much of a slowdown as it used to be. Pooky was behind the counter with Eugene, while Beth was due to arrive at any moment, which would free me up to leave. The dining area was clean, with only a couple of people sitting at the tables. The smell of fresh coffee was in the air, and it made me long for a cup of my own.

With the rearranging of Dad's bookshelf complete, I had a few minutes to spare. I pulled out my phone, did a quick search, considered, and then dialed, stepping back behind the shelves so as not to disturb anyone.

The phone rang so many times that I was about to hang up, when a tired, raspy male voice answered with a terse, "What?"

I hesitated, then asked, "Is this Beers and Rears?" cringing at saying the name out loud.

A heavy sigh. "It is. What do you want this early in the freaking morning? Do you know what time it is?"

"Almost noon." I realized belatedly that the question was rhetorical, but it was too late now.

A grunt, then, "Are you going to tell me why you woke me up, or are you just going to sit there, making dumb comments?"

I wanted to reach through the phone and slap the person on the other end of the line, but I restrained myself. "I'm looking for Ivan McGraw," I said, doing my best to keep my voice semi-pleasant, though it was a struggle.

"Well, you found him."

I opened my mouth, closed it again. Then blurted, "You sleep at your bar?"

Ivan said something rather unflattering under his breath, but not so far under that I didn't hear it before he then said, "I work late. I've got a bunk in the back for nights when it's a challenge to get home, if you know what I mean? Why are you calling here, anyway? We don't open for hours, and I have no idea who you are."

"Krissy Hancock," I said. "I was hoping to talk to you about Bucky Sweeny."

There was a long pause. I waited it out, curious to see what Ivan might say unprompted.

"Kristy Hancock? You're that coffee lady Bucky was working with, right?"

"Krissy. And yes, that's me."

Another long pause, then, "Since I'm up, I might as well get breakfast. If you want to meet me at the Banyon Tree, I can't stop you. Might be nice to have some company, who knows? I'll be there in, oh, let's say an hour. Need time to clean up after last night." He chuckled in a way that made my skin crawl. "We can talk about Bucky or whatever it is you want to discuss then. I've got nothing to hide."

"Sure," I said. "I'll see you there."

"Mmm-hmm."

And then he was gone.

That had gone . . . surprisingly better than I'd anticipated it would. I'd expected Ivan to be more evasive. And while I wasn't too keen on spending time at the Banyon Tree, I'd much rather talk to Ivan there than at his bar.

I pocketed my phone and headed for the stairs just as Todd Melville entered. Just like the last time he'd been to Death by Coffee, he paused just inside the door and took a deep breath. He held it a heartbeat, as if waiting for his allergies to kick in, and when they didn't, he practically skipped to the counter.

Okay, I *had* to know . . .

"Todd," I said, approaching him. He was a regular, though we didn't talk all that much. He was usually masked and ready to bolt for the door the moment his coffee was in hand since he was horribly allergic to cats, and even when Trouble wasn't around, he often suffered from the residual fur and dander in the air. "You look good."

He turned to me with a smile. "I feel great." Another deep breath and a grin. He was short, balding, and wore less-than-fashionable clothing, but that didn't make him any less pleasant to be around.

"Trouble is upstairs," I said, looking him up and down. "It doesn't seem to be bothering you today."

"It doesn't, does it?" His grin widened. "I'm on a new allergy medicine. Well, two of them, to be precise. I get a monthly shot, and now I also have a new prescription that I take daily. It's new and wonderful, and I can *breathe*. I never knew what *air* smelled like before." He laughed. "I was always so stuffed up, it's a wonder I've survived this long."

Pooky handed over his coffee with a smile. Todd took a sip and then just about melted through the floor.

"I apologize if I ever caused you trouble," he said. "I felt so miserable all the time, I'm sure I wasn't the most pleasant person to be around."

"You were fine," I said. "But I'm glad you're feeling better."

"Thank you." He raised his coffee in salute. "I'm going to go to the park today. That's something else I've avoided because of the flowers and pollen and *everything*." He laughed. "I'll see you soon."

"Have fun," I said, unable to keep my own smile at bay. He looked so happy, it was infectious.

Todd strode out the door, standing taller than I'd ever seen him. It was amazing how something as simple as allergy medication could change a person's life.

I checked the time, but I still had close to an hour before my meetup with Ivan. Besides, the Banyon Tree wasn't that all that far away, so I went ahead and cleaned up the recently vacated tables. That done, I made a pass through the restrooms, checked the trash bins to make sure they didn't need to be emptied, and was about to grab my things and head out when the door opened and Justin entered with Beth Milner at his side. They were chatting amicably, and when Justin saw me, he broke off to come my way, while Beth headed around the counter to clock in.

"Justin?" I said, curious. "Did Vicki have you scheduled to work today?"

"Nah," he said, waving me off. "I was in the neighborhood and saw you through the window, so I thought I'd stop in so I could thank you."

"Thank me? For what?"

"For getting me this job. And a job for Jo."

"I told you that you two would have a place here."

"Yeah, well . . ." He shrugged, looked chagrined. "People say things all the time. Not all of them follow through."

Boy, did I know it. "We're glad to have you," I said, and then, "Is Kari going to put in her application?" As far as I was aware, she still had yet to apply.

Some of the cheer left Justin's expression. "I doubt it. I don't think it has anything to do with you or anyone who works here. Kari's just . . ."

"Kari," I finished for him.

"Yeah. This isn't the sort of place where she'd feel comfortable. And I'm not sure the people she served would be too thrilled by her either."

A part of me was disappointed, while another was relieved. Kari Collins might not have been Death by Coffee material, but that didn't mean I wouldn't have welcomed her with open arms. Beth hadn't started out as one of my favorite people, and look at her now. Everyone deserved a chance, even people as grumpy as Kari.

"Anyway," Justin said, "I just wanted to pop in real quick. I've talked to a few people here, and everyone seems great." He turned to look back at Beth, who was pretending that she wasn't listening. He cleared his throat and tried to hide his smile. "So, yeah, anyway."

Justin, despite saying he wasn't staying, headed for the counter. When I left a moment later, he and Beth were chatting in a way that made me wonder if he'd truly happened by, or if he'd had another reason for coming to Death by Coffee.

But my curiosity would have to wait.

J&E's Banyon Tree looked like a diner, which, of course, it was. Rockabilly music played over the speakers as I entered, shoulders hunched against my fear of being rebuffed. I saw one of the owners, Judith Banyon, the moment I was through the doors. She shot me a look, but then surprised me by not chasing me out like she was wont to do. Instead, she turned away and headed for the back.

"Hi, Krissy," Shannon Pardue said, flashing me a smile as she approached, carafe of coffee in hand. Recently a single mom, Shannon and I had begun to grow closer. She was looking less worn down, less overwhelmed, which I was glad to see.

"Hi, Shannon. I'm here to meet someone. You don't happen to know Ivan McGraw, do you?"

Her face clouded over. "Oh, yeah, I do. He's over there." She hooked a thumb toward a scrawny man with gray-spotted stubble and hair that looked as if he hadn't bothered to comb it in a decade. "What do you want with *him*?"

"He knew a friend of mine who died," I said.

Shannon opened her mouth in an *ah* expression and then nodded his way. "Have fun. I'm going to stick to my side of the diner, if it's all the same to you."

With that ringing endorsement for Ivan fresh in my head, I walked over to where he was seated. He glanced up, made a quick assessment of me, and then motioned to the chair across from him.

"Krissy, yeah?" Spoken through a mouthful of runny eggs and too-done toast.

"Yep." I sat.

"Gonna have to make this quick. Got a call about some prospects I need to make a decision on." He didn't extrapolate on that, for which I was glad. "Whatcha wanna know?"

I was more than happy to jump right in. "You called Bucky the day he died."

Ivan stabbed a sausage, shoved the entire thing into his mouth. He spoke as he chewed. "I did."

"And you were seen outside Bucky's a few days beforehand. I was told Bucky shoved you, that you two might have been arguing."

"We were. He did." Ivan used a slice of toast to mop up the remainder of his egg. "I also called him a few unkind names, and no, I don't regret doing so."

"You were also seen meeting with Jaqueline Lyon."

Ivan chuckled, continued to wolf down his food and talk through it. "You've been talking a lot about me and my business, haven't you? I wish I knew more about you so I could return the favor."

"Bucky died," I pointed out. "Your name keeps cropping up."

A swig of orange juice, followed by a coffee chaser. "All right, I'm going to lay it out for you best as I can. As soon as I'm done talking, I'm paying my bill and leaving, so you'd best listen, all right? I'm not going to repeat myself, here or elsewhere, you get me?"

I nodded, biting back a snarky response. He was willing to talk, so no sense in poking the proverbial bear, though I was annoyed he'd agreed to meet and was already bailing.

Ivan wiped his mouth and hands with a napkin before leaning his elbows on the table and raising his fingers, checking off points as he came to them.

"Yes, Bucky and I had our issues. We fought, but not about his bar or how he runs his business. That's none of mine, as they say. You wanna know who stirred the pot, tried to get us all to fight amongst ourselves, go talk to Ruth Camden. She loves that sort of thing. It makes her happy to see everyone else squirm."

I almost spoke up, saying I *had* talked to Ruth, but I realized that Ivan wouldn't appreciate the interruption or care.

"I called him that day to warn him. He didn't like it. It's the same reason why I was talking to him outside his place. I warned him, he shoved me because he didn't like what I had to say. It's also why I talked to Jaqueline, because if Bucky wouldn't believe me, then perhaps she could talk some sense into him."

"What were you warning him about?" I asked, unable to keep quiet any longer.

Ivan waved over his waitress, pointed at the table. Without a word, she rushed to get his bill.

"I think it's pretty clear that someone wanted Bucky dead, yeah? I mean, the guy ended up that way, so it makes sense. I tried to tell him. Turns out, I was right."

"About what?"

He scratched his cheek, waited for his check to arrive, then handed the waitress a twenty before she could scurry away. "Keep the change, hot cheeks."

There was a moment when I was positive his waitress was going to slap him, but instead, she took his money and left. Ivan chuckled, as if being insulting and getting away with it was some sort of accomplishment.

He turned to me, smug as could be, and then hit me with it. "Someone at Bucky's Tavern wanted him dead so they could take over the business. And before you ask, no, I don't know for certain who that might be, but I have my suspicions. We all know who slithered into his good graces right before he passed, so . . ." He spread his hands.

Kandice Vaughn.

"What makes you think it was someone from his bar?" I asked. I wanted Ivan to be wrong, and not just because I didn't like him. I knew those people. I didn't want to think of any of them as a killer.

And could I truly trust the word of a man like Ivan McGraw? Or Dwayne Morris, for that matter?

Ivan stood, brushed crumbs from his lap. "Someone told me, that's how I knew."

My heart did one of those slow, dramatic *thump*s as I asked, "Who?"

Ivan paused, seemed to consider it before speaking.

"Who told me that someone wanted Bucky dead? You wouldn't believe me if I told you."

"Try me," I said.

Ivan smiled. It wasn't a pleasant expression, but one that spoke of a man who enjoyed having the upper hand, even in something like this. "Geno Lyon, that's who."

My eyes widened in surprise, which caused him to laugh.

"See, I knew you wouldn't believe me."

"Geno Lyon told *you* that someone at Bucky's Tavern wanted to kill *Bucky*?" I asked, the disbelief clear in my voice. "How would *he* know?"

"You'd have to ask him that," Ivan said, making as if to leave, though he still lingered. "I'm pretty sure someone else told him, someone close to the situation. Geno said that Bucky refused to listen to him, so he came to me. Don't know why, don't really care. I did my part." He leaned toward me, made sure I looked him in the eye when he spoke next. "It's too bad that Bucky didn't listen to me. If he had, he might still be alive today."

23

After a quick lunch—at the Banyon Tree, no less—and some heavy debating on what to do next, I climbed into my car, pulled out my phone, and tried to reach Paul. When that went to voicemail, I opted for Buchannan. And when *that* failed, I tried one last number, fully expecting to be shunted to voicemail again for the trifecta.

"Krissy?" Lena's voice came out sounding like her mouth was full. "What's up?"

"I'm sorry. Did I catch you at lunch?" I started my car.

"If you can call it that. I'm sitting in my cruiser, eating some sort of sandwich that I'm pretty sure shouldn't exist. At least not on purpose."

As I started driving, I asked, "Did your mom make it?"

"Becca did. I think she's on a health kick because there's mashed olives in this thing. I mean, who does that?" She made a gagging sound. "She made extra to share, probably because she didn't want to suffer alone. I'd like to say I was thankful to be included, but . . . ugh."

On a normal day, I would have laughed, but today was anything but. "I'm sorry to bother you while you're eating, but I tried both Paul and Buchannan, and they didn't answer."

"I'm not surprised," she said. "They've been busy. Did something happen?"

"It's about Bucky's murder." I paused, considered. "I think."

"Tell me."

"I really don't want to interrupt your lunch. It might not be important."

"Let me be the judge of that," Lena said, sounding as if she'd hunt me down and force me to spill if I continued to resist.

Still, I hesitated. Yes, Lena was a police officer like Paul and Buchannan. Telling her would be just like telling them.

But it was *Lena*. The skateboarding, purple-haired girl who'd worked at Death by Coffee since we'd opened. Even though I *knew* she'd gone through her training and was a full-fledged officer of the law, my brain kept wanting to put her back in the coffee-girl box that she'd outgrown long ago.

"Krissy," Lena said, tone serious. "If this is about the murder, you should tell me. If I can't handle it myself, I'll make sure Detective Buchannan hears about it." A pause. "And I'll leave your name out of it if that's what you want."

"No." I took a deep breath. "Ivan McGraw told me that someone told Geno that someone at Bucky's Tavern was trying to get rid of Bucky." Whew, say that three times fast. "I'm kind of hazy on why he'd go to a competitor like Ivan with this information, but maybe he couldn't think of anyone else who would listen to him. I don't even know why this mystery person went to Geno in the first place, or if this is all some elaborate lie meant to confuse me."

"And you have no idea who the original source of this information might be?"

"Well, actually, there might be someone." I frowned. "There was this woman . . ." I went on to explain about the woman who'd approached me at Geraldo's. "I don't know who she is or how she connects to Bucky or even if she has anything to do with what Ivan told me, but—"

"Where are you?" Lena asked, cutting in before I could tell her about Skinny's video of Bucky and the woman.

"In my car," I said. "Why?"

"Let me guess. You're planning on talking to Geno Lyon?"

I was surprised, but supposed I shouldn't have been. "Maybe?"

Lena made a sound half between a laugh and a snort. "Maybe, my foot. You should let Detective Buchannan handle this."

She was right, but when did I ever let the police handle something I could do myself? I could be wrong about Geno. Ivan could have lied to me. Dwayne could have as well. This whole thing could be a simple case of jealous business competitors poisoning the competition and talking to Geno Lyon would get me nowhere.

But what if Ivan was telling the truth?

"I know," I said. "But I'm almost there, and there's always a chance he might talk to me. I imagine Buchannan's already talked to him anyway."

"He has, but—"

"You could meet me there," I said, cutting her off. "Back me up or whatever. Or I'll back you up. Either way, we could make it like we're just following up on stuff, a sort of casual conversation."

Silence on the other end of the line.

"Bucky left everything to Kandice Vaughn. There's concern that she might have had reason to kill him, and if Geno knows something . . ."

"He should be asked about it."

I turned down a residential street not far from the Lyons' home. "I know it's a long shot, but if she *did* kill him for his bar, it would be better to find out *before* she signs all the papers."

"Because it might be hard to untangle that mess afterward," Lena said, thoughtful.

"So . . . you'll meet me?" I asked.

"I'm already on the way." A pause. "Just . . . wait for me, okay? John will skin us both alive if he finds out I let you talk to a suspect without supervision. He's already not going to like it that you were involved at all. Though he knows that no one can stop you when you set your mind to something."

"I'll wait," I promised her. A huge weight felt lifted from my shoulders knowing that she'd be there. "I'll see you in a few."

"This is going to be fun." Deadpan, and then she clicked off.

I tossed my phone into the passenger seat. I was almost to Geno's, and the nerves were starting to kick in. What would I do if he said that Kandice really was trying to get rid of Bucky? I liked Kandice. I didn't want to think her capable of murder.

I thought about Grant with his family troubles and how he'd given Bucky that coffee, which could very well have been poisoned. I considered how it could have been someone from the kitchen, or maybe Jazz. Or, yes, Kandice. And then there was the woman who'd tried to approach me at dinner, who'd appeared in Skinny's video. Ivan, as I feared, could also be misleading me. He could have poisoned Bucky or paid someone to do it. Or perhaps Dwayne did it. Or Jaqueline. Or Ruth Camden. Even Geno Lyon himself.

There were so many suspects, I had no idea what to think, and I wasn't sure talking to Geno would help.

The first thing I noticed when I pulled up in front of the Lyons' house was that Jaqueline's truck was gone. My disappointment was brief, because the garage door was open and inside was another car, one I took for Geno's. I figured that if both the Lyons had left, then they wouldn't have left the garage door hanging wide open, even if it was considered a safe neighborhood. And since it was Jaqueline's vehicle that was missing, I suspected Geno was the one who'd stayed behind.

Or maybe that was just wishful thinking.

I glanced in the rearview mirror, but Lena had yet to arrive. I drummed my fingers on the steering wheel and found myself reaching for the car door. I pulled my hand back and forced myself to wait, even though I was anxious to get this over with.

"Come on, Lena," I muttered, eyes going back to the rearview mirror and the empty road behind me. I picked up my phone and debated on calling her to get an ETA, but I opted to try Paul again instead. Straight to voicemail.

Of course. I heaved a sigh, then opened a text to him, figuring I could at least message him to tell him what was going on. He might be too busy to answer his phone, but perhaps he *could* check a text.

A knock on the passenger window startled a yelp from me. I nearly dropped my phone in surprise as I looked up to find an angry male face staring in at me. Mustached, with dark, beady eyes, the man made a motion for me to roll down my window, old-school style.

I pressed the automatic window button and opened my mouth to speak, but he beat me to it.

"Go away," the man shouted into my car. "My wife and I have had enough of your sort pestering us."

"Geno Lyon?" I asked.

"You know well enough who I am," he said, hands gripping the car door hard enough that his knuckles were white. "I'm tired of the harassing calls and visits at all hours of the daggone day. Things are already bad enough without you pestering us for sound bites."

The light bulb clicked on in my head. "I'm not a reporter."

His eyes narrowed at me.

"Really," I said. "My name is Krissy Hancock. I was working with Bucky on the Irish coffee he sold at his bar."

The man—Geno, I assumed—stepped back with a frown. "Then, what are you doing here?" His attention jerked away from me before I could answer as a police cruiser pulled up behind my car.

Lena.

We both climbed out of our respective vehicles and joined Geno in his driveway.

"What's going on?" he asked, taking a step toward his house like he desperately wanted to make a run for it.

"We're sorry to bother you, Mr. Lyon," Lena said. "I'm Officer Allison, and this is my associate, Ms. Hancock. We're looking into the death of Bucky Sweeny, and we've received information that you may know something about it."

I glanced at her, surprised. She'd sounded so . . . official. It was the first time I'd ever heard her sound like that, and I was rather impressed by it.

"I've spoken with a police officer already," Geno said, narrowing his eyes. He was clearly suspicious, despite the fact that Lena had arrived in a police cruiser and was wearing a uniform. I imagine it had something to do with her purple hair. "A detective."

"Detective Buchannan," she supplied.

"I think that's it. I already told him everything I know and have nothing to add."

I couldn't help it. I broke my silence and asked, "Which is what?"

Before he could answer, Lena stepped forward. "Maybe

we could discuss this inside?" She gave him a reassuring smile. "Wouldn't want the neighbors to gossip."

I immediately thought of Georgina McCully up the street and thought, *Too late*, but I kept my mouth shut.

Geno looked between us, then sighed. "I suppose that'd be all right."

He led us up the driveway, into the house. The front door opened into a small living room. The floor was carpeted and looked as if it hadn't been swept in a few weeks. He dumped an armload of laundry from the couch onto the floor and motioned for us to sit.

"I don't know what else I can tell you," he said, crossing his arms, and then, seeming to realize that he was towering over us, he dropped into a listing recliner. "Like I said before, I already talked to the police."

"You were concerned about Bucky's safety?" Lena asked.

"'Concerned' might be the wrong word," Geno said. "I mean, I didn't want anything to happen to him or anything. We've had our differences, of course. Jaqueline . . . well, you know how it is? Exes and such."

"What made you think someone was after Bucky?" Lena asked.

Geno shrugged, looked away. "A woman called me and told me that someone from that bar of his wanted to take over the business."

"By killing him?" I asked.

Another shrug. "I suppose that's what happened, didn't it? I mean, he's dead and all. When I first got the call, I wasn't sure what she was getting at. She was kind of cryptic, to be honest with you. Wouldn't name names or anything. Just kind of told me to talk to Bucky and warn him."

"Did you?" Lena asked.

"I tried. He didn't want to listen."

Which was what Ivan had said. "What can you tell me about the woman who called you?" I asked. "Could it have been Kandice Vaughn?"

He shook his head. "I don't know Kandice all that well, but that wasn't her voice," he said. "This person was younger, maybe even a girl. Teenager, perhaps. Maybe older, but couldn't be by much."

Like the woman at Geraldo's. I was more convinced than ever that she was at the center of Bucky's murder.

"Why did she call you?" Lena asked.

"Heck if I know," Geno said. "It came out of the blue. I've never spoken with this person before, nor have I since. All I know is that she told me that she'd tried to talk to Bucky and he wouldn't listen to her. I tried to tell *her* that Bucky and me weren't on talking terms, but she begged, so I did what I could."

"Including talking to Ivan McGraw?" I asked.

Geno laughed. "That man is something else." He shook his head. "But yeah. I told him about what this woman had said. Don't know why I did it, to be honest with you. I suppose it was the way she'd sounded, all scared and certain-like. I didn't want to let her down, and I thought that if anyone would know about something going on at Bucky's, it might be someone in the business, you know? It's not like I could go to one of the employees, since one of them was supposedly after him."

"Did you talk to your wife about it?" Lena asked. "She and Mr. Sweeny were once close, were they not?"

"Yeah, no." Geno scowled. "I wasn't about to saddle her with anything involving Bucky Sweeny. Those two were done and had nothing to do with one another these days, and I didn't want to bring them back together by laying this on her."

I wondered if he was jealous of the relationship or if it had something to do with the poisoning he'd suffered all those years ago.

"When was the last time you talked to Mr. Sweeny?" Lena asked.

"I suppose it was during the parade on St. Patrick's Day," Geno said. "He staggered up to me while I was waiting for Jaqueline to get back from pulling one of the acts. He accused me of meddling. He didn't like the fact that I'd gone to Ivan with what he considered his business, and he made sure I knew it."

I realized that meant that when I'd seen Bucky during the parade, he'd been going to talk to Geno, not Jaqueline or Ivan or anyone else. By then, he was already sick from the poison, so I wasn't sure it mattered where he was going, but it was nice to know. It filled in another piece of the puzzle, albeit a small one.

"Are you certain you didn't see or talk to him after that?" Lena asked. "Perhaps you saw him talking with someone else later that night?"

Geno rubbed at his jaw, looked almost worried.

"Mr. Lyon," Lena pressed, catching it, just as I had. "You saw him, didn't you?"

"Well, I suppose I did," Geno said. "I guess you

could say I followed him later that night. Not for any ill intent, mind you. We crossed paths, and while we didn't speak, I saw how *bad* he looked. It got me feeling worried, like that woman who'd called might have been right and something was up with him. I didn't think poison right away, but somewhere in my subconscious, I'm sure it crossed my mind."

"Because you were poisoned before and recognized the symptoms?" I asked.

Geno shot me a look, nodded. "I suppose that might have been it. I just know that he didn't look right, and I took it upon myself to keep an eye on him. I was on my way out of the Weasel when he came staggering in. He and Dwayne Morris had words, then Bucky went down. I left a few minutes later since Jaqueline was waiting for me in her truck."

So, Geno was the man Caitlin saw that night. Another box checked.

"You left, even though you were worried about him?" Lena asked.

"What was I supposed to do?" Geno snapped. "I wasn't his caretaker. Dwayne helped him up and, I assume, sent him on his way. I don't know how or why Bucky ended up here, but I can say that he wasn't in the truck when we left the Weasel. Maybe Dwayne drove him here, maybe he wandered here on his own. Jaqueline and I had nothing to do with his death, you understand?"

I did. And, strangely, like with Ivan and Dwayne before him, I believed what he was telling me.

"Do you think Kandice Vaughn was the person after Bucky's Tavern?" I asked.

Geno met my eye and surprised me by saying, "No, ma'am, I do not."

"Why's that?" Lena asked.

"Because," Geno replied, crossing his arms and sitting back, "when that woman called me, she never gave me a name, but she did let slip that the person wasn't female. I specifically remember her saying that *he* wanted to get rid of Bucky, not *she*."

24

"I don't know what to believe anymore," I groused as I slumped in my chair at Scream for Ice Cream. I pushed my nearly full bowl across the table in a huff. My stomach was in knots, and not even vanilla ice cream could ease it.

Lena took a bite of her own mint cookie dough and then pointed and twirled her spoon at me. "Evidence has been hard to come by. Detective Buchannan has been complaining about it since this whole thing started."

"He's been investigating, hasn't he?" I asked, knowing he had, but I was feeling petty.

"He has," Lena said. "We all have, to some capacity. So far, every path has led to a dead end. I don't know all the details since I'm just a peon, but I've gleaned a few things here and there."

"You're more than that."

"Yeah, well, I don't get told much of anything, so it sometimes feels like it." She took another bite and savored it before continuing. "I know that Detective Buchannan has gone to all the bars, has talked to everyone at Bucky's. He's spoken with Geno and Jaqueline Lyon. Who does that leave?"

I considered it. "Skinny?"

Lena made a face, telling me she knew of Skinny Jefferson's history. "I don't know for certain, but if he's involved somehow, I'm sure Detective Buchannan has spoken to him too."

I slumped further in my chair. Any farther and I'd slip to the floor, but I was feeling dejected. Lost.

"Bucky opened his tavern, and the other bar owners didn't like it," I said, speaking my thoughts aloud in the hopes that it might help me better sort through them. "He starts seeing his bartender, Kandice Vaughn, sometime after he opens."

"Who initiated the romance?" Lena asked.

"No clue." It was something I should have asked Kandice the last time we'd spoken, but to tell you the truth, it had never crossed my mind. "So, they're dating, and Bucky has his stomach issues, something everyone knows about. There's a rumor that he's seeing Jaqueline Lyon on the side, that they'd rekindled their relationship, but that doesn't seem to be the case."

"According to Jaqueline and Geno Lyon," Lena pointed out.

I conceded the point. "Jaqueline is involved somehow. She was seen talking with Ivan McGraw and Dwayne Morris on separate occasions. That can't be a coincidence."

"Right." Lena held her spoon in front of her. The ice cream there was slowly melting and dripping back into the bowl. "Wouldn't that point to Jaqueline Lyon as being Bucky's likely poisoner? He *was* found in her truck."

"You'd think," I said. "But I don't think so. It doesn't feel right." As if how I felt about something was evidence enough. "Ivan had called Bucky the day he died. Afterward, Bucky went to talk to Geno. I saw him heading that way during the parade. Later, Bucky makes the rounds, goes to Dwayne's, where he collapsed. Dwayne said he sent Bucky on his way, and to some extent, Geno corroborated that."

"Which leads Bucky to being found in Jaqueline's truck," Lena said. "What if Bucky *was* seeing Jaqueline on the side and Geno found out about it? He could have poisoned him, and then Bucky, realizing what had happened, went to confront him."

It made some sense, but . . . poison? That didn't seem like something a jealous husband would do.

"Jazz Day said he thought Bucky might have been trying to poison Geno and accidentally poisoned himself," I said. "Geno was poisoned before, so there's precedent there."

"I wish I knew what Bucky was poisoned with," Lena said. "It would help determine where he might have come into contact with it and when. But if Detective Buchannan has gotten the results of the tests he requested, he hasn't told me about them."

"What about Geno? Do you know how he was poisoned all those years ago?"

Lena shook her head, frowned. "I wish I knew who

this woman was who'd called Geno Lyon. If she was worried about someone coming after Bucky, then there's a good chance that she knows who killed him."

I hated to think it, but Grant was looking more and more like Bucky's killer. He was struggling with money, was estranged from his family. He'd all but admitted that he would have liked to run the bar, as it was likely the only way his family would accept him again after whatever mistakes he'd made in his youth.

I *really* wanted to talk to the woman who'd approached me again, but how could I find her?

"I think I've seen her," I said.

Lena set her spoon back down and shoved her own bowl away. "You've seen the woman who called Geno? When? *Who*?"

"I don't know her name," I admitted. "She approached me at Geraldo's while I was out to dinner with Paul, Vicki, and Mason. She waited until I was alone and tried to talk to me, but she was so nervous, she didn't say much."

"Okay." Lena considered that, then asked, "What *did* she say?"

"Only that she didn't want the police to get involved. She practically panicked when I suggested it."

"And you have no idea who she was?"

I shook my head as the image of the woman's face floated through my mind. I could see her standing there at the table, nervous as could be, seemingly afraid to look at me directly.

And then I saw her as she stared into the camera.

"Wait," I said, a bubbling of excitement growing. "Skinny!"

Lena groaned. "Him again?"

"He filmed her. On St. Patrick's Day, after the parade. She showed up at Bucky's to talk to Bucky. Skinny caught their interaction on video. Or some of it, anyway." I stood. "You could run facial recognition software on it and find out who she is!"

"Right," Lena said with a snort. "Because we're that high tech at the department."

I slumped back down into my chair, frustrated. The woman *had* to be the key. She'd come to me, acting as if she had information on Bucky to share. Geno said the person who'd called him was a younger woman. It didn't take a genius to realize that they were likely the same person.

I could always go to Kandice, Jazz, and Grant and ask them if they knew who she might be. Perhaps get a still photo from the video and pass it around. If she worked for Ruth or Ivan or Dwayne, I could go to them as well. But if she was involved in Bucky's death somehow, would they even tell me?

"Hey?" Lena said. She was standing with her hand on the door, as if she was about to leave. I hadn't even seen her move. "Are you coming?"

I frowned and stood. "Where?"

"To Skinny's," she said, pushing her way out the door. "I want to see this video."

Skinny Jefferson was surprised to see us, but he didn't appear unhappy about it as he led us into his house and to his computer.

"I expected to hear from someone eventually," he

said, clicking through various screens so quickly, I couldn't make heads or tails of them. "And since Krissy was interested in the clip you're asking about, I went ahead and fiddled with it some and tried to get a good still of the woman, just in case it's important enough that someone came for it." He glanced back at us. "It's important, right?"

"It might be," Lena said. She stood at near attention, hands behind her back, which was ramrod straight. I didn't know if she was trying to project authority, or if it had to do with Skinny's less-than-kosher reputation. I'd tried to explain his change in priorities to her on the way over, but I supposed it was hard to accept that he'd changed until you'd seen it more than once.

A few more *click*s, and then he stepped back. "There," he said, a proud smile on his face. "Cleaned it up good, if I do say so myself."

The still was indeed of the woman who'd approached me at Geraldo's. Bucky's face was mostly a blur in the image, but that was okay. We already knew what *he* looked like.

Lena leaned forward to get a close look at the woman's face. She was silent for a good ten, fifteen seconds, before she spoke under her breath, too low for me to make out.

"What was that?" I asked.

"I know her," she said, straightening. When she turned, she looked almost shell-shocked. "I went to school with her. She was a couple grades ahead of me, but I swear that's her."

"Who?" I asked, excitement growing.

But Lena was already moving toward the door, phone

in her hand. I mouthed, *"Thank you,"* to Skinny, and then hurried after her while she typed. Outside, she held up a finger to me, then took two quick steps away as she brought the phone to her ear. She spoke quietly and briskly to someone on the other end of the line, waited for about thirty seconds, and then hung up with a smile.

"Got it."

"Got what?" I asked.

She started for her cruiser. "The woman in that video? Her name is Mara Wilson. I have her address."

I desperately wanted to ask questions as Lena drove us to Mara's place of residence, but I was afraid that if I did, she'd decide to drop me off at my car and go alone. She was a police officer, and I was . . . well, I was a civilian who spent far too much time acting like I belonged in places I most definitely did not.

As she drove, I did a mental rewind, trying to remember where I'd come across the name "Mara Wilson" before. Even though I knew her face from the video and our encounter at Geraldo's, I was struggling to put the face with the name, so I was pretty sure I hadn't met her before, even casually.

We pulled up in front of a small rental a short time later. A car sat out front. Like the house, it was old, but well-tended. There was no porch to speak of, nor was there anything of interest in the front yard, other than a slightly raised, circular flower bed full of dead plants.

Lena got out of the car, and after some debate, I joined her. She glanced at me, but didn't tell me to stay behind like Paul or Buchannan would have. Together, we approached the door.

"I'll do the talking," Lena said as she knocked. "But if something comes up that rings a bell for you, don't hesitate to speak up." She glanced at me. "It's so strange giving *you* orders. I should have you make me a coffee when this is done."

"Sure. And I'll make sure you get a doughnut too, Officer."

"Ha-ha." She rolled her eyes, then grinned. "But I won't say no to a long john if you have one."

The door opened, and there she was. Mara Wilson, looking as nervous as ever. I was once more struck by how she looked familiar, yet I still couldn't place her beyond the video and when I'd seen her at Geraldo's. Looking at her now, I thought it had to do with her dark blue eyes, the way they bore into me whenever her gaze passed my way.

"H-hello?" Mara said, voice breaking on the stuttered word.

"Hi, Mara." Lena flashed her a smile. "I don't know if you remember me, but—"

"I do. Lena. From school, right?" Her gaze drifted to me, stayed there. "I'm sorry I bothered you last night. If that's why you're here, I didn't mean—"

"No, I didn't mind," I said. "You could have stayed."

"May we come in?" Lena asked. "I'd like to discuss Bucky Sweeny with you."

Mara's hand tightened on the door briefly before she stepped back. Lena and I shared a look, and then we entered the apartment.

The place was tidy, and as noted before, small, but since it appeared as if Mara lived alone, it was more than big enough for her. A pair of cat dishes sat on the floor, and I recognized the dry food in one as the same brand I fed Misfit. Of the cat, however, there was no sign.

Mara led us into the living room, where Lena and I sat side by side on a two-person love seat. Mara took the recliner and angled herself so she could look at us. I noted she kept her hands in her lap, and she kept plucking at her thumbnail in nervous agitation.

"You're not in any trouble," Lena said, noticing the same thing I had. "In fact, I'm hoping you might be able to help me understand a few things. Get *me* out of trouble, if you want to think of it that way." Her smile wasn't quite forced, but I could tell she was putting it on to ease Mara's mind.

"It's about Bucky?" Mara asked.

Lena nodded and then removed her cap so she could run her fingers through her purple hair. I assumed it was another method of making our visit feel less official for the frightened woman.

Some of the tension *did* bleed out of Mara's shoulders, but not much. "I . . . I'm not sure what I can say."

Lena glanced at me, giving me permission to speak.

"Just tell us what you wanted to say when you approached me at Geraldo's," I said, following Lena's example and keeping my voice light and kind and a smile on my face.

Mara dropped her head to look at her hands. "I can't."

"You said you tried to warn Bucky," I said, hoping I was remembering right. "About what?" And while I knew, I also didn't want to lead her on.

"He . . ." She swallowed and shook her head. "I'm sorry, I . . . I just can't."

"Why not?" Lena asked, leaning forward. "If you're afraid of someone, we can protect you."

Mara's flinch told me that Lena had hit the nail on the head.

Seconds passed. I could *feel* Mara's desire to speak, yet she remained stubbornly silent. And while I couldn't see any wounds on her, any physical indication of abuse, something told me that there were internal ones, the kind inflicted by threats and harsh words. I'd seen it before, with other women, some of whom had become friends over the years.

"How about you start by telling us what you and Bucky were talking about on St. Patrick's Day?" I suggested. "Someone filmed the two of you together. Bucky wasn't happy about that."

Mara glanced up briefly, went back to staring at her hands. "He wasn't."

I waited for more, but it didn't come, so I pressed. "Did you two kiss? It was suggested—"

"No!" Her eyes widened. "I mean, he kissed my cheek, but not in the way you're implying. I've known him for a long time, since I was little. I . . . We . . ." She closed her eyes, took a deep breath, and when she let it out, she started speaking slowly, methodically. "I was there to warn him. I'd tried for days, but he didn't want to believe me."

Lena opened her mouth, likely to ask Mara what it was she'd warned Bucky about, but I nudged her with my elbow before she could. This was something Mara needed to get out on her own.

"I tried," Mara said after a moment, blinking back tears. "I really did. But I was warned not to get involved, to keep my mouth shut or—" She sucked in a breath as if remembering the harsh tone used, the threat that wasn't just implied, but promised. "Bucky was angry about that man filming us because he was protecting me. He knew I was upset, that I was scared that my warning would get out, that it would get back to my uncle."

Lena and I shared yet another look. A sense of dread started working through me as the pieces started to connect.

"He died because he didn't believe me," Mara said as the tears started flowing. "Even when I told him what I'd seen, he didn't believe me. He said I must be mistaken, that he'd smooth everything over, but he didn't, and look what happened." She looked up, met my eye pleadingly. "I tried to talk to others, to let them know, to get the word out, but it didn't help. Bucky was stubborn. Trusting. And . . ." She shoved her fists into her eye sockets, teeth clenched in frustration.

"What did you see?" I asked as gently as I could. "What made you think something bad was going to happen to Bucky?"

Mara dropped her hands. Her eyes were red and wet. "I didn't know how he was going to do it. I just knew that my uncle wanted to be rid of Bucky, that he believed he could run things better than Bucky ever could."

So, Geno and Ivan were right, and the whole thing had to do with ownership of the tavern.

Lena pressed her hands together, almost as if begging. "Mara? Who's your uncle?"

Mara opened her mouth and closed it a few times. It was obvious she *wanted* to tell us, but something was stopping her. The threats. The fear of hurting a family member, even one who would go so far as to murder someone.

Her red, swollen eyes met mine, and suddenly, I knew.

I'd thought from the start I'd recognized her, but it wasn't *her* I'd recognized, but her eyes. Those dark blue eyes of hers were near-identical to another set of eyes I *did* know. I wasn't sure why it had taken me so long to realize it.

I said his name in a puff of exhaled breath. "Jazz."

Mara blinked rapidly and nodded. "I'm . . . I'm afraid," she whispered.

"Don't worry, Mara. We'll protect you," Lena said, rising.

"I'm not afraid for me." Mara took a trembling breath, seemed to center herself. "Uncle Jazz might not like that I told, but he wouldn't hurt me. Not physically. But he desperately wanted Bucky's Tavern. He wanted it so badly that he killed Bucky for it." Her gaze settled on me, firmed. "I'm afraid he's desperate enough that now that Kandice owns the bar, he's going to go after her next."

25

I watched through the windshield of the police cruiser as Officer Lena Allison paced, phone to her ear, in front of Mara Wilson's home. Mara stood at the door, arms crossed over her chest, fear etched across her features. Agitation had me wanting to leap out of the car to hurry Lena along, but she wasn't the reason we were still sitting there, mere moments after Mara all but said Kandice's life was in danger.

With frustration etched across her face, Lena jammed her phone into her pocket and threw herself into the car next to me with a mild curse under her breath.

"Well?" I asked, even though I already knew the answer from her body language.

"Detective Buchannan is being a stubborn—" She made a face indicating that what went through her head was better left unsaid. "He didn't answer, so I left a message with the department. Hopefully someone there will have better luck reaching him."

I could feel the seconds ticking away in the back of my mind, and I feared those seconds could very well be Kandice Vaughn's last. Maybe I was being overly dramatic, but if Mara was right and her uncle Jazz had poisoned Bucky so he could take over the bar, what was stopping him from doing the same to Kandice? She could already be suffering from the effects as we sat there.

"We have to do something," I said. "We need to warn Kandice. Find Jazz. *Something*."

"Do you have Ms. Vaughn's number?" Lena asked.

I grabbed my phone and dialed. Straight to voicemail. "No answer," I said. "Big surprise there."

"Do you know where she lives?"

"No, but—" Before I could finish speaking, Lena was already making another call. She spoke quickly and concisely. A few minutes later, and we were on the way to Kandice's home.

My leg jiggled up and down as I rode along, mentally rewinding the last week over and over in my head, looking for signs that Jazz had wanted Bucky dead, that he'd had his sights set on the bar. All I kept seeing was Jazz's sad eyes. The calm way he explained how Bucky must have been planning on killing Geno and accidentally poisoned himself instead.

All lies.

But what if Mara was wrong about what her uncle intended? Jazz could have said that he could do a better job than Bucky at running the tavern, but people said stuff like that all the time, especially if they were frustrated. That didn't mean those same people would *kill* anyone. It was idle talk, nothing more.

Yet, even if I believed that Mara was overreacting, that *I* was overreacting, someone *had* poisoned Bucky Sweeny. And she'd said she'd seen something, though she hadn't explained *what*. I refused to believe that Mara was so confused that she'd accuse her own uncle of murder without being sure.

Lena pulled up in front of Kandice's house a short time later. One look and I knew no one was home, yet I climbed out with Lena and waited while she knocked on the door and called Kandice's name. After a few minutes of that, we were right back into her cruiser.

"Bucky's Tavern," I said, buckling in. "She owns the place now, so she could be there."

Lena nodded, and we were again on our way. Kandice could be anywhere—including locked in Jazz's trunk. She could be out shopping, or sitting down with the lawyers, talking about Bucky's will. There didn't have to be a sinister reason as to why she wasn't home and why she hadn't answered her phone.

Speaking of which . . . I tried her on her cell once again, just in case. It went straight to voicemail. Dead battery? Or had her phone been turned off? Broken?

I was relieved to note that Kandice's car was in the lot at Bucky's Tavern, sitting right beside Grant's own vehicle, when we arrived. What was even more of a relief was that Jazz's car wasn't there. It'd be far easier to ask her about him without him lurking in the background.

We entered Bucky's Tavern to a blast of upbeat pop

rock blaring over the speakers. Grant was standing behind the bar, sorting through a box of brand-new beer
glasses—likely replacements for the ones Kandice had
broken.

"Krissy?" he said, jumping in surprise as I approached.
"I didn't see you come in." His gaze flickered to Lena,
dressed in full uniform. "What's going on?"

"Where's Kandice?" I asked, scanning the other-
wise-empty bar. "Is she in the back?"

"No." Spoken slowly. "She's not here."

I frowned as I turned back to him. "Her car is out
front."

"I know." Grant set a glass down. I noted it had
BUCKY'S TAVERN emblazoned on it. I assumed that meant
Kandice was keeping the name. "She *was* here for a little while, but then she had something she needed to do,
so she left."

"Where is Ms. Vaughn now?" Lena asked.

Grant's brow furrowed. "Is something wrong with
Kandice?" he asked. "She didn't . . ." He swallowed,
unable to say what he was thinking.

"She might be in danger," I said. "Please, Grant.
Where is Kandice?"

He took a deep breath and leaned on the bar. "She
went to Bucky's house to get her things. She said she
needed to get it over with so she could finally move
forward with her life or something like that."

Both Lena and I spun toward the door. I made it two
steps before I turned back around and asked, "If she
went to Bucky's, then why's her car still here?"

"She didn't want to go alone," Grant said. "So Jazz
went with her."

My adrenaline spiked, but I kept myself outwardly calm as I walked back to Lena's cruiser. I climbed into the passenger's seat, buckled in, and waited, entire body thrumming, as Lena got in next to me. She sat there a heartbeat, hands on the wheel, then started the car, turned on the sirens, and we were off.

She didn't drive like a maniac, but she didn't go slow either. No, we didn't know for sure that Jazz had any ill intent toward Kandice, but why take chances? Just because he'd allegedly poisoned Bucky didn't mean he would do the same to Kandice.

And while that could mean he didn't intend to kill her, it could also mean he might take a more direct, immediate approach to his problem.

Lena turned off the siren as she turned down the road leading to Bucky's former home. I could see Jazz's car sitting out front, which meant that whatever he was planning, he'd at least been true to his word and brought Kandice to gather her things. Lena parked behind his car, cutting off an easy escape. Together, we approached the door to Bucky's—Kandice's now, I supposed—house.

"Jazz Day?" Lena called, knocking on the door with the back of her hand. "It's Officer Allsion with the Pine Hills Police Department. I'd like to speak with you for a moment."

There was a beat of silence punctuated by a heavy *thump* of my heart. And then Kandice called out, "It's open."

"Same as before," Lena said to me before opening the door and leading the way inside.

I'm not sure what I'd expected to find when I entered, but Jazz and Kandice standing in the middle of the living room, each with a cup of something steaming in hand, wasn't it.

Still, the sight of the mug had my nerves bouncing. "Don't drink that," I said, a little more forcefully than I'd intended.

Kandice's brow furrowed. "What?" She looked down, into her mug. "It's tea."

Jazz appeared just as perplexed. "I made it myself. We didn't use anything of Bucky's, other than the mugs, if that's what you're worried about." His eyes widened. "Unless you think the poison came from the mugs themselves?"

"Everyone, stay calm," Lena said. "Let's just set the tea aside, and then we can talk about it, all right?"

Jazz complied immediately, while Kandice was slow in lowering hers. A box sat on the floor next to her. It was filled with her personal items and a few other objects that I assumed might hold sentimental value to her.

"What's going on?" Kandice asked. "Was there a break in the case?" She hugged herself, as if bracing herself against the answer.

I looked to Lena, desperate to plow forward with my usual gusto, but I allowed her to take the lead as she wanted.

"First, tell me why you two are here," she said.

"I came for my things." Kandice nudged the box next to her with her foot. "I was told by the detective in charge of Bucky's case that it would be okay if I retrieved them."

"And I'm here as moral support," Jazz said. "I'm

glad I came, too. It was . . . overwhelming for her—for the both of us. When Kandice became shaky, I retrieved a box of tea I keep in my car for situations like this. And, as I said before, the mugs did belong to Bucky, so if I wasn't supposed to do that, I apologize."

I *really* wanted to ask him if he'd poisoned her tea, but I knew that would only escalate the situation unnecessarily. It would also put him on the defensive, which was something none of us wanted.

"What's going on?" Kandice asked again, her agitation growing. "Please tell me you caught the person who hurt Bucky. I . . . I'm not sure how much longer I can take this."

"Not yet," Lena said before her gaze swiveled to Jazz. "But we did talk to Mara Wilson. That's your niece, Mr. Day, is it not?"

A brief hesitation, and then, "Yes, that is correct. Do you know if she took her medication before you spoke with her?"

"Her medication?" I asked.

Jazz sighed. "Mara gets paranoid. Delusional, even. It's been a problem with her for years. I told you she had issues, as does my sister. Allie has always been resistant to getting Mara the help she needs, which is why I stepped in. They both took offense to my interference, but Mara had been better as of late."

Beside him, Kandice frowned, seemingly perplexed.

"Did you know about that?" I asked her.

"No, but . . ."

"Mara was at Bucky's on the night of his death," I said. "She was with him when he threw Skinny out of the bar." I watched Kandice as I said it. "But you knew that, didn't you?"

Her nod was slow. "I knew she was upset," she said, glancing at Jazz. "I didn't want to make things worse for her. I didn't know she was on medication, but I *did* know something was bothering her enough that she was constantly hounding Bucky. He never told me what it was she was so upset about, but I could see it."

Jazz's sigh was heavy. "I tried to keep her away from all of this," he said. "She told me that she feared for Bucky's life, that she thought someone was after him." He *cluck*ed his tongue, shook his head. "I thought it was one of her delusions, but perhaps she was right, since someone *did* poison him."

"You said you thought Bucky poisoned himself," I pointed out.

"Yes, I did," he admitted, eyes flicking toward Kandice before leveling on me. "He wanted Geno gone. And I do believe that Jaqueline put him up to it, even if it was done subtly." He nodded slowly, shaking his index finger. "You know, it might be possible that it wasn't Jaqueline's doing, but Mara's. I hate to say it, but if she's been off her medication, her paranoia might have pushed her to make such a drastic move."

"What are you saying exactly?" Lena asked. "Are you saying *Mara* put Bucky up to poisoning Geno? And that he accidentally poisoned himself in the process?"

Jazz made a pained expression. "It sounds insane, I know, but it wouldn't entirely be out of character for her," he said. "I hate to think that Mara could have had anything to do with Bucky's death, but now, seeing how she was following after him, talking to everyone . . ." He spread his hands. "It fits."

Did it?

I mean, yes, Bucky had died from a poison of some kind. But to think that Mara Wilson had done it after spending so much time telling him that Jazz was after him? That didn't make much sense to me. Even the idea that Bucky had tried to poison Geno, and had flubbed it up so badly that he'd made himself sick instead, had never sat right with me.

"I don't believe it," Kandice said with a shake of her head. "Mara wouldn't have hurt Bucky. She wouldn't have asked him to hurt anyone either. I . . . I tried to protect her because she's always been so scared. It's why I never said that I saw her at Bucky's that night. If the police came knocking on her door, I was afraid of what it would do to her."

"She showed up at Geraldo's," I said. "She tried to tell me something, but then got spooked. And she was pretty scared when we went to her house earlier."

"It's more proof that she is off her meds," Jazz said. "She came to you because she was becoming paranoid to the point that she probably thought *I* was responsible for killing Bucky. She's done something similar with my sister before. We kept it quiet, but now, I'm starting to wonder if we should have done more. It's clear the medication isn't helping her. She must have gone to Bucky that night and—"

"Wait," I said, holding up my hands. "Just hold on a second."

"Krissy?" Lena asked, but I barely heard her. My mind was racing through what I knew, piecing together the timeline as best as I could with what information I had.

"Someone poisoned Bucky either early on St. Patrick's Day or the night before," I said. "Not after. Not when Mara was talking with him. Not at the Weasel."

"Yes, but she—" Jazz started, but I held up a finger at him to silence him.

"She'd been talking to people, telling them that someone was after Bucky's Tavern, that they wanted to get rid of Bucky. No one believed her, and that included Bucky himself. He didn't want to think that someone he knew would want to hurt him, whether it be by taking his bar or by attacking him in some way."

Jazz opened his mouth, likely with another, *"Yes, but,"* but I talked over him.

"Something happened—something she heard or something she saw, I don't know—but Mara ended up going to Bucky after the parade, but he was already sick by then. He left Bucky's later, went to Dwayne at the Whistling Wet Weasel, where he collapsed. From there, he left and wasn't seen again until he was found in the back of Jaqueline's truck."

I let that simmer a moment. What had Mara said to Bucky specifically? She'd said she'd warned him, but had she mentioned Jazz by name? I found it likely. She might not have named names when she'd talked to Ivan, but with Bucky, chances were good she would have, or at least hinted at it enough that he'd know whom to be wary of.

From there, he went to the Weasel, spoke with Dwayne. I still wasn't clear on what he'd hoped to accomplish there. By then, he was extremely sick, so he might not even have known why he'd gone. Either way, he left, and then he had to have gone *somewhere*.

Then, quite suddenly, I realized where.

"Bucky was so sick that night, he struggled to stay upright," I said. "He collapsed at the Weasel, which probably clued him in that he was sicker than he realized. Up until then, he'd acted like it was his intestinal issues that was the culprit, and I suppose, in a way, it was."

"He'd always had a bad stomach." Kandice said it like a lament.

"I think he realized then that Mara was right, that someone close to him was indeed trying to kill him," I said. "He might even have realized *where* he'd been when he'd first started feeling ill. He could have decided to go back there, to confront the person Mara had warned him about."

I let that hang for a long moment, my eyes never leaving Jazz's own. He stared back, completely at ease, and that's when I knew I had him.

"He went to your house," I said. "You didn't kick a hole in your wall like you told me you had. Bucky fell and hit his head there, didn't he?"

"That's preposterous," Jazz said. "You have no proof that he was anywhere near my place before or after he got sick."

"He was, though," Kandice said. "The night before St. Patrick's Day. He went to see you to talk about the business. He told me that he had some concerns, but he didn't want to bother me with them."

Jazz started to speak, stopped. Tried again, and came up empty once more.

"I bet there's DNA evidence in the wall," I said, looking to Lena. "He fell hard enough to put a hole in it. There were marks on his head and shoulders when he was found in Jaqueline's truck, which means there might be hair or other evidence left in the hole. Buchannan thought his wounds came from when he collapsed, but they didn't. They came from when he fell at Jazz's."

"We could get samples," Lena said. "Even if the site was cleaned up, we'll be able to find something if it's there."

Whether that was true or not, I didn't know.

In the end, it didn't matter, because the strength went out of Jazz's legs then, and he collapsed into Bucky's chair, hands falling limp between his knees.

"Mara saw me," he said. He didn't sound anxious. In fact, he sounded quietly *angry.* "Always snooping. Always trying to be a part of everything." His fists clenched, but he didn't lunge at anyone or attempt to make a run for it. "I told her to stay quiet, that if she didn't . . ."

"That you'd kill her too," I said, unable to keep the bitterness from my tone.

Jazz glanced up and smiled in that way of his. So relaxed, so unaffected. So . . . dead inside.

"I am the only one who would have been able to keep that place alive," he said. "Kandice will run it into the ground, just like Bucky was going to. There was really only one way to stop him. I did what I had to do." He lowered his head, and as Lena stepped forward to cuff him, he repeated it: "I did what I had to do."

26

I got out of the car with only a slight wince. Both of my legs were burning and felt like they were made of loose rubber that didn't want to support my weight, let alone move me forward. After my run with Cassie, I'd felt great. After showering and then sitting in my car for the ten minutes it took to reach my destination . . . not so much.

"There you are, dear," Rita Jablonski said, coming out of the Pine Hills Police Station as I was about to enter. "I expected you to be here already."

"Sorry," I said. "I had to get cleaned up before—"

"Yes, well, I can't stay and talk," Rita said, cutting me off with a wave of her hand. "I've got to get back home so I can make plans for my upcoming trip."

"You're going on a trip?" I asked, surprised. "Where are you going?"

"Where *won't* I go?" She paused, going wistful a moment, before snapping back to herself. "Plans haven't fully been set as of yet. It's why I need to sit down and think things through." A smile spread across her face. "Though I do expect I'll be paying a visit to that father of yours. Who knows? Maybe I spend a day or two there, really get to know him."

I pretended I didn't hear that. "I'm glad for you," I said, and I meant it. Because, yeah, Rita deserved to live her life any way she saw fit.

Well, most ways. She could leave Dad out of it, and I'd be okay with that.

"Now, while I suspect I'll be traveling for quite a while, don't be thinking I will be missing your wedding. I've got that marked on my calendar and everything." She gave herself a sharp nod. "You won't be getting rid of me that easily, Krissy Hancock!"

I laughed. "No, I didn't expect I would be."

"Good." She blinked in a way that told me she was fighting back tears. "I'll see you around then. So much to do!"

And with that, she quick-stepped her way to her car.

I watched her go, feeling . . . I wasn't quite sure *what* I was feeling. Rita was a fixture in Pine Hills. Having her gone, even for a week or two here and there, would be strange.

Almost as strange as Patricia Dalton *not* being the police chief, yet here we were.

I turned and entered the police station, putting Rita out of my mind for now.

The lobby was full to bursting with cops, most of whom were in their civilian clothes, with only a handful of them dressed in their uniforms. There were a few other faces around the room, some of whom I recognized. Old retired cops. People close to the department, but who weren't a part of it. Kinda like me.

I saw Paul standing off to the side with Lena, Becca, and Detective Buchannan, but I didn't head their way. Instead, I crossed the room to where Chief Patricia Dalton stood in front of the remains of a cake I'd seen ahead of time or else I wouldn't have known it had an image of an old lady sitting in a rocking chair, wineglass in hand, with the words "retirement plans" in bold letters above her head. Patricia saw me coming and handed over a plate with a piece of cake already on it.

"Thank you," I said, taking it. I might be exercising until my legs fell off to get in better shape for my wedding, but that didn't mean I would turn away free cake. "Good turnout."

She glanced around the room, snorted. "They're just glad to see me gone is all."

"Right," I said with a roll of my eyes. "You know they're going to miss you. *I'm* going to miss you."

"I'm not dead yet," she said, though she did so good-naturedly. "But thank you. I expect to still be associated with this place over the coming months, but not too much. I need the break. Besides . . ." She leaned closer to me. "I've got to make sure you and my son go through with this wedding thing. No backing out now."

"I'd never even *think* about it," I said, turning to face Paul, who was watching us, curiosity etched across his features. "Do you remember that you're the one who gave me Paul's number?" I asked her. "If it wasn't for you, we'd never have gotten together." Or, at least, it would have happened far differently.

She laughed. "I do." She nudged me with her elbow. "Goes to show that I always make the right decision. Remember that."

Before I could respond, she turned and walked over to join a group of former police officers.

"I will," I promised, before carrying my cake over to the four cops I knew best. "Nice party," I said.

"Chief hates it," Paul said with a chuckle. "She wanted her announcement to be the end of it. No party. No big farewell. I wasn't about to let that happen."

"She's going to make you pay for it later," Lena told him.

"She deserves a party," Becca Garrison added.

Buchannan merely nodded, and was that . . . a *tear*?

"She's a big part of what makes this place special," Paul went on. "It's not going to be the same without her."

No, it wasn't. I took a bite of cake, only mildly regretting cheating on my kind-of, sort-of diet. "I thought she might drag it out a bit," I said once I swallowed. "You know, tell everyone that she's retiring and then stick around for another year or two."

"That sounds like her," Paul said.

"I bet she would have too," Garrison said. "But this last murder . . ."

"It was like it finally became enough for her," Paul said. "She decided she was done, and that was that."

A flash of melancholy shot through me. "I wish it hadn't taken Bucky's death to push her out."

"She wasn't *pushed*," Paul said. "But I understand what you mean."

"Lena should get some credit," I said. "Maybe even a promotion since she caught Bucky's killer."

"Did I?" she asked with a smile. "I distinctly remember you being there."

I ignored Buchannan's scowl as I said, "Yeah, but you're the one who recognized Mara. Without her, we might not have realized that Jazz was her uncle, that he was the one who'd set his sights on Bucky's Tavern."

"He lied, you know?" Lena said. "About Mara being on medication."

"I'm not surprised."

"Actually," Buchannan said, cutting into the conversation, "Ms. Wilson *was* once on medication, but she stopped it over a year ago. It seems like Mr. Day convinced some out-of-town quack of a doctor to prescribe it for her. He didn't realize she wasn't on it any longer."

"Wait. She didn't need it?" I asked.

"Nope," Garrison said. "It kept her docile. Her mom—Jazz's sister, Allie—is . . . not great. Jazz stepped in and took control of the family situation. He was a dominant force in both their lives, and there was little either woman could do about it."

I could only imagine what that was like. I realized

now, after thinking about it, that all the times I'd seen him smile or laugh or show emotion of any sort, it had been fake. I wasn't sure Jazz Day even *had* real emotions of any kind.

"When we sat him down, Jazz admitted to everything," Lena went on. "He poisoned Bucky the night before St. Patrick's Day, using sugar cubes he'd prepared ahead of time. He dropped them into Bucky's tea, convinced him to drink it to calm down. I'm sure he told him that same story about Mara being off her medication and that she was paranoid and not to believe her."

I shuddered, thinking back to when I'd sat at his table, drinking his tea, using his sugar cubes. Jazz had been right about how easily he could have poisoned me, had all but told me he'd done so to Bucky that very day.

"Bucky realized what had happened and went to confront him about it," Lena said. "By the time he got there, however, it was too late to do anything for him. He died there, in Jazz's house."

"And Jazz didn't even panic," Garrison added. "He simply waited until no one was around, popped him into the back of his car, and took him to the Lyons' so he could put him in Jaqueline's truck. No one saw him do it, not the neighbors, not Jaqueline or Geno."

"But why tell me that Bucky had poisoned himself?" I asked. "Why not just blame Jaqueline?"

"He couldn't defend himself," Buchannan said. "He didn't know who had an alibi, so why risk it? He knew the story of the Lyons' history with poison and decided to use it."

"Because of Geno," I said.

"Because of Geno," Lena confirmed. "If he'd said that Bucky poisoned himself, who would contradict him? He thought Mara was cowed. Figured that no one would even *think* that he could be responsible, even if she did speak out against him. He figured everyone would assume it had to do with the Lyons, and if they didn't, they'd think Kandice was responsible."

"Which we did for a time," Buchannan said with a scowl.

"Apparently, Bucky had told Jazz months ago that if something were to happen to him, he wanted Jazz to take over the bar," Lena said. "Instead of waiting around for that to happen, Jazz decided to give Bucky a push."

"He didn't realize that Bucky had changed his will," Paul added, putting his arm around me and squeezing. "If he'd known, he might not have killed him."

"Or he'd have taken out Kandice first," Garrison said. "Or driven a wedge between them so that Bucky would change it back."

We all stood there and considered that. Half my cake was gone, and I no longer wanted the rest of it. I set it aside on a nearby desk.

"Ruth said Bucky had secrets," I said. "Do we know what she was talking about?"

"No idea," Paul said. "But from what we know of her, it's likely she was making stuff up, just to stir the pot. Let's just say that Ruth Camden has a history of causing trouble without lifting a finger herself."

"She'd whisper a few words in the right ears and then watch the fireworks as they happened," Garrison said.

"And," Lena added, "it turns out that she had gotten together with the other bar owners and convinced them to put pressure on Kandice to sell *them* the bar. Some sort of collective."

Which was why they'd gone to Bucky's together after his death. Not because they wanted to pay their condolences, but because they wanted to take advantage of the situation.

"What about Dwayne?" I asked. "Why was he meeting with Jaqueline?"

They all shared a look.

"What?" I asked, looking from face to face and getting nothing. "Did I miss something?"

"Let's just say that Jaqueline and Geno Lyon won't be sharing a bed anytime soon," Paul said.

"She might not have been cheating on her husband with Bucky, but that didn't mean she was honoring her vows," Garrison added.

Which meant he'd lied to me. Was I surprised? Not really. I found it funny that out of the three bar owners, only Ivan McGraw seemed to have told the full truth. Go figure.

"By the way," I said, wanting to change the subject, "it looks like we're going to be buying Death by Java!"

My pronouncement was met with blank stares.

"It's a bookstore café in California modeled after Death by Coffee," Paul supplied.

"We're still working out the final details, but Vicki

and I will be the official owners in just a few weeks, maybe a month."

"That's great," Lena said, stepping forward and giving me a hug. "Who's going to manage it?"

"Well . . ."

Before I could come up with an answer I didn't have, someone across the room called for a speech, putting a blessed end to our conversation. We turned to face where Chief Patricia Dalton stood, red-faced and looking for all the world like she wanted to be anywhere else. She took a deep breath, let it out in a sigh, and when she spoke, she did so in the clipped, annoyed way she so often spoke in.

"Thank you all for being here," Chief Dalton said. "I might not like it, but I appreciate this whole shebang. You've made me feel as if I might actually be missed."

Someone clapped, which infected the room. I found myself close to tears as everyone joined in, clapping and hooting loudly. Chief Dalton waited it out before continuing.

"I suspect whoever takes over my role will do a fine job." Her eyes flicked over to where Paul and the rest of us stood. "Might even be better in some ways. I've been here forever, and a part of me knows that because of that, our department may have stagnated some. My stepping down will allow you to grow, to move into a newer, brighter future." She cleared her throat, wiped a hand quickly across her eye. "I gave a lot to this place, and I'll leave some of my soul here when I'm gone. But I don't regret it. And, yeah, I'll miss it." A pause. "Miss you."

Paul sniffled next to me, while Buchannan coughed into his hand.

Chief Dalton scanned the room, tearless. Stoic.

"That's all I've got. My last command for you all is to have a little more fun, then get back to work."

A cheer went up around the room.

And then, for one last time, we did as we were told.

Visit our website at
KensingtonBooks.com
to sign up for our newsletters, read
more from your favorite authors, see
books by series, view reading group
guides, and more!

BOOK ▐▐▐▐ CLUB
BETWEEN THE CHAPTERS

Become a Part of Our
Between the Chapters Book Club
Community and Join the Conversation

Betweenthechapters.net

DEATH BY IRISH COFFEE

"Paul," I said, trying to keep the desperation out of my voice. "What's going on?"

A beat passed when he didn't react to my question. Then his gaze swiveled to meet mine, and he said, "We're not certain Bucky Sweeny died of natural causes."

I slow-blinked. Spoke just as slowly. "You're not sure it was natural causes? What does that even mean?"

"It means that some things have come up." He sighed, sat back. "At first glance, it did indeed appear as if Bucky Sweeny had too much to drink, got sick, and then collapsed into the back of the Lyons' pickup truck. He'd sustained no wounds, other than the mild bruising on his shoulder and head that could be explained away easily enough, especially if he was so sick that he fell a few times. But none of his injuries could have accounted for his death, not even remotely."

I absorbed that, then asked, "And on second glance?"

"We think he might have been poisoned."

I stared. "Poisoned?" And then a new, panic-infused thought. "From the Irish coffee . . ."

Books by Alex Erickson

Bookstore Café Mysteries
DEATH BY COFFEE
DEATH BY TEA
DEATH BY PUMPKIN SPICE
DEATH BY VANILLA LATTE
DEATH BY EGGNOG
DEATH BY ESPRESSO
DEATH BY CAFÉ MOCHA
DEATH BY FRENCH ROAST
DEATH BY HOT APPLE CIDER
DEATH BY SPICED CHAI
DEATH BY ICED COFFEE
DEATH BY PEPPERMINT CAPPUCCINO
DEATH BY CARAMEL MACCHIATO
DEATH BY JAVA
DEATH BY IRISH COFFEE
CHRISTMAS COCOA MURDER
(with Carlene O'Connor and Maddie Day)

Furever Pets Mysteries
THE POMERANIAN ALWAYS BARKS TWICE
DIAL 'M' FOR MAINE COON

Cat Yoga Mysteries
A POSE BEFORE DYING
A PURRFECT DATE

Published by Kensington Publishing Corp.